The
Forgotten
Guide to
Happiness

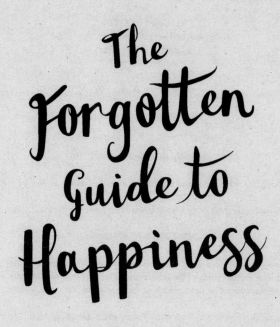

The Forgotten Guide to Happiness

SOPHIE JENKINS

avon.

Published by AVON
A division of HarperCollins*Publishers* Ltd
1 London Bridge Street
London SE1 9GF

www.harpercollins.co.uk

A Paperback Original 2018

4

Copyright © Sophie Jenkins 2018

Sophie Jenkins asserts the moral right to be identified as the author of this work.

A catalogue copy of this book is available from the British Library.

ISBN: 978-0-00-828180-9

Typeset in Minion 11.5/14.5 pt by Palimpsest Book Production Limited,
Falkirk, Stirlingshire

Printed and bound in UK by CPI Group (UK) Ltd, Croydon CR0 4YY

MIX
Paper from
responsible sources
FSC™ C007454

This book is produced from independently certified FSC™ paper to ensure responsible forest management.

For more information visit: www.harpercollins.co.uk/green

To Paul and Joe, Elaine, Pat, William and George,
for humour, happiness, tolerance and joy;
and for Rowena, with love

How I thought my story ended . . .

After months on the road in her camper van, she was coming to her journey's end, to the place where it had begun. In the distance the city sparkled. Marco drove through the outskirts of north London and the leafy suburban streets, into Highgate Village with its Victorian and Georgian houses, and down Highgate West Hill where he bumped up the kerb and parked up next to a red-bricked mansion block with a green wooden gate flanked by dark hedges. The engine cooled and ticked.

'This is it.' Marco took the key out of the ignition and kissed her, his mouth warm on hers. 'We're home, Lauren,' he said softly, watching her, his eyes dark with love.

The word took her breath away. She looked up at the building with its warm, lighted windows.

She thought back to the moment everything had changed. The moment he'd asked her to go back with him.

'I hoped you might be ready to come home now,' he'd said, squeezing her hand. 'Come home with me.'

'Home?' For a moment she'd felt as if she was stepping on quicksand; that off-balance terror and the thrill of excitement.

'Lauren, I love your independence. You're the most self-contained woman I've ever met. You and me, we're two of a kind, don't you think? You can have all the freedom you need and I'll be away some of the time anyway. It will be like it is now except I won't have to rely on a tracker to find you.'

'That's crazy!' she'd said. Put together all the time they'd known each other and it amounted to a few weeks at the most.

'I know,' he'd said cheerfully, taking it as a compliment.

And now, for the first time, they weren't parting with promises to keep in touch, promises that faded as time passed. Home was togetherness and warmth and permanence and, after nine months of travelling, the word was like a forgotten dream and she was filled with sudden happiness.

Their adventure wasn't over.

It was just about to begin.

CHAPTER ONE

The Sequel

Some days start off looking hopeful: it's August, the sun is out, the birds are singing, people are smiling – this was one of those days. I was waiting with anticipation for my literary agent Kitty Golding to let me into her apartment block. She lives in the penthouse of a modern architectural block bordering Regent's Park, which is five storeys high and glass-fronted, giving it the effect of a doll's house. On the ground floor, the white sofa had its back to the window and I could see the top of a head of black, curly hair – could be a man or woman, girl, boy or dog. I was itching to reach in and rearrange the furniture.

The intercom clicked into life. 'Come on up, Lana.' The door clunked open, and I got into the lift which took me up to my agent's floor.

Kitty was waiting for me, smiling faintly. Early forties, lean, glossy black hair, wearing a lime-and-heather-coloured boiled-wool dress.

She held the door open, and I smiled back at her and went into her office. The glass wall looked out at the sky and the rooftops above the busy street below. The other three walls were lined with books. Mine was easy to spot: *Love Crazy*, with LANA GREEN emblazoned along the spine.

I headed for a low tan and chrome chair, and for a disconcerting second I had the sensation of plummeting – the chair was lower than it looked. I tugged at my red skirt: I could see my fake-tanned knees in close-up.

Kitty took the chair opposite me, gripping the armrests and lowering herself in a sort of triceps dip. She picked up the typescript of my sequel, *Heartbreak*, from the glass table and flicked through a few pages, nodding thoughtfully.

'Nice paper.' She looked up. Her gaze met mine, and held.

The feeling of anticipation was similar to the early days of a relationship: expectation mingled with excitement. Kitty doesn't show much emotion – she leaves that to editors – but I was waiting for my high-five moment.

Kitty tapped my novel. 'As you know, I *love* your writing. You can *write*; there's no doubt about that.'

'Thanks,' I said.

Kitty hooked her pale fingers into the string of lime beads around her neck. She took a deep breath and let it out long and slow. 'But we've got a problem.'

'Oh?' I hadn't been expecting the *but*. 'Is it too long?'

'No – well, maybe a touch. It's not that. The question is, Lana, what's the hook?'

I did some quick-thinking. 'The hook is that this is the sequel to *Love Crazy*,' I said after a moment.

'That's not a hook,' Kitty said.

'Okay.' I had another try. 'The hook is how love turns to heartache.'

'Yes. Heartache. That's what the problem is. It's the storyline.'

'Eh? What's wrong with it?'

'Frankly, it's depressing. The last few days I've had this dark

4

shadow over me and' – she hoisted my typescript up as evidence – 'it's this book. It's bleak.'

Couldn't argue with that. 'Well' – I shrugged – 'that's the story. It's about the break-up. It broke my heart.' I was starting to feel nervous. No one likes criticism. 'That's why it's bleak.'

'It's not just bleak; it's bitter.'

'Yeah. That's what I was trying to get across.'

Kitty sighed and changed position. She studied the neat tan shoe dangling on her toes and looked up again. 'Lana, no one wants to sit down with a book that makes them feel bitter. Bitterness is not appealing,' she said. 'What's happening with your blog?'

'I was getting so much hate mail I stopped posting.'

'You see? Sad; now that's something else. Sad, you can get away with, at a push. So, maybe you could have your hero die of something?'

'Yes, I could do that!' I leant forward eagerly. 'Trust me, I've imagined it – Mark Bridges is hanging off a cliff and I could save him, but I don't, and at the funeral, although I'm wearing black, I'm ecstatic that he's been smashed to a bloody pulp on the jagged rocks.'

Kitty screwed her nose up. 'No, that's a different genre altogether. Look – think of your first book. *Writer falls for photo-journalist.* You've got lots of conflict but plenty of pay-off, too – and that ending, with Lauren and Marco moving in together, and that last line . . .' Kitty pinched her fingers together, waving the words at me like a tiny banner. '". . . Their adventure wasn't over. It was just about to begin."'

Woah, was I wrong about that.

'You've already given us the happy ending,' Kitty said, 'and the sequel should go on from there. It should be about their continuing adventures. Forget about the fact Mark Bridges abandoned you for a Swedish girl—'

'Helga,' I said gloomily; her name hurt like a curse.

'Whatever – that's between you and him. Leave real life out of it. We're talking fiction here. This isn't about you and Mark Bridges, it's about Lauren and Marco, the couple your readers love. We want the adventure, the lifestyle, the feel-good factor.'

'Feel-good factor?'

'So let's talk about what happens next. Maybe Lauren and Marco start a family,' she suggested.

I looked at her in dismay. 'You want me to write about having a fictitious baby?'

'That's it! Remember, your book is about living the dream. No one wants to read about how it all went wrong and you didn't get out of bed for a month – they can look to their own lives for that sort of thing.'

I stared at her bleakly. What kind of insanity would that be, writing as if Mark and I were still together, in love, and then switching off the PC and coming back to the desperate hideousness of reality? I couldn't do it. The whole idea made me ill.

I gripped the chair tightly. 'Kitty, could you just tell me, before we start thinking about new ideas, is there anything at all about this book that you do like? Apart from the paper?'

She thought about it for a few moments, obviously troubled by her own integrity. Personally, I don't mind a lie if it's told in a good cause.

'The problem is, it's too real,' she said at last.

'But the first book was real!'

'Broadly speaking, yes; but you fictionalised it, you made a romance of it, whereas this one' – she laid her palms on it – 'to be honest, it reads like a misery memoir. Lana, I want you to see this' – she spanked the typescript with the flat of her hand – 'as a catharsis, a healing process, a way of getting all your angst out of your system.'

'But – you don't like *any* of it? There's nothing I can keep?'

Kitty sighed – the only thing worse than receiving bad news was giving bad news. 'Okay. Forget about writing a sequel. Put this book behind you and start again with something new. Start afresh. Invent a hero. You're a writer. Be creative! Find that little spark of hope!'

I tried. I looked inside my head for a spark of hope. It was very dark in there. There was no glimmer of light at all. Opening my eyes, I said in desperation, 'I don't know where I'm supposed to get that from when there isn't any. I'm not sure I even believe in love any more. What if it's all a myth?'

I expected her to get panicky right along with me, but she stayed calm.

'We need to think about your publishers, you know,' she said gently. 'Anthea feels that *Heartbreak* is not suitable for your established readership. Those are her exact words.'

Ohhhhh.

Don't ask me why I hadn't considered this before. I'd got the idea the publishers were buying my writing, when actually they were buying the romance. I hadn't realised that until now.

To be fair, Kitty had asked me at regular intervals to show her the sequel, but had I? Nooooo. Had I even given her a synopsis? Nooooo.

Why not? Well – I was convinced she would love it: the Dream turns into a Nightmare. It was *real*. I honestly thought Kitty would be moved to tears; I didn't expect to make her depressed.

I burned with shame. Second novels are notoriously difficult to write. Kitty was strumming the rubber bands binding my four hundred sheets of good quality paper together while she waited for me to work it out for myself.

'Okay,' I said. 'What are my options?'

'Either you can start again . . .'

'Or?'

'You can pay back the advance.'

'*Or?*' I prompted in a panic, because I was broke and the promise of a payment was one of the major factors why today had started off perfect.

Kitty raised her eyebrows and shrugged. On the *or* front, that was it.

Generally, you have to be thin-skinned to be a writer, so you can be insightful and all that, but you have to be thick-skinned too, because no one in the history of the written word has ever written anything that *everyone* likes.

Still; rejection does put you off, even if you're trying to be philosophical about it.

The truth is, I like being a writer. I don't like the actual writing, which is hard work, but the rest of it – lunches, interviews, festivals – is great fun and I recommend it.

I looked around. On the shelves were books with bright covers. By the law of averages, some of them had to be bad – trust me, plenty of bad books get published. And how depressing was this – mine was *too* bad even by those standards.

I imagined starting on a new book. In the right genre. A contemporary romantic novel.

I pushed myself out of the low chair and walked right up to the glass window, pretending to walk off the edge, which is what I felt like doing. Pressed up against the pane, I couldn't go any further and neither could my thoughts. Way down below, a man was looking up at the building. I could see his face, his shoulders and his feet. What could he see? A blonde-haired doll standing in the doll's house?

Hope flared – I could write about *him!* – and faded.

Once upon a time I had looked at all men with interest; and then I found Mark and I stopped looking. The end.

My breath clouded the window and I was just about to wipe it with my hand when Kitty said, 'Don't do that! It's just been cleaned.' She glanced at her watch. 'I have a lunch at one.'

I hugged myself in panic at being dismissed. 'What do I do now? I need the "on delivery" money. I've got an overdraft. I've got bills to pay!'

Kitty brightened. 'Good! That's your incentive! Now we've got something to work with. Let's forget about paying back the advance for the moment,' she said briskly. 'We'll extend the deadline. You come up with a new story and we'll talk it over. Love, and it goes wrong, but they get back together, happy ending. Find the characters, the emotions, the dialogue and we can stick a plot in later.' She smiled. 'Okay?'

I'm very susceptible to suggestion, so I nodded back. 'Okay.'

She stood up and I realised we were done.

'I'll give you the typescript back,' she said. 'You can recycle the paper.'

She gave me a Tesco carrier bag to take it away in.

When I left her apartment I had a day-drinking feeling of light-headedness.

My book on rejection had been rejected.

CHAPTER TWO

Heroic Attributes

Heading towards Camden Town, I decided to avoid the markets and the tourists by calling in the York and Albany for a drink. If you feel drunk and you drink, it makes you feel less drunk, like homeopathy. But I realised it was exactly the kind of place that Kitty might be going to for lunch. A bit further on, just off Delancey Street, is the Edinboro Castle, a place she would never set foot in, so I walked on and went into the bar, swinging my heavy Tesco bag. It was so dark it was like being momentarily blinded.

I took my wine out into the glare of the beer garden and sat at a table all to myself under a silver birch where I could think up a plan with no distractions.

A shadow fell over me. 'Is this seat taken?'

'Yes,' I said automatically. Looking up, I saw a guy wearing a bright orange Nike sweatshirt and faded jeans. He had messy dark hair but, despite being unshaven, he had a friendly, open face with straight dark eyebrows and clear grey eyes. Realising I was being 'difficult', as my parents liked to put it, I quickly apologised. 'Sorry, that was rude.' Suddenly, having company wasn't such a bad idea, even if it was with a stranger. 'No. Help yourself.'

'Cheers.' He smiled, sat down and put his lager in front of him.

His smile looked like the smile of a man who has had an easy life, which is a good foundation for a warm character. People who have an easy life assume the best and tend to be generous and optimistic – I haven't googled this or anything; it's just my opinion, based on experience.

On the downside, I do remember reading that optimistic people die younger because when they're ill they take it for granted it's something trivial. But it's not as if the optimistic people I knew were dying in droves, so it wasn't much of a negative, currently.

As I was pondering on these facts about him, which I later discovered I'd got completely wrong, the sun slid out of the shadow of the pub and shone through my wine glass, throwing a radioactive reflection onto the wooden table. A phone rang.

We both sprang to life and patted ourselves down, but it wasn't mine, it was his.

'Jack Buchanan,' he said. And then he frowned. '*What?*'

I heard the disappointment in his voice.

He listened for a few moments and then said, 'I don't understand. *Embroidery* scissors? What are they? How big are they? Well – okay, so she bit him, but what did he do to her? Yeah, well – how hard could she bite? She hasn't even got a full set of teeth,' he said with increasing indignation. 'I don't see how biting him makes her vulnerable. It's the bar manager who's vulnerable. Why don't you put *him* in a home?' He listened a bit longer and then said gloomily, 'Thursday. At two.' He ended the call and shook his head. All the happiness had gone out of him and he looked weary and troubled.

If you're going through a bad time and you're with someone

who is happy, it makes you feel ten times worse. Conversely, if you're going through a bad time and you're with someone who is also struggling, things start to look a lot brighter.

'Dog trouble?' I asked.

He looked at me blankly. 'What?' His eyes were grey and distant. Then he saw where I was coming from, and said, 'No. It's my stepmother, actually.'

I'd been trying to work out where the embroidery scissors came into it, and it made more sense now. A warm and friendly feeling came over me, the sort you get when you see a man on his own with a baby. I hadn't realised you could get the same effect with stepmothers, but there we are – my mission as a writer is to observe and report; something I learned from my journalism days.

'She bit someone? I couldn't help hearing.'

'She's been going to that bar for years,' he said bitterly. 'Now social services have got involved. You know what that means.'

'Yes, I do,' I said. Our two problems were very different, but who had the worse one? He had a feral relative and I had a whole novel to write. Just at that moment, a yellow birch leaf dropped into my wine glass. It didn't exactly tip the scales but I did start feeling got at.

Jack Buchanan watched me fish it out. 'Can I get you another one?' he asked as I flicked it under the table.

'Thanks!' But like a warning vision I saw the whole week speeding by. 'Better not, though. I've got to write a book. Well, an outline. I know Stephen King did all his best work while he was drinking but it doesn't really work for me – it comes out gibberish, or sentimental.'

'You write books? Who are you?'

'Lana Green,' I said.

'Ah . . .' he responded. He rubbed the stubble on his chin. 'Sorry.'

'That's all right. You're not my target market.'

'So what's your book going to be about?' he asked.

'It's got to be a romantic novel. Love, and it goes wrong, they get back together, happy ending.'

He laughed. 'Well, that seems easy enough.'

'Yeah, it's not.'

'Subdivide it into where, why, what and how.'

'It's not as simple as that.'

'No, I suppose it isn't,' he reflected. 'Otherwise everybody would be doing it.'

'Don't get me started on that,' I said, 'because it seems as if everybody *is* doing it. Comedians write children's books, models write romances, chat-show hosts write drama – it's really annoying. How would they like it if I started doing stand-up, or hosted a chat show, or got famous for my boob jobs? People should stick to one occupation per person. On principle, I don't buy any fiction written by people who are famous in other fields.'

Jack Buchanan laughed; it suited him. He had a face that was made for happiness. 'My stepmother does a bit of writing.'

Incredible. 'See what I mean?' I looked at my watch. Half the day had gone already and I had work to do. 'I'd better go. I've got to find myself a hero.'

'And I've got to go back and do some firefighting.'

That was interesting. 'You're a firefighter?'

'Metaphorically speaking. I have an IT company. Tell you what, you can write about me, if you like,' he said helpfully.

I grinned. 'No offence, but you're not hero material.'

'Why's that?' He looked hurt.

'Sorry.' As usual I wished I'd kept my thoughts to myself. 'I didn't mean it to come out like that. You seem perfectly nice and . . .' I couldn't point out that he was also scruffy and worked in IT and was worried about his stepmother, so I took another approach. 'Are you fearless? And incurably romantic? Are you self-assured to the point of arrogance?'

Jack Buchanan rubbed his jaw and thought about it. 'No. Not really.'

'Mmm. Worth a shot, though. And I appreciate the offer,' I added, and finished my drink. 'Good luck with your step-mother.' I stood and picked up the Tesco bag. It was heavier than I remembered, but my head was clear.

'Hey, Lana?'

As I turned back, he shielded his eyes from the sun and looked up at me. In the shadow of his hand his eyes were a cool, clear grey. I couldn't read the expression in them.

'So, that's what makes a good husband, is it?' he asked. 'Being fearless and stuff?'

I hadn't thought of it like that before. 'Probably not, except in books.' The Tesco bag was surprisingly heavy as I cradled it in my arms. 'A hero and a husband are entirely different things.'

CHAPTER THREE

Reflections

If we could edit our own lives, there are plenty of things in mine that I would delete and rewrite, but looking back, the way I said goodbye to Mark is the main one I would change. It was more than a year since we'd first met up while I was travelling. We'd been living together for almost four amazing months and for me, our relationship was still exciting and new. But the day he was due to leave for his assignment in the Bahamas I was part of a panel of authors at the British Library, so we said our farewells at the flat. His blond hair was still wet from the shower and he kissed me long and hard and as I looked into his brown eyes I was thinking, *I really have to go now*. Mark never closed his eyes when we kissed and I kept mine open too because the kiss was deeper that way. It was a kiss to remember him by.

But my mind was more on the time than the kiss, because I was nervous and I didn't want to be late for the panel. I loosened the hug but he was still holding me tight.

'I wish you were coming with me,' he said into my hair.

'Yes.' I should have said *me too*, but that would have been hypocritical. I'd chosen to stay behind because I had *Love*

Crazy to promote and the book meant everything to me. Being a novelist had been a lifelong dream since the age of six when I'd self-published a slightly derivative story on coloured paper, which my mother had immediately ruined by correcting the mistakes in black felt-tip.

We had one final kiss before I hurriedly left the flat, but at the door something made me turn back. I told him reassuringly, 'It's not as if you'll be away for long.'

He nodded.

It turned out to be a clear example of dramatic irony.

I'd forgotten what it was like, being alone. After living with Mark, the solitude was more empty than I remembered and I missed him more than I'd imagined. It wasn't just physical; I missed his presence too, and without his energy I felt lethargic and aimless, as if I was ill. To begin with, we spoke to each other most days but when I went to Penrith to do workshops for the Romantic Novelists' Association's conference, we messaged instead. I used my time productively and wrote drafts of short stories, planned the outline of my next novel, updated my blog and received humorous tweets from my followers on how to keep busy while Mark was away.

I counted down the days until finally it was time to get my legs waxed, my eyebrows threaded and my hair blow-dried and, feeling good, I took the train to Heathrow to welcome him back. The idea was to surprise him.

His flight was due to land at 11 am and I got there earlier than I'd expected so I bought a sandwich and a coffee. As I ate my sandwich I studied the people around me on my side of the barrier; the drivers holding up names, the girls checking their phones, the family groups distracting bored children, the parents watching hopefully. I watched the passengers coming into the arrivals hall. Some looked tanned and energised, others were tired, doggedly pushing trolleys, but happiest of all were the eager travellers who came through knowing somebody was there to greet them.

And as I watched, each reunion almost brought tears to my eyes. I imagined what it must be like to get off a long flight and see someone who loved you waiting to welcome you home.

For Mark, that someone was me.

Glancing at the indicator board, I saw that his flight had landed and I felt the thrill of excitement. I threw away my cup and sandwich wrapper, wiped my hands with a lemon wipe and edged nearer to the barrier until I found myself standing next to an elderly man in a navy blazer who was holding a bouquet of lilies. Their heavy sweet scent was so strong that I turned to look at him.

He smiled back at me. I had a warm feeling of connection; we were two different generations there for the same loving purpose.

I could see the faint shape of people beyond the sliding doors and suddenly the travellers were coming through in a rush with their Virgin Atlantic tags. The old man and I pressed ourselves against the barriers, scanning faces. My heart was beating hard as I searched for Mark and the people came through in wave after wave and then the cabin crew came through with their wheelie bags and the crush around us gradually eased as the drivers met up with their passengers and the divided families became whole again and after a while, out of the original welcoming committee, it was just the old man and me.

We gave each other a wry, philosophical shrug. Well – it hadn't gone the way I'd imagined but I thought about it logically. The airline could have lost Mark's bags and he could be still in baggage claim. Or maybe he'd left his passport on the plane and then had to be accompanied back to look for it. Or I'd missed him in the crowd. Of three possible options, I considered that was the worst scenario, the one that ruined everything.

With a beep-beep-beep, an airport golf cart came through the automatic doors carrying an old lady with fierce red hair and my elderly companion knocked his flowers on the barrier as he ducked under it, showering me with pollen, and greeted her with a kiss.

That just left me.

My mood had changed completely by this time; I was dulled by the anticlimax. Even if Mark had just at that moment come through the doors I could only have managed to express relief. The thrill of the surprise element had gone. So I phoned him.

When he answered, he sounded groggy. 'Hello?'

'Mark, where are you? Are you okay?' I asked urgently.

There was silence. It seemed to go on forever. I recognised it as the silence of a storyteller wondering where to start.

'Yeah,' he said finally. 'I was going to call you.'

I didn't like the sound of that at all. 'I'm at Heathrow,' I said indignantly, as if it would make a difference.

'Okay,' he said warily. 'What's the time?'

I looked up at the indicator board. 'Ten past twelve.' A new crowd of meeters and greeters was gathering and I edged my way through them towards the relative quietness of a bureau de change. 'Ten past seven, your time,' I added, because at that point I knew without a doubt that he was still in the Bahamas and that he hadn't caught the flight after all. 'What's going on?'

'Listen,' he said, 'I'm staying on here a bit longer.'

I felt so instantly bad, so painfully crushed by unhappiness that I just wanted to know the worst so that I could stop feeling this utter dread about what he was going to say. But at the same time, I was terribly scared to hear it.

'Mark, just tell me, is this it?'

Again, the long pause.

I waited helplessly for the judgement.

'Look, I'll call you later,' he said finally, and he cut me off.

Back home, waiting for the call, I obsessively went through his texts and checked his Instagram and Facebook pages and studied the pictures he'd posted of the free-diver, Helga. I rang his parents, Judy and Stephen, hoping that they could tell me what was going on, but although Judy greeted me warmly she was vague and said she believed he was working. I left messages pleading with him to phone me.

He finally did get in touch, jolting me awake from a restless sleep a couple of weeks later. From the background noise it sounded as if he was in a bar. He was remorseful, but he told me he was staying in Long Island a bit longer because this was a good assignment, and it might turn out to be one of his best.

If he'd left it there, it would have been easier to live with. But he went on to say that there had been too much pressure on us being the perfect couple and he didn't like the way people assumed they knew him because of Marco in *Love Crazy*. He said I'd written things that were meant to be private. He needed some space because we'd rushed into living together, he said, forgetting it was his idea in the first place.

I listened to his familiar voice against the drunken tumult of the background noise and stared at the shadows on the ceiling.

'So it's my fault?' I didn't say it indignantly but more out of self-knowledge. I couldn't make people like me, and the fact that he'd left me didn't come as a surprise. My pillow was damp. I hadn't realised I was crying.

'I'll call you when I get back,' he said.

But as the time went by, every buzz and ping of my phone ignited hope and then plunged me back into a depression which drained the colour from my life. When I first wrote in my blog about his non-appearance at the airport the supportive messages helped a lot, but people don't have a great tolerance for relentless misery. *Love Crazy* was in the bestseller lists and the vitriolic responses I got for ruining the dream of happy ever after resulted in my total withdrawal from social media. I gave up the blog and poured my emotions into *Heartbreak*.

And look how that worked out.

As I closed the door to my flat behind me, Mark's black and red Trek bike cast its shadow on the wall like a Banksy stencil. I hung my red jacket on the handlebars. I'd bought the bike for him when I got the first payment for *Love Crazy* and it was currently my most expensive coat rack.

I was in the hall, still standing by the bike, still holding the heavy Tesco bag and listening intently because I sensed something strange about the flat; something off-kilter. I crept towards the lounge, caught a glimpse of movement, a flash of blue and red, and I froze. But no. It was the reflection of the Tesco bag. Still, I waited and listened.

Despite what thriller writers want you to believe, no woman in her right mind goes into her flat, senses something suspicious and calls out, 'Hello? Anyone there?' No – the thing to do is to be alert, and at the faintest sound, run back out of the door as fast as you can. This is writing what you know. However, I want to point out that writing what you know doesn't mean everything you know is worth writing about. I was holding the evidence right here. Just because a story is true doesn't make it a good story.

I looked out onto Parliament Hill Fields. I could hear the distant repetitive *thwok* from the tennis courts. My desk was cluttered with pens, mugs and pages, just as I'd left it that morning when I was full of optimism. The table was clear. The cushions on the lemon sofa were plumped. All seemed as it should, but it felt wrong.

I put my typescript on the table and went cautiously into the shady bedroom. Duvet crumpled, blinds still shut. And suddenly I realised what was different. When I'd left that morning, *Heartbreak* was a literary tragedy that was going to support me and help me pay my bills. Now it was a worthless cliché. I'd been dumped by a guy; simple as that.

Here I was, surrounded like Miss Havisham by the relics of our love story – his unwanted bike, his discarded clothes, the last fumes of his aftershave. Stripped of literary worth, they were meaningless. No story here; nothing to look at, stand back, stand back.

Writing *Heartbreak*, I'd imagined Mark reading it and rushing back, begging for forgiveness, appalled at the pain he'd caused me. Now I realised he would have resented me for making him feel bad. Who wants a book that makes you feel bad? As Kitty said, that's the sort of thing we can do for ourselves.

Well, I'd finally got the message.

It was like taking yellow sunglasses off and seeing the dull hue of reality.

House keys, bike, clothes, me.

Who leaves all that behind? Someone who doesn't want them any more, that's who.

CHAPTER FOUR

Catalysts for Change

Next morning I woke up, hungover, with my pillow over my head, fighting for air. I'd slept badly all night, just on the edge of unconsciousness, and rolled over, relieved to see dawn bleeding into the room. I felt shabby, with a pounding headache that made me squint. Even with the curtains closed, the room seemed unreasonably bright.

My failure crowded me in and I got out of bed, walking on a lean. Glancing at the empty bottle and the greasy pizza box, depression clung to me like a cold, wet cleansing cloth.

The letterbox rattled and there in the hall lay a letter from my publishers, forwarded to me by Kitty.

I tore it open, hoping that the publishers had made a mistake and they wanted *Heartbreak* after all, but no. Still, it was the next best thing. It was a royalty cheque.

For five pounds and seventy-one pence.

I studied it carefully. How could that be right? I pointed at each word as I read it, hoping I was delusional. But no.

How had this happened? I was now officially broke.

Fresh panic made my heartbeat thud chaotically around my skull like a squash ball.

I held my head in my hands to steady it and I sat at the table and suddenly recalled that I'd had some drunken inspiration for a new plot. Trembling, I checked my notebook in case I had become Stephen King under the influence. I'd written: *Mopeds. Virgin. Stern letter. £10,000-ish.* There might be a story there somewhere but I couldn't remember what it was.

I got dressed and decided to address the main problem, insolvency, by going to visit my bank.

I had to wait to see an advisor. I sat on one of three seats by a low orange partition that acted as a wall for the desks behind it. The light buzzed like a bee in a jar. Although there were three desks set at angles, only one was occupied so I settled down to wait, and with nothing else to do I watched the advisor, a thin man with vertically gelled hair, greet his client, an old, bald Asian guy with an anxious expression. He sat down cautiously and pushed a paper across the table.

'Is this your name?' the advisor asked him.

The old man leant forward and confirmed it in a low voice.

'What's your address?' the advisor asked, studying the screen.

The old man sensed my interest and glanced at me crossly. He turned back to the advisor and huddled further across the desk, like a man with something to hide – an exam paper, for example.

'In Hong Kong?'

The advisor paused. 'No, UK.'

'No address in UK,' the old man said sternly.

'There's nothing here under this name. But then how—'

The old man scribbled something down. 'Try this way,' he instructed.

Triple-tapping of the keyboard, and then . . . 'Sorry. I'm not finding it. If you have your account number—'

26

'I give you my money! Hundreds! Thousands!' the old man cried out in panic.

Imagine that! What a nightmare! Putting all your money in a bank and suddenly they've got no record of you.

A slim, blonde woman stood over me. 'Are you waiting to see an advisor?'

'Yes,' I said, so I don't know how the story turned out.

Better than mine, I hope.

We walked over to one of the empty desks. 'How can I help you?' she asked warmly as I sat down, which led me into a false sense of security. She reminded me of Meryl Streep, with her glasses and her up-do, so I told her the whole sorry story about my book being turned down. As the horror of it came back afresh, I asked her for an overdraft to keep me going until I wrote another novel and got my advance.

She turned her attention from me to the screen. 'You already have an unauthorised overdraft which is costing you five pounds a day,' she said blandly.

'Five pounds a *day*? No wonder I've got no money. If you could just authorise that overdraft so that I don't have to throw money away, that will be great.' I was showing her how astute I was, financially speaking.

'You have already exceeded your overdraft limit.'

'Well, I'd like to extend it. It's just temporary, until I get my advance.'

'What date are you expecting to receive that?' she asked, fingers poised so she could type it in.

I was starting to feel uneasy. 'I don't have an exact date because I have to write a new storyline first but I'll do it as soon as possible, obviously.'

She frowned and I remembered I didn't actually like Meryl Streep much.

'Approximately how long will it take?' she asked. Her voice was a couple of degrees colder.

'Well . . .' I began, getting panicky – it was giving me writer's block just thinking about it, 'I actually know two authors who've written a whole book in a fortnight.' One of them is a woman with an overactive thyroid. If I ever have to have an illness, that's the one I'd choose because it revs you up – the body is working perpetual overtime and you can get a lot done with that spare energy. An overactive thyroid is like natural cocaine. On the minus side, like cocaine, it makes you more prone to having a heart attack, but I'm just saying, if.

She lowered her fingers and turned her attention from the screen to me. 'You're saying you'll only get paid once you've written a new book?'

'Yes.' I shouldn't have poured my heart out to her – bad mistake. I thought she'd feel sorry for me, but here she was holding it against me already.

She looked at her screen again. 'You currently don't have sufficient funds to cover your direct debits.'

'Exactly! That's why I'm here.'

She was so frosty you would have thought I was asking her to lend me money out of her own pocket. Where was the compassion, the eagerness to help?

After a bit more tapping and clicking, she said, 'As you have reached your overdraft limit, we can't extend it. A limit is a *limit*,' she explained, enunciating clearly.

It was the way she said it that annoyed me. 'Hey, I know what a limit is! Words are my life!' Knowing how ridiculous I sounded, but I was desperate. This wasn't going at all the way I'd imagined. I hadn't realised that banks love you when you have money, and they go off you when you don't, like the worst sort of friends. 'So what do I do now? If you stop my direct debits I won't be able to pay my rent and I'll be homeless. Is that what you want?'

'I would like to remind you not to raise your voice.' She pointed to a sign by the window which read: *Abuse of advisors will not be tolerated.*

I'd always wondered why that notice was there, and now I knew. I jumped to my feet in frustration.

'Well you're not getting this,' I said, waving my royalty cheque. Impulsively, I tore it up and threw the bits over the table. My heart was pumping hard as I walked towards the stairs.

One day's overdraft money lost in a pointless gesture. I immediately regretted it.

Back home, I lay on the lemon sofa and realised to my dismay I was going to have to ring my mother for help. She lives in Loano, Italy. (Literally, the last resort.) She can detect laziness even over the phone so as I pressed her number I sat on the edge of my desk so as to sound alert and also to enjoy the view which in all probability wasn't going to be mine for much longer.

'*Pronto!*' she answered impatiently.

'Mum? It's me. Lana,' I added for clarity.

'Oh, this *is* a surprise,' she said.

She'd been a teacher, and then a head teacher, and after the divorce she'd taken early retirement and gone to the Italian Riviera to boss a whole new country around for a change. I can spot a teacher a mile off. They're the ones telling people off.

I took a deep breath and once again I felt the burning shame of failure. 'Listen, I've got something to tell you. My new book got turned down yesterday.'

'*Got?* You mean it *was* turned down.'

See?

Now that she'd corrected my grammar, she waited for me to go on.

'Well, that's it,' I said. 'That's what I wanted to tell you.'

'Oh,' she said thoughtfully. 'Perhaps now is a good time to think about doing something else.'

'But I don't want to.' My voice started to rise. Right. Be calm. Regroup. Clear throat. 'I didn't call you for advice. The point is, without Mark, I can't afford next month's rent.'

She was silent for a long moment. 'You're calling to borrow money?'

'Yes, please. It's just until I come up with a new story.'

'Why don't you try asking the bank?'

Desperation made me flippant. 'I have tried them, and now I'm trying you.'

'I see.' She managed to put a surprising amount of disapproval into that short sentence.

When I was little, someone gave her a book by Libby Purves called *How (Not) to Be a Perfect Mother*, and she's stuck rigidly to the concept ever since.

After a long silence, she sighed deeply. 'Do you want to come and stay here for a while?'

Did I? It wasn't the solution I would have chosen, but it was still a solution and I grasped it, trying not to sound too eager.

'I sort of do,' I said.

'Sort of do?'

'Is that not grammatically correct?'

'Come then, if that's what you'd like.'

Honestly, no wonder I prefer making things up to real life. 'But would you like me to come? You know, with enthusiasm?'

'You're my daughter,' she said, which wasn't really an answer.

I probably expect too much of her. She's never been a Cath Kidston, cupcake-baking type of mother. If I went to stay it would like having twenty-four-hour private tuition from her. And from her point of view, she would be wasting her teaching skills on a bratty and reluctant pupil. We love each other but we don't *get* each other in the slightest.

I'm guessing this was going through her mind, too. 'Why don't you go back to journalism?' she suggested.

'Definitely not! I hated that job. I hated visiting people when they were at their worst. I hated court reports, and seeing the looks on their families' faces as their men were described as being of "bad character". I loathed the whole *Crufts Doc in Dog Collar Shock* thing. Yuk!'

'In that case, have you thought about teaching creative writing?' she suggested.

'Hah! Those that can't, teach,' I said bitterly, managing to insult us both in one sentence. I'd turned down a job as tutor at the London Literary Society a few months previously on the grounds I was too busy writing my sequel. Well, I'd had money then; I could afford to.

'Actually, you make a far better teacher if you *can* do a thing,' my mother said, 'and despite your current setback you're a published, successful author. Capitalise on it.'

'Yee-ees.' I've never fancied teaching because I'm no good at telling people what to do but I didn't argue because she'd just said I was a successful author – the first time she'd ever acknowledged it. It gave me a bit of a lift, to be honest. 'Thanks, I'll think about it.'

'Good!'

Before I could say anything else, she hung up.

I always forget that about her, that she comes to the end of a call and hangs up. Mind you, it does away with the closing awkwardness of *lovely to talk to you, yes, same, see you soon, yeah great, have a good day, call me, I will, lots of love, etc.*, but it still takes me by surprise.

I stood by the window and imagined getting a job.

It would just be for money, I told myself.

I would still write in my spare time.

Getting a job. The phrase broke my heart; the fading dreams of an ex-writer, the brave face – *yeah, but it's only temporary, I'm working on another book, going for literary this time . . .* dragging that lie out for a few years until people gave up asking me how the novel was coming along.

Still, I was forced to face reality and so I began to update my CV. I was sadly deficient in most employment skills such as bar-tending or barista work, but I was willing to learn.

Shortly after that, my father unexpectedly rang me to tell me the Chelsea score. I only support them because he does, not because I have any particular interest in football, but he used to take me to the home games when we lived in Fulham and I think of those days with a certain nostalgia. Since we had lost touch with the minutiae of each other's daily lives and we had taboo subjects like Jo-Ann and my mother to avoid, I liked our footballing chats.

He gave me his personal version of the match report and a scathing overview of the incompetency of the manager and, just as we were on our goodbyes, he said, 'Your mother called.' He lowered his voice. 'She's worried about you. I'm sorry they didn't like your new book.'

'Oh.' I felt both touched by the concern and surprised my parents were on speaking terms since the news of Jo-Ann's pregnancy, at the age of forty-five. 'Don't be,' I said. 'It's probably for the best. I'd have been like Gwyneth Paltrow, telling the world about my perfect life, and then in book two, oh, by the way, my perfect man has only gone and uncoupled me. I'd be that woman at literary parties who people whisper about out of the corner of their mouths – *her first book was amazing but he left her, you know, and she never got back on form.*' Tears filled my eyes. Self-pity is seductive, but it makes you pitiful.

'That's the spirit,' my father chuckled. 'I'm glad you're staying positive. Look, darling, you can come here until you find your feet.'

My spirits lifted. 'Really?'

'Of course. Just a moment,' he said quickly. He muffled the phone. I could hear Jo-Ann talking indignantly with an offended 'Excuse me . . . seriously . . . don't I have a say in it?' and my father replying in a low stern voice, 'Daughter . . . bad patch . . . least you can do . . .' Didn't he know the phone had a mute button?

The truth was, I couldn't imagine moving in with Dad and Jo-Ann. Nothing wrong with her, and probably they'd grown out of the constantly touching stage by now, but she was home all day and how would I find the space to write?

I was ready to hang up when my father's voice came clear again. He was slightly out of breath after the argument. 'Sorry about that.'

'It's okay. Thanks for the offer, Dad,' I said briskly, 'but I'll manage.'

'Oh . . . well done!' he said, sighing with relief as if he'd just kicked his work shoes off. Yeah, that Jo-Ann. She pinched. 'The next game's on Sunday; Spurs at home. Speak to you then.'

I got off the desk. My left leg had gone numb.

Checking through my emails, I found the one from Carol Burrows at London Lit offering me a job.

I composed a reply and told her I'd been reconsidering her generous offer of tutorial work of a few months previously, and I was now in a position to take her up on it and give something back to the community. (Coming up with a line like this is one of the benefits of writing fiction.)

Carol Burrows phoned me about ten minutes later to ask me if we could meet for lunch, adding apologetically that it would have to be in the college canteen – which was a relief, because canteens I could just about afford, if it turned out I was paying.

The London Literary Society is down Euston Road so I had a quick shower, dressed in the red suit, took a hardback copy of *Love Crazy* as a thank you, which was all I had to offer, walked to Kentish Town and caught the tube to Euston.

Carol Burrows was waiting for me by the barrier to the car park, wearing a fluttery green print tea dress and a leather biker jacket. She was her fifties and her curly brown hair was cut in a wedge; she looked feminine, stern and erudite, as if she belonged to the Bloomsbury set. After she'd given me a visitor's pass to hang around my neck we went inside, straight to the canteen. She had a burrito and chips and tea and I had fish and chips and a Diet Coke, and as she paid I helpfully carried the tray to a table.

'The full-time post of creative writing tutor has been filled,' she said, drawing up her chair.

'When? Since I spoke to you this morning?'

'No, a while ago.'

I changed my mind about giving her my book, but then she said, 'We're looking for someone to take an evening course. It's for writers who want to progress towards publication.'

'Hmm.' I opened my Coke can. Pffft!

She smiled, and delicately cut a chip into three with her knife and fork. Her eyes met mine. 'We all feel it would be a great fillip for the college to have you here.'

Philip? Oh yeah. I felt better already. 'How much would be . . .' I'd caught her way of speaking, '. . . the salary?'

When she told me, it sounded fair enough, until she added 'pro rata'.

34

Whatever happened I realised I was going to have to get rid of the flat and find somewhere else to live. I felt ill again. But at least this was guaranteed money in my hand, I reasoned, squirting ketchup on my plate. And it wasn't totally a copout. It was still about writing, still creative, and possibly – here's the smart bit – I might get inspiration from my students.

Readers sometimes feel that taking things from life is cheating, and that fiction should be something a writer has completely invented from some mysterious source deep in the imagination, but the truth is, all stories come from reality. Take Hemingway, for instance. He plunged straight into the action. Married young, fought wars, replaced his wives, insulted his friends and found himself with plenty of material to keep him published for years. Of course, his friends stopped talking to him once they recognised themselves in his books and he made his ex-wives utterly miserable and in the end he shot himself, but that's not the point. The point is, he got what he wanted, which was fame.

I might also get some new ideas from my students. This is not in any way plagiarism. Plagiarism is the 'stealing and publication of another author's language, thoughts, ideas or expressions and passing them off as one's own', according to Wikipedia and I'm giving the source so as not to be accused of plagiarism, which would be a horrible irony.

'There is some paperwork involved with the course in the form of progress sheets and end-of-term assessments,' Carol said, her delicate hands fluttering, 'but nothing too arduous.'

'I was expecting that,' I lied. Assessments were another name for school reports. 'I will take the job.'

She spent the rest of lunchtime asking for my professional opinion on books I hadn't read. Some I hadn't even heard of. I bluffed and mumbled around my food, pulling adjectives out of the air and even said that one of them was 'too wordy', which to my surprise she agreed with.

When we'd finished, she escorted me to the office, took my photograph, gave me my staff pass, showed me the fire escapes and the location of the library as she was contractually bound to do, and by the time we said goodbye I was feeling optimistic.

I'd had a hot lunch and found myself a job. Things were looking up.

CHAPTER FIVE

Writer's Block

Despite the trauma and conflict of my private life – like failure, disappointment and penury, which are all the traditional ingredients of a decent book – I still hadn't managed to come up with an idea for a heart-warming story. And I knew why. The one essential ingredient for writing was missing: boredom.

Boredom stimulates the imagination in a way that nothing else can. The mind hates a void with its intimations of mortality. On the minus side, if unchecked, it can fill itself with any old junk, as I found out the day I booked a session in a flotation tank at a central London spa for creative purposes.

I'd gone there to find my muse.

Trisha Ashley, a writer I admire, has a vain, bad-tempered, leather-clad muse named Lucifer and I thought it was time I got one for myself.

At the spa, surrounded by rolled-up towels, dizzied by rose petals and incense sticks, I listened as Michaela-in-the-white-uniform explained the process to me. The flotation tank was like a large water-filled cupboard. The lights would dim to black, the music would gradually fade to silence, and sensory deprivation would promote vivid colours, auditory hallucinations and creative ideas, the effects of which would last up to two weeks, until it was time for a top-up.

Michaela held the door while I climbed in and she promised to be back at five forty-five.

It was the longest forty minutes of my life.

Alone in the dark, once the music stopped and the white right angle of light around the door disappeared, I lost sense of the walls around me and suddenly felt as if I was drifting alone in a black sea. With sharks. No colour or auditory hallucinations, just the prickling awareness of large creatures biding their time beneath me. Nudging me. Getting a sense of what they were dealing with. To reassure myself, I groped for the walls to get my bearings and got saltwater in my eyes. It stung. I forced myself to relax but as I breathed out deeply I lost buoyancy and sank lower into the water and it flooded into my ear. How much water can an ear hold before it starts to weigh down your head, pulling you under?

Eyes throbbing, mind wandering, I realised I'd been in there longer than forty minutes. The water was getting cold. It had been quiet for a long time. I imagined Michaela forgetting all about me and taking off her white jacket, locking up and going home while I lay uncomfortably suspended in the thick and silent dark. She might only remember me when she was fighting to get on the tube. And what if she had a date? Yes, I was suddenly certain she did. That's why she forgot about me. If the date went well she might not remember me until morning, when she came in and found me hypothermic in the ice-cold water, half eaten by sharks.

On the scale of panic, from nought to ten, I was at this point about a five. I got to my knees and felt for the door handle, for reassurance. It wasn't where I expected it to be so I methodically smoothed my hands over the general area, panic rising swiftly to a seven when I couldn't find it. But why would there be a handle on the inside anyway? Michaela was supposed to be there. She'd promised to let me out.

My perception swiftly altered. I was no longer a tiny soul in limitless space. I was fully grown and locked in a watery cupboard getting claustrophobic.

'Help!' I shouted, deafening myself. 'Help!'

A bright light shone over me.

'You okay?' Michaela asked quizzically from behind me.

'You came back!' I said, crawling out.

'You've got another thirty minutes,' she said.

I looked at the clock and she was right, but nothing in the world would have induced me to go back in there. I haven't bothered looking for a muse since.

I threw my energy into cleaning the flat mostly for mercenary reasons – I needed the deposit money back. When Mark and I moved in, we'd photographed every flaw, every scuff on the skirting board, every chipped tile in the bathroom, because if there's one thing landlords hate, it's returning the deposit.

The creative power of boredom is something that the non-writer doesn't appreciate. They see you sitting there with your feet on the desk, staring out of the window, and assume that you have knocked off for the day, and ask what's for lunch. Obviously you're not ready to make lunch because you're writing. Then the person will point out that you're not writing, you're sitting there doing nothing. So you explain that the creative force is all going on up here, and you point to your head, and then they will tell you to take your creative force with them to the nearest McDonald's because they're starving.

After the argument, you find you've lost your train of thought completely.

Anyway, as well as cleaning I cancelled my phone contract

and walked to Camden and bought a cheap pay-as-you-go phone. Over a McCoffee I texted my new number to Kitty, my parents and Carol Burrows and once I'd done that I walked back home and sat at my desk and tried to think of good characters for my book. Characters are more important than plot. When you finish a book that you've really enjoyed, you never miss the plot. Nobody ever says that they enjoy the plot trajectory and wish they could have more of it; no, it's the characters that you long for. That feeling of closing the jacket knowing they've gone off without you and you're left alone as they disappear into the distance; that's the feeling that feeds a reader and forces her to find another book to get involved in.

I couldn't think of any character to write about. I wondered if I had writer's block. Herman Melville got it after writing *Moby-Dick*. Hemingway was terrified by it. F. Scott Fitzgerald suffered enormously with it. What if I was a one-book wonder like Margaret Mitchell, who, after writing *Gone with the Wind*, got run over in the street without having ever written a sequel?

The problem with writing is, the only way to be a writer is to write. This might seem obvious, but there are a lot of people who want to be writers without writing. They go on motivational courses and spend whole fortnights at writers' retreats in Crete or in timber lodges in Dorset, having food delivered while they wait for inspiration to strike. They join the BBC Book Club and ask authors interesting questions and take notes and listen to the broadcast a few weeks later. They go on holiday for research purposes and generally have a really good time without writing enough words to make a short story. I should know; I was currently one of these people.

Slightly depressed, I spent that evening googling house shares. I could afford to live in Barcelona and Malaga (but imagine the commute). I could share a bathroom with two vegetarians and a salamander in Ealing. I could hot-bed with students in Bethnal Green if I didn't mind going nocturnal and sleeping through the day.

And then I came across a website called the Caring Share.

The deal was, I could live with an old person for practically nothing and in return I would spend eight hours a week keeping them company and generally being helpful by doing 'light household duties', something I did anyway, for free. The website looked inviting – patterned china and cupcakes and old people with grateful white smiles. It was like moving in with Granny. I could offer advice on crossword clues.

I typed in my details. For references, I cited Kitty and Anthea, who could at least vouch for the fact I was honest and literate.

In anticipation, I advertised my possessions on Gumtree with the proviso 'Must Collect', and over the next two weeks I sold the lemon sofa and armchair, my IKEA desk and the small beech foldaway table with the four chairs that slotted into it.

It was like dismantling a dream, emptying that flat. Each night the place was hollower and less mine. The landlord brought people round to see it and the couples would stand by the window, arms around each other, taking in the view, and I wanted to kill them. And one day, scaffolding went up, and the safety netting bathed the flat in an alien green hue, like living in a pond.

The red and black Trek bike was still in the hall. I couldn't bring myself to sell it, even though it was the most valuable thing I possessed. It was a symbol of success; and I wondered if I could save money by riding it.

I carried it downstairs. It was very light – it weighed practically nothing. This is, in cycling terms, a sign of quality, apparently.

The night was cold, the kind of cold you get opening a fridge door, and in the west the turquoise sky was streaked with dirty dark blue clouds. I tucked my scarf into my parka and wheeled the bike onto the Heath, the wheel ticking, the chain clanking against my leg.

I couldn't sit on the seat because it was too high so I held onto a bollard for balance and pedalled a few yards, sitting on the crossbar. It really was a lovely bike. I dismounted in a controlled fall by a speed bump and wheeled it virtuously along the path which says 'No Cycling' and took it for a walk before I went back to the flat.

When Mark and I moved in together, I'd imagined life was going to get better and better and better; all summits and no valleys; I'd imagined us soaring relentlessly upwards, propelled by happiness, trailing fame and fortune.

I hadn't imagined it coming to this, being here alone, clearing the place out by myself.

Love. What was it all about?

I thought about my dad and Jo-Ann's unlikely alliance and whether love amounted to nothing more than finding someone you could watch Netflix with.

That's what dating apps should be about – matching up couples and box sets. 'I have *The Wire* and I'll raise you *Better Call Saul*.' 'I have *Happy Valley* and *Miranda*. Sorry. It's not going to work out.'

A few days later I was delighted to get a call from the Caring Share about a place in Knightsbridge with a widow named Mrs Leadbetter who had room in her apartment for someone mature. Was I mature? I reassured them about my maturity and general common sense and I agreed to go there that afternoon to meet Mrs Leadbetter in person.

Knightsbridge! Harvey Nicks and Harrods! I was instantly cheered by the news. I've always wanted to live in Knightsbridge

– who wouldn't? We could go walking in Hyde Park. And forget the baking, we could go out for afternoon tea.

Mrs Leadbetter's flat was in a small sixties block at the back of Harrods, in an architectural style totally different from its neighbours.

I buzzed her bell and she told me to come up in the lift. It was a very small lift with no mirrors. Personally, I like a mirror in a lift. It's the last chance to prepare before meeting someone, but as this one didn't have one I had to hope for the best.

Mrs Leadbetter was waiting for me by her open door. She looked very old and withered, with thinning white hair over a candy-pink scalp, but her navy velour tracksuit and white trainers gave her a jaunty air of sportsmanship. She was scrutinising me with the same thoroughness.

'You're too young,' she said.

'I'm not that young,' I reassured her. 'It's just good genes.'

She studied my face. 'Are you over fifty-five?'

'No.' My genes are not *that* good.

'I need someone over fifty-five to come with me to the Over Fifty-Five Club. I told the Caring Share I wanted someone mature.'

'Oh . . . I thought they meant sensible.'

'Come in anyway. You might as well have a cup of tea while you're here. Have you come far?'

'Parliament Hill Fields.'

'I used to watch the Blitz from there,' she said. 'It was like Bonfire Night every night.'

I was right. She was very old.

Her sofa was draped with a cream mohair throw, and as I sat down the hairs magnetically attached themselves to my black trousers.

Mrs Leadbetter made the tea and sat next to me with the perky curiosity of the elderly. 'Tell me something, why would a good-looking girl like you want to live with an old dear like me?' she asked.

So I told her the whole tragic story from the beginning and felt depressed again.

She was sympathetic about my rejected book and my lost love and she offered some advice. 'Find yourself a husband with a house and a good job.'

'It's not that easy these days to find someone to love you.'

She looked surprised. 'Don't worry about looking for someone to love *you*. Find someone to love,' she said.

'Yeah – I've tried that and it didn't work,' I told her.

As I said goodbye I felt disappointed that my room with her hadn't worked out. I wanted to be settled; I wanted to go *home* again – wherever that was.

The following evening I went to see a bedsit in Mornington Crescent.

Mornington Crescent is that inconvenient stop between Camden Town and Euston on the Northern line, Charing Cross branch, and a road at the wrong end of Camden High Street. However, it had a charm of its own and, what's more, a Burma Railway Memorial.

I got there at six. It was a wet night and the rain made golden haloes around the street lights.

The building had the faded ghost of a sign stencilled above the front door: 'The Grand Hotel'. A flake of red paint peeled off the front door as I banged the knocker, not a good sign, and I heard footsteps thudding down the stairs.

This thin guy opened it, shirtless, early twenties, smoking and toting a Spanish guitar. 'Hey! I'm Louis, come on up,' he said, taking me up the uncarpeted stairs to the first floor.

On the landing, the energy-saving light was losing the battle against the dark.

With a flourish, Louis showed me into what he described grandly as 'a place to call your own', which was thoroughly deodorised by cigarette smoke. Strung across the room was a pink sheet hanging from curtain wire, which, with a candle behind it, cast a rosy glow.

'See that partition? Behind there it's all mine. This here is your end,' he said, hoisting his jeans from his hips to his waist and pointing to an alcove fitted with a single bed and an orange Anglepoise lamp. 'Want to take a look? Get an idea of the potential?'

He pulled back the 'partition'. Most of his end was taken up with a king-size mattress. Beer cans doubled up as tables – handy for his phone charger and that sort of thing.

'You can do what you like with your own space,' he said cheerfully. 'Knock yourself out. Feel free.'

The one thing that kept me standing there was the fact that I could afford it.

'And this way to the ensuite,' Louis announced, quite the joker. He threw open the bathroom door.

I looked around, which took all of two seconds. 'It's not quite what I was looking for,' I told him. 'Basically, we'd be sharing a room.'

'It's cheap though, isn't it?' he pointed out, to tempt me. 'See, what it is, my girlfriend's just left me and I need someone to share the rent.' He played a plaintive chord on his guitar.

We had more in common than I thought.

'Not keen on the partition, am I right?'

'Right.' I stood there thinking: this is what it's like to have no options. I'd never experienced it before; never want to again. 'No offence, but I'll keep looking.'

'No worries,' he said philosophically, and he stood cheerfully on the gloomy landing and strummed an accompaniment on his guitar as I descended the stairs.

I caught the bus home.

The evening stretched ahead, long and empty, and I opened the window, breathing in the cool night air to calm myself – fresh air costs nothing. Through the green netting I saw two buses idling at the terminus, their destination, Victoria, all lit up. Behind them the Heath was dark and humped with bushes. A drunk meandered along the pavement, shouting hoarsely into the night.

I was anxious, restless with adrenaline and at a loose end. I wanted to move time on, to fast-forward to happier days when all would be well again. I wanted the hard stuff to be over. I wanted to leave the flat now and move somewhere safe. I wanted it all done with and finished.

In this restless frame of mind, I wandered into the bedroom and opened Mark's end of the wardrobe for the first time in months.

His clothes queued calmly on the brass rail in tasteful, ice-cream colours of cream and beige. His Paul Smith suits, shirts, moleskin trousers, khaki cargo pants, all radiating the faint smell of his aftershave. My throat tightened and my heart softened. Mark's stuff. I'd loved those clothes when he'd loved them. I'd loved them when he loved me.

I took a shirt out of the wardrobe and held it up – it was creased around the tails, where he'd tucked it in. I sniffed it and then put it around my shoulders and tied the arms around my neck, as if he was hugging me from behind. The sleeves were cool and soft. I could smell his deodorant on them.

Angry at my self-indulgent sentimentality, I dashed into the kitchen, tearing a bin bag off a roll. I unhooked his clothes, setting the coat hangers jangling, and stuffed them into it like the rubbish that they were. I put my coat on, slung the bag over my shoulder and headed to the Oxfam Clothing Bank near the Forum in Kentish Town. Shifting the heavy bag to the other shoulder, I passed the school, still lit up. On the top floor, a man in a high-vis jacket was operating a floor-polisher with one hand. I slowed down by the rug shop – the Orientalist has a life-sized model of a camel outside. It's been there for years and nobody has stolen it or vandalised it or even put a traffic cone on its head, which tells you something.

My destination, the recycling bins, were surrounded by interesting stuff – a folded buggy, a clothes airer, and some lengths of pine which, reconstituted, could be a bookcase. Refusing to be diverted I opened the lid and, with a grunt, hoisted the bin bag up to stuff it in and hesitated on the brink.

Just do it.

Listened to the *thwump* of its soft landing.

I flexed my shoulders and caught my breath. Then I looked inside the bin, suffering from sudden separation anxiety, but the bin bag was lost in the dark. Too late.

CHAPTER SIX

Plateau

I had reached what publishers call a plateau. I couldn't write. My worries took up all the space. Time was going by and I still had no story.

Little did I know I was about to experience a turning point. Publishers like these – the more the better.

It was sunny, one of those autumn days when the sun is still warm on the skin but the shadows are chilly, and I thought the fresh air might stimulate my brain. I was walking on the Heath, distracted from my reflections by a parakeet screeching overhead like a haunted door in the kind of horror film that goes straight to DVD.

Parakeets are everywhere now, flying around with their long pointy tails and screaming hysterically, but really, it's all show because they have little to scream about. Parakeets in London have no natural predators. Is it because they're green and look too vegetarian for raptors? I walked past the boating pond. The ducks were fighting over a M&S prawn sandwich. You know that research that concluded ducks prefer kale? Not in London, they don't. London birds prefer fast food. But only the gulls eat chilli.

My phone rang and it was Kitty, asking how the writing was coming along.

I watched the ducks moving their squabbles into the reeds. 'I'm still at the planning stage,' I said.

'Well,' she said, 'keep at it. The reason I rang is, I got a call. Someone's looking for you.'

'Who?'

'He didn't give his name. He said he was your hero and you'd know who he was.'

I felt as if I'd been Tasered.

And then I felt a sudden rush of euphoria.

Thank you, God! 'Did he leave a number?'

'He did. Shall I text it to you?'

'Yes please.' I stood on the Heath flooded with happiness and laughing to myself. Mark was looking for me. I'd changed my phone number but he'd tracked me down. He *cared*! I stared at my phone and when the message pinged it was like having a winning lottery ticket in my hand.

I'd *known* this was going to happen!

It was preordained and I was generous in my happiness, gloating over my good fortune, smiling at people as they passed me. It felt like the glory of life had suddenly been revealed to me! I walked up Kite Hill and the grass was greener, the sky bluer, the passers-by more glamorous than they'd ever been before. I was seeing everything with new eyes.

I leant against a tree, feeling the cold bark through my jacket, filled with gratitude at my good fortune. I thought of Mark's Trek bike fondly. What amazing good luck it was that I hadn't sold it! I realised at that moment that I'd misunderstood my motivation. I hadn't kept it because it was his; I'd kept it *for* him.

I dialled the number. The phone rang, once, twice; my heart was thundering and then:

CHAPTER SEVEN

Turning Point

'Jack Buchanan.'

What the? *Who?*

What kind of trick was this?

My glittering bauble of happiness shattered into bits, irrevocably broken.

I squashed my bag against my face and screamed into it. It had all been a delusion. I was such an *idiot*. The worst thing about losing an imaginary future is that the lights go out and you stare into the blackness and you can't see anything there. There's no destination. It is a bleak and frightening feeling. Time heals, they say, without adding that it moves in a slow and arduous way, like sludge, and the only way to time-travel is to sleep.

'Hello? Hello?'

'It's Lana Green,' I said, unable to hide my frustration. 'My agent said you were trying to get hold of me.'

'Yes! I don't know if you remember me – I met you at the Edinboro Castle. You're a writer in need of a hero. I'm the dark-haired guy in the orange sweatshirt. I put that in Rush-Hour Crush. Don't you read the *Metro*?'

'What do you want?' I asked, too disappointed to make an effort, watching dogs snuffle past my line of vision.

For some reason my lack of interest and gloomy tones didn't put him off.

'I emailed you on your author's website but when you didn't reply I called your agent because she was in the acknowledgements. Listen. I've been paragliding.'

'So?'

'So, if you're still looking for a hero, I'm reapplying for the role.'

'I don't want—'

'I've never done anything like that in my life. I've never felt so alive! Or,' he added soberly, 'so close to death. Look on YouTube if you don't believe me.'

'I do believe you.' *I just don't care.*

'Well look at it anyway. By the way, just want to reassure you I haven't suddenly grown boobs – that's a water balloon down my shirt.'

It was like being licked by a labrador. 'Jack, I'm not—'

'Yes, I know, you're going to say that going paragliding once is not enough.'

'Actually that's not what I was going to say.'

'Good! Let's pick a date. I'll try my best to be aloof. What are you doing on Saturday?'

There is nothing worse than a person who is trying to engage you in conversation when you don't feel like talking. Just at that moment I would have given anything for aloofness. It's what gave Mark an air of superiority.

Women think that the one quality they want in a man is someone they can talk with. Bad mistake. Nowhere in the whole history of romantic fiction has a woman fallen in love with a talker. Talking is what girl friends are for. My advice is, always go for a man you fancy the pants off, it's as simple as that.

52

However – what was there to lose? He might even buy me lunch and I'd get a free meal out of it.

'All right,' I sighed. 'I'll bring my notebook.'

'Great! Twelve o'clock at the Edinboro Castle,' he declared. Then he added in an undertone, 'How did that sound?'

I smiled despite myself. 'Decisive and masterful,' I said.

CHAPTER EIGHT

Words, Words, Words

Some people never forget a face. I'm not one of them. I couldn't remember what Jack Buchanan looked like, other than the general impression of a person who'd just got out of bed. But when I got off the bus in Delancey Street he was leaning against the white gatepost of the Edinboro Castle. He was wearing a lime-green jacket, his dark hair ruffling in the breeze.

'Hey!' he said, taking his hands out of his pockets.

'Yeah, hey!'

'You came!' He grinned at me.

I was surprised that he thought I wouldn't. It wasn't as if I had anything better to do or any other invitations, but there's nothing quite as satisfying as exceeding someone's expectations.

'How is your new book coming along?' he asked.

'Basically . . . not well. To get creative, you need to be ill or bored.'

'Is that so?'

'Andrew Motion drinks Lemsip when he's writing. It's to fool his mind into believing he's got a cold.' Just behind Jack

I could see the menus pinned to the gateposts in gilt frames. I have a lot of faith in a menu in a gilt frame. 'Are we going in?'

'Well, what I thought was, we could walk to the Hub Sports Pavilion, have a coffee and then go to the boating lake and hire a boat. I'll row.'

I fancied a glass of wine and something to eat in the pub, but I had to give him credit for coming up with a plan.

'Or,' he said, 'we could hire a pedalo, but that doesn't seem the kind of thing a hero would do, right?'

I thought it over as we turned the corner and walked past the flower shop through the scent of lilies. A train rumbled beneath us.

'True. A hero would have a jet ski.'

He laughed. 'Yes. I read your book.'

'You did? I can't believe you bought it!'

'Well . . . I didn't exactly buy it. My stepmother took it from the library. But it has given me a rough idea of what you're looking for in a hero.'

The suspense was killing me. 'So what did you think of it?' I asked casually.

'Time-consuming,' he said. 'Not the book – I mean, love in general.'

I looked at him curiously. 'You've never been in love, have you?'

'Me? No. All that uncertainty, does she love me or not, and then the misunderstandings and other complications . . . I thought you got the title perfectly: *Love Crazy* – I like the way you identified it as a kind of insanity that makes people behave completely out of character. I'm more of a logical thinker. I like things to be straightforward.'

'You got all that from my book?'

'Nah. Mostly from life. My parents broke up when I was young.'

'Yeah? Mine too.'

'How old were you?'

'Eighteen. You?'

'Eight. It killed my mother.'

Mine, too, I almost said but then I looked up and his face was expressionless, as if he didn't want his thoughts to show, so I held back my comment in case he meant it literally.

Of course, when I asked him what he thought of the book, what I actually wanted to know was whether he'd enjoyed it. Writers are strangely needy that way. Last year I went to the Radio Four book club and sat next to a woman named Minna Howard, who was also a writer (it was research, in case we were ever asked to do it ourselves), and the highly acclaimed guest author David Mitchell responded to her praise with such warmth and delight that I was convinced he was her ex-lover. Turned out she'd never seen him before in her life. He was just deeply grateful for her kind words.

We crossed at the lights and stepped into bright sunlight at Gloucester Gate. The sky was a pale, frigid blue. Attached to the railings was a plaque showing St Pancras being attacked by pumas. We crossed at the stone grotto drinking fountains where Matilda the bronze milkmaid posed with her bucket and he asked: 'So, what happened to Marco Ferrari?'

I blushed. Well this was uncomfortable. When I'd written *Love Crazy* I'd assumed Mark and I would be together forever so I'd never imagined this situation arising – going out with a guy who knew all about my past.

I've always been obsessed with telling the truth and, although I see it as a positive character trait, other people don't necessarily see it as a good thing. But I've stuck with it because it's become my way of rebelling. No one can argue with the truth.

The way I looked at it, this meant that I was also going to

have to explain that Mark had dumped me and it was way too soon to disillusion him – I always prefer people to get disillusioned with me in their own good time.

However, the habit of a lifetime is hard to break.

'We broke up,' I said, and glanced up at him, blinking – in the sunlight his lime-green jacket was hard on the eyes.

'I knew it!' Jack said. 'So, what happened? Did you get bored with all that adventure and the excitement?'

I liked the way he assumed I'd been the one to end it. 'We'd always kept our independence; I guess it was an extreme version of that.'

He pressed the button on the crossing. 'Independence to the point of separation?' He gave me a look that was both incredulous and empathetic at the same time. 'And now you're looking for a new hero to write about.'

I wanted to say something witty and trivial in reply. We crossed the road and while I was working on it, Jack said, 'So, with the pedalo you really need two to pedal, that's why I thought we could get a rowing boat and I could row you by myself.'

'Have you rowed before?'

'No, but I watch the boat race every year and I think it's all about the rhythm. Brisk and steady.'

I laughed. There was an endearing quality about him; something normal and nice, and trust me, they weren't attributes that I ever thought I'd rate in a guy. We walked in step alongside the Zoological Society of London's railings, keeping a respectable distance away from each other.

Ahead of us was the park. In the golden glow of the autumn sunshine, the grass was bright green, and the trees striped it with muted shadows. A glossy brown boxer dog bounded across our path chasing pigeons and two children raced their brightly coloured scooters towards us with speed and aplomb.

Joggers overtook mothers pushing buggies and I thought about Jack's comment that love was time-consuming. I was just going to ask him about it when his phone started to ring right at that moment.

He took it out of his jacket, stared at the number and frowned. For a moment I thought he wasn't going to answer it. He let it ring a couple more times and then he sighed.

'Sorry, Lana, I'd better take this.'

'Go ahead.'

I did that polite thing of staring at the horse chestnut trees in the distance and pretending not to listen as he said, 'Hello? Nancy. Slow down – what do you mean, a lot of men? John the police officer?' He flicked a glance at me. 'Okay, okay, put him on. Hello? Yes,' he said irritably, 'I can hear that she's fine. No, I'm not worried.'

He turned his back to me as he looked across the park. 'A *sex* offender? What's he done? What do you mean you can't tell me? Okay. Put Nancy back on. Hi, Nancy, it's Jack again. Listen, I'm out with a friend at the moment. I'll call you later.' His face was set as he turned back to me and tucked his phone away.

Obviously I was intrigued by what I'd heard. I hadn't been a journalist for five years without knowing a good story when I heard one.

'Problem?' I asked lightly.

'My stepmother's had a drink with a sex offender. That's all they would tell me.'

'How did she know he was a sex offender? And how did the police get involved?'

'Don't ask me.' He shrugged. 'This always happens,' he said grimly. 'Every time. It's as if – anyway, forget it, let's crack on. Do you mind if we miss out the coffee and go straight to the boating lake?'

He strode off up the Broad Walk without waiting for an answer and I hurried to catch up with him as he cut across the grass.

I grabbed his arm. 'Look, Jack, we don't have to do the boating thing. We can go another day, I don't mind.'

'No,' he said stubbornly, 'it's fine. I've *planned* it.' But he stopped walking, his eyes narrowed with indecision. He rubbed his hands over his face and his grey eyes met mine and held. 'I'm sorry. You're right. I *should* go.'

'Yes.' I was more disappointed than I'd expected. He was easy to be with and he made me smile, but I could see the relief in his face and I knew that for once I'd said the right thing. 'I hope you get things sorted out.'

Behind the railings, through gaps in the foliage, I could see the penguins standing at the edge of their blue pool, bracing themselves to dive, wings held at the ready before taking the plunge. 'Well, thanks. It's been—'

'You could come with me,' he said.

'Really?' Our day out wasn't over! 'Okay.' I didn't need asking twice.

We turned around and headed the other way, towards the road. The crossing beeped and the cars stood at bay and the green man showed, and we walked over the canal together even though the fake date was over and we weren't going boating any more.

We caught the C11 bus from Adelaide Road and stood in the wheelchair area, crushed together. He was taller than Mark and I was eye-level with his throat. It was a nice throat; smooth and strong.

'Your stepmother – did she break up your parents' marriage?'

'Yes. She was pretty ruthless about it. And my father was weak.'

'How did she get to be your responsibility?'

He gave a brief laugh. 'After my mother died I went to live with her and my dad. Then he died, so now it's just Nancy and me. She was in her late fifties when she and my dad met so she doesn't have children of her own.'

I thought about the way he'd said that heartbreak had killed his mother. But despite all that, he was still looking out for Nancy. I tried to imagine being that dutiful towards Jo-Ann and failed miserably.

We got off at South End Green and walked up South Hill Park. The house was four-storey, red-bricked Victorian; it backed onto the other side of Parliament Hill Fields. I could probably see it from my window. A police car was parked up against the kerb. Jack rang the doorbell and a community police support officer answered the door; she had short dark hair and an attitude that indicated we shouldn't mess with her.

'We've taken a statement,' she told Jack in the hallway.

To the side of the chandelier above her head loomed a huge oil painting of an old lady with a skinny black and white dog. They were looking into an empty cupboard with some dismay. It seemed a strange choice of picture. I had built up an image of Nancy as an older woman clinging onto her youth with yoga, Pilates and Botox; I'd imagined she'd go for something more modern, an abstract.

'She seems fine, but she's vulnerable.'

'She's eighty,' Jack said.

'Yes, but she's got no sense of self-preservation. She started a fight with a police officer who tried to take away her drink.'

I suppressed a smirk – but too late.

'One day someone is going to hit her back,' the CPSO warned me.

'You don't know that,' Jack said. 'You're just seeing the worst-case scenario.'

'Trust me, this came close to being that scenario.'

'I still don't understand what happened. What's the big deal?' Jack asked.

'I can't say.'

'Well now, *you* can't tell me and *she* can't tell me. Fuh . . . lipping . . .'

'Okay, the guy's a gerontophile. Rules of his licence – don't engage with old ladies AT ALL. But they were in a pub having a drink, which is engaging, so we arrested him.'

In the background a lavatory flushed, and then a belligerent voice called out: 'Who's there? What are you all doing, conspiring in my hall?'

Jack's stepmother hurried towards us, dressed in a burst of colour – a yolk-yellow cardigan and a yellow, grey and black skirt.

To my astonishment I recognised her immediately. She was Nancy Ellis Hall, the novelist. My mother and I had gone to listen to her at the Hay Festival when she was shortlisted for the Orange Prize and she had signed a book for us with the inscription 'Be what you are'; which pleased my mother enormously, although she said it didn't apply to me.

I could have sworn Jack had just said his stepmother 'wrote a bit'.

I was suddenly self-conscious standing in the hallway at such an awkward moment, with a police officer and some kind of sex scandal going on – I still wasn't sure how the police had come into it.

'You! Who *are* you?' she asked me crossly, pointing her finger inches from my face.

'Lana Green,' I said, thinking she might recognise the name as she'd taken my book out of the library. I felt a shiver of intense happiness. Nancy Ellis Hall had read my book!

'What have you come as?'

I didn't understand the question, but I had a stab at it anyway. 'A visitor.'

'Oh. In that case, come on in and sit in the parlour, said the spider to the fly. Not you,' she said to Jack.

'Nancy, it's me.'

'Oh! Well you'd better watch yourself because they will be after you if you talk to me. I met a nice young man today, and these policemen sprang out of nowhere while we were having a drink and took him away.'

'*VUL-NER-ABLE*,' the CPSO mouthed from behind her.

'And she' – Nancy turned and pointed at the officer – 'was jealous because he was taking an interest in me.'

'I was *not* jealous. That man is a known offender,' the officer said tightly.

'Don't be ridiculous! He didn't offend me in the slightest. And that constable tried to take my glass of wine before I'd finished it.' She turned to me crossly. 'What have you got to say about that?'

'Very bad-mannered of him,' I said.

'Exactly. They think they know better, but I've been – what have I been?' she asked Jack.

'A novelist and a feminist,' Jack said.

'Exactly.' Her mood lifted. 'I'm awfully good at it, you know,' she said happily, and as she smiled I noticed the gaps in her teeth.

The officer's phone rang. 'I'll take this outside,' she said. 'John!'

The police officer appeared from another room. He seemed to know Jack. He said he'd taken a statement from Mrs Ellis Hall and he raised his eyebrows meaningfully – although exactly what it meant I wasn't sure – and that they would be in touch.

'So, this guy you arrested, what's happening with him now?' Jack asked.

'Sorry,' John replied. 'I can't tell you anything at this point.' He was interrupted by Nancy Ellis Hall trying to shoo him out of the door with sweeping movements.

'Off you go! Off you go!'

Once the officers had left, shutting the door firmly behind them, she turned back to look at us with intense curiosity. 'Are you two sweethearts?'

Jack glanced at me. 'Potentially,' he replied.

Unexpectedly, I blushed. Potentially? It's always nice to get a compliment.

'In that case, I'm so glad you've dropped by,' she said graciously. 'I do feel I add to the happiness of the occasion.'

While Jack made the tea, Nancy Ellis Hall took me into her parlour. It was a writer's paradise.

The room was large and high-ceilinged, with books everywhere, decorated in a dusty pink with polished mahogany furniture bearing silver-framed photographs. My heart leapt to see her posing with Beryl Bainbridge in a cloud of cigarette smoke and sitting in a field at Hay, sandwiched between an elderly Molly Keane and Germaine Greer. She had a leatherbound, gold-tooled visitors' book. And there was a colour photograph in an oval frame of her cheek to cheek with a young, dark-haired man who looked familiar but whose name I didn't know.

'Who's this?' I asked her, pointing to it.

'Yes . . .' She picked it up and looked at it closely. 'Yes, now I'll tell you exactly who it is. This is a lonely young man that I met in a bookshop. The police officers came in, hundreds of them, and pounced on him, and they tried to take my wine from me.' She put the frame back on the table and sat in the armchair. 'Ooh!' she said, admiring her own yellow-patterned skirt as though she was seeing it for the first time.

'Mrs Ellis Hall,' I said. 'Can I ask you, are you writing anything at the moment?'

'Yes. Yes you can,' she replied.

I waited for her to elaborate, but she was still looking at me patiently. 'Go ahead,' she prompted.

'Er – are you working on a new book?'

'Yes! I have all my notes. I never throw anything away.'

'What's your advice on how to start a new book? What's the secret?'

She didn't even have to think about it. 'Words, words, words!' she said, waving her hand in a dramatic flourish.

Jack opened the door with his foot and came in with three mugs rattling on a tray. The three of us sat on the largest, softest sofa and while we drank our coffee Nancy told us the story of the interrupted drink with a stranger a few more times, with creative variations; editing it in the retelling. Then she began to tear squares from a peach toilet roll, counting each one carefully, like a meditation.

I looked around at the bookshelves, hoping to see the library copy of my own book so that I could ask her opinion of it. I spotted it on top of a small pile of Jiffy bags. Just a minute – was that a photograph of a young Kingsley Amis?

My heart soared. I loved this room. And I loved her. She was an inspiration, and surrounded by literature I was, for the first time in a long while, fired up with the urge to write.

Words, words, words!

Jack was quiet when we left.

The sun was low and golden and it was cold in the blue shadows of the buildings. He turned his jacket collar up and shoved his hands into his pockets.

'What did you think?' he asked as we walked past Hampstead Heath station on our way to the bus stop.

'You didn't tell me she was Nancy Ellis Hall the novelist; you just said she wrote a bit,' I said indignantly.

'I didn't know if you'd have heard of her. She hasn't been published for years.'

'My mother was a fan, being a feminist and things. She signed a book for us once. Wow . . . So she's taken to biting people.'

He gave me a strange look. 'She hasn't taken it up as a hobby. She just gets frustrated when she can't find the words. It's the illness.'

'What's wrong with her?'

'She's got dementia.' He pressed his hand over his forehead. 'It's here, this is where the damage is. In the frontal lobe.'

'Dementia.' I couldn't associate the word with the woman I'd just met. It didn't fit my idea of it as a disease that gradually erodes the personality, the sense of self. Nancy Ellis Hall was *all* personality. 'Apart from a bit of repetition she seems perfectly fine. I mean – she's even writing a new book,' I said.

'She's always writing,' Jack said with a flicker of a smile. 'She gets edgy when she doesn't.'

'I know the feeling,' I said ruefully. 'It wears off after a while.' I couldn't wait to tell my mother that I'd been in her house. 'She's lively, isn't she?'

'That she is.' He looked at me, his eyes troubled. 'Do you think she's vulnerable?'

'Not particularly – I can't imagine anyone being brave enough to mug her.'

'That's the problem,' he said sadly. 'She isn't scared of anyone. And according to the CPSOs, it makes her vulnerable. If she stayed in all the time, being fearful, that would be fine. How does that make any sense?'

I shook my head in sympathy.

'All their worries are theoretical anyway,' he went on. 'People are nicer than you think – they can see that she's odd and generally they make allowances for her. And that guy she met, she didn't take him home, they went for a drink in the pub. She's not stupid and she's done nothing wrong. Police officers, they see bad things happening all the time and I get that. But most people live perfectly safe lives.' He glanced at me. 'You know what the secret is?'

'No. What?'

'Always keep under the radar.'

We stood by the bus stop and watched the bus creep slowly down the hill towards us in the line of traffic. I was going home – it was too late to go boating now.

'Where do you live?' I asked him.

'Mornington Terrace,' he said. 'You?'

'Parliament Hill Fields. The other side of the Heath from Nancy's.' We were heading in opposite directions.

The C11 bus pulled up alongside us, gusting hot air from the brakes.

'I'm sorry our fake date didn't work out,' he said.

The bus stopped and the doors slid open. I tapped my Oyster card and turned round to wave goodbye. Didn't work out? He had a famous literary stepmother!

I gave him my brightest smile to remember me by, because: 'There's always a next time,' I said.

CHAPTER NINE

A New Dawn

After that small and intense burst of excitement, I was back to my depressing real life again.

By September my footsteps echoed hollowly in the bare flat and it no longer felt like home. I'd also sold the wardrobe, so I moved the Trek bike from the hall into the bedroom to use as a clothing rail. I was writing, sitting, eating and sleeping on my bed. The whole thing gave me a strong sense of nostalgic déjà vu – it was like being in the camper van again.

Potential tenants were turning up with tape measures and questions about the energy rating and how often the bins were emptied and whether the bedroom was soundproof – what were they thinking of doing in there?

I answered their questions resentfully. Especially annoying were the couples who stood happily radiating hearts in the middle of the room, holding hands and trying to imagine what the place would look like without me in it.

In one of the interludes I sat on my bed and opened my laptop and found an email from Carol Burrows with details of the Towards Publication: Romantic Prose class which was starting the following week. I downloaded the attachment. It was a list of names, but names are sometimes all you need. Call me name-ist, but take Joan Parker for instance. She had to be over seventy, right? And Arthur Shepherd; he's going to be over seventy-five – or under ten. I didn't have much to go on with Kathryn Smart and Neveen Barsome, but that was the least of my worries because I realised I only had four students.

Four.

That felt like failure in itself. It seemed I wasn't such a fillip after all.

I lay on top of my bed with my hands behind my head and stared at a piece of silver tinsel that looked like a spider, left over from the previous tenants. I blew at it and a moment later it quivered frantically. I closed my eyes and listened to the night noises: a police siren, a helicopter circling the Heath. This was it; this was rock bottom.

I went into fight or flight mode and let the tears roll. Despite scientific research which has proven that crying ensures high levels of stress hormones don't overwhelm the system, I didn't feel any better for it and after twenty minutes or so I gave it up as a bad job.

As a diversion, I opened my laptop and looked up the video of Jack Buchanan on YouTube. There he was with the harness strapped on him, a grey cliff edge ahead of him and a forest below, talking into the camera.

'Are you ready, Joe? How to be a hero, part one. This,' he said, his face filling the screen, 'is a balloon full of dye. We're going to drop it on the target. I've been told to put it some-where safe. Which,' he said, tucking it into his sweater, 'is apparently down here.' He grinned into the lens. 'Okay, this is it.'

Jack was strapped in front of another guy and they ran up

to the cliff edge and with a triumphant yell they tumbled off it. The parachute billowed in a blur of colour, jerking them up, swaying and getting smaller, Jack's screams fading, and they flew over the autumnal trees in silence apart from the low chuckling of the cameraman tracking their progress.

It made me smile. Actually, smiling is a much better antidote to misery than crying. I've never read any scientific research on why cheering up makes a person feel so much better than losing protein from tears – I suppose it's not obscure enough to publish a paper on.

I googled Jack Buchanan and found a lot of entries for a Scottish actor who'd died in 1957. Then I remembered he had an IT company, and I found him at AFB, Apps for Business. There was a red-filtered photograph of a modern office with a group of people looking engaged, Jack in profile.

All those hours that we'd been together and he hadn't mentioned it. Usually that's the first thing a guy talks about – he sets out his credentials; occupation, car, house. Not Jack. I knew his cynical views on love and a bit about his slightly dysfunctional family and I'd met his famous, ruthless stepmother but I knew almost nothing about his daily life.

Balancing my laptop on my knees, I looked up Nancy Ellis Hall's entry on Wikipedia. At the top of the entry there was a picture of Nancy with her chin in her hand in a way that was meant to denote deep creative thought. Her face was tilted away from the photographer, but her eyes were fixed firmly on the camera. Her direct look subverted the pose of the dreamy author. It was the one they used on the jacket of *The Dent in the Pillow*, which she'd signed for my mother and me: 'Be what you are'.

Her bestsellers, written in the 70s and 80s during the second wave of feminism, were mostly about problems particular to

71

women – lack of affordable childcare, discrimination in the workplace, subservience to men. She was the ideal liberation feminist, living life on her own terms without a man to clean up for or be undermined by; totally liberated from sexual culture – the main theme of *A Dent in the Pillow*, published in 1996.

Which made what followed next all the more surprising.

At the age of fifty-eight, Nancy Ellis Hall fell in love for the first time. Richard Buchanan, her love interest, was thirty-four, married, with a young son. His wife, Penelope, had brought him to Nancy's book-reading in Foyles in the hope that Nancy's message of liberation would get through to him.

It wasn't her best plan, as it turned out.

Richard and Nancy quickly became inseparable and his marriage ended in acrimony. For many of her followers, that was not just a sexual betrayal but a betrayal of the sisterhood; sales of her books plummeted and she gave up being published to – how's this for a surprise twist? – devote her time to her new husband.

Penelope Buchanan died four years later of heart disease and Richard Buchanan died suddenly in 2013.

I read it through again, thinking of the 'young son', Jack. Jack had as much reason to hate Nancy as his mother did, but here he was, years later, looking out for her. I understood where his cynicism about love stemmed from. Four lives left in bits. What I didn't understand was his ongoing kindness towards the woman who had caused the damage.

It was a long time since I'd taken an interest in anything outside my own problems but suddenly, despite everything, I had a vaguely hopeful feeling, the kind that comes after a bout of illness, the realisation that there might be a future for me after all. New ideas seemed to shimmer out of reach but not too distantly.

Meeting Nancy suddenly seemed propitious, significant, like some catalyst in the novel-writing process that I hadn't been aware of before. Life wasn't easy. It was full of surprises, like the gun on the mantelpiece whose importance only becomes apparent later in the narrative. Me being the gun, obviously.

So what, Green? chipped in my self-esteem at this point. *Where are you going with this?*

Well, I didn't know yet.

But look at these coincidences. Coincidences are not really encouraged in fiction; they're seen as a bit of a copout. However, I'd met Jack in the Edinboro Castle because my book got turned down and then I'd met Nancy, who years before had signed our book, because she was involved in an incident on our first fake date. And since seeing Jack's video, I liked the whole concept of 'How to Be a Hero'. It was a great title. See what I mean? I had all the ingredients of *something*. It was up to me what story I told.

Lack of money meant that I had no one to talk to and no distractions for three days and as a result I came up with a decent and upbeat outline of the story about this nice guy who wants to be a hero.

Writing lifted me out of my bare, comfortless surroundings and I realised this was obviously why writers traditionally thrive in an attic – what else is there to do?

CHAPTER TEN

Perseverance

On my first evening as tutor at the London Literary Society I wanted to look professional but approachable, and humble but superior. That was the look I was going for. I wore my red suit (my only suit) and leopard-print flats to walk to the college. It took longer than I thought and it started to rain. Never trust a weather forecast. I took a short cut via Euston station, dodged the six-lane traffic on Euston Road and ran to the London Lit building. Flashing my pass at the security guy who waved me past, I hurried to meeting room nine on the ground floor.

Result! I was the first there. I hung my jacket on the radiator to dry and collapsed on the long grey table with relief, damp, breathless, my heart beating so fast I could feel it in my eyeballs, and in a mild state of panic.

Room nine was a long, thin room. The table had grey plastic chairs placed around it. The walls were painted a stylish but gloomy French blue, and there was a round red clock on the wall with red hands and a startlingly loud tick that made me think of Edgar Allen Poe. I sat at the end of the table, like a CEO. But then I changed position and decided to sit in the middle. I had planned the session carefully. My approach was going to be that we were all in this writing business together, equals in the creative process. I was going to emphasise the power of perseverance and then we would take a look at the various works in progress.

I opened my bag and took out my spiral notebook and Berol pens. I flattened my sheet of A4 and studied the names of my students. In an optimistic frame of mind I saw that just having four students had its good points. I would have enough time to listen to everyone's work. And at the end of it I would only have to read four assignments and submit four reports; and it wasn't as if I was getting paid per head.

I could hear people laughing in the corridor. I smiled to myself and sat up all alert and welcoming and watched them walk straight past my door. Another little group came by and went past and they too sounded jolly. I wondered which course they were going to. Clown school, maybe? I knew a girl who went to clown school. She was five foot one and she was paired with a seven-foot-tall professional clown, and there you have visual humour without even trying.

Interspersed in the clatter-clatter of heels I heard the thud of leather soles on laminate and a tall thin bearded man in a leather jacket looked into the room. The jacket looked expensive and gave him the aura of an ageing rock star.

'Oh, hello,' he said. 'Is this the Romantic Prose class, do you know?'

'Yes it is,' I said, putting my welcoming smile back on.

'So; we're the first,' he said cheerfully, pulling out a seat. 'Nice to meet someone else who likes to be early.'

'Actually, I'm Lana Green,' I said quickly before there was some horrible misunderstanding in which he confided that he didn't like *Love Crazy* but he wanted to be published and that's why he was here.

'Oh!' said my student. He held out his hand and I shook it. 'I'm Arthur Shepherd.' He hesitated for a moment, then he said, 'Call me Turo. Arthur's an old man's name, as my girl-friend keeps pointing out.'

'Turo.'

It was hard to tell exactly how old he was because of the greying beard. His eyes were a surprising deep blue, like the sky at twilight. Despite the jacket, he seemed more like an Arthur than a Turo. Arthur is a gentle name. He seemed gentle.

'What are you writing?'

'Historical,' he said, taking off his leather jacket. 'Second World War.' He said with sudden feeling, 'I thank God every day that I didn't have to go to war. My generation has been lucky that way.'

It was a magnificent statement, being grateful for something you hadn't had to do.

'I've never thought of it like that,' I said.

Turo stroked his beard and looked around at the empty room. 'How many of us will there be?'

'Four.'

'Is that all? I thought there would be more.'

I was just about to explain the benefits of a small group to him when a girl with a red velvet coat twinkling with mirrors came into the doorway. Her black hair was in braids and she looked as if she had stepped out of a fairy story – she had the traumatised air of someone who had been lost in the woods for a while. She glanced at the two of us in alarm and then took a step back to check the door number.

'Romantic Prose?' I asked.

For a moment she didn't answer. She stood on the threshold. 'Is it just us?' she said anxiously. 'I thought it would be a bigger class.'

I looked up at the red clock, at the flick of the seconds. 'It's not quite seven yet,' I pointed out.

Someone came up behind her.

'Excuse *me*! You're blocking the way!'

'Oh! Sorry!'

A grey-haired woman pushed past her wearing a purple knitted beanie. She had a disappointed face – her eyes and her mouth drooped, like one of those drawings that you can turn upside down and suddenly they're all smiley. She sat next to Turo, one empty chair between them.

'Joan Parker.'

'Turo,' he said, holding out his hand.

She shook it briefly. 'That's an unusual name,' she said.

'It's short for Arturo,' he replied.

'Are you Italian?'

'No, but my girlfriend is.'

'It's lucky for you that your parents had the foresight to give you an Italian name,' she remarked wryly.

He looked at her, unamused. 'My parents christened me Arthur.'

'Very wise. I don't know why you'd want to change it. You look more like an Arthur than a Turo. Tu-ro,' she said, listening to the word as if trying to make something better from the sound of it. She shook her head and gave up.

The girl in red with the dark hair seemed reassured by the new arrival and she finally sat down. 'A is the beginning of the alphabet,' she pointed out. 'T is almost at the end?'

'And?' Joan asked.

For a moment I thought the girl was going to shy away back into the corridor, but to my surprise she laughed. 'I'm Kathryn,' she said, sitting next to Joan.

'And I'm Lana Green,' I ventured, holding my hand up, hoping it was obvious; but one has to be modest about these things just in case.

The three of them looked up at me as if they expected me to say something profound.

It was like being at an interview. My mind went blank. I tried to think of something intelligent to say to impress them. I looked at the clock.

'It's nearly seven,' I observed.

Luckily my last student came in just then; a plump, middle-aged, dark-haired woman in a trouser suit: Neveen.

I always like to start exactly on time these days. When I first did talks, I would start a little late just in case there were latecomers. But then I found out that latecomers can sometimes be really late and it didn't seem fair to make the ones who come on time wait. Why should they be punished? Anyway, some people are always late for everything, which is passive-aggressive, if you ask me.

'Hello!' said I, the bestselling author, cheerfully. 'I'm Lana Green and it's a pleasure to be here with you on your journey towards publication. It's not always an easy journey,' I added truthfully, 'but if there's one great quality that makes a writer, it's not genius or vocabulary, it's perseverance.'

When I'd first been offered the role, I'd had some ideas of who my students would be, based on the demographic of my readers and the fact we were doing Romantic Prose. They would be young, good-looking and ambitious, with love on their minds; old enough to be looking for a soulmate and young enough to be scared of not finding one. I'd imagined them tweeting from my class until I trended. I'd planned this course for them. It was too late to change it now.

'How long did it take you to write your book?' Turo asked.

'Nine months,' I said.

'What had you written before that?'

'I was a reporter, and when I lost my job I went travelling and started my blog and that led to a book deal.'

'So, in what sense of the word did you need perseverance?'

'Good question.' Obviously I hadn't needed perseverance, personally, because *Love Crazy* came easily enough, but I needed it now and I was pretty sure that *they* would too. I was trying to be encouraging. 'Many aspiring writers find it very hard to finish a story. I mean it in that sense. You mustn't give up.'

'Did you find it difficult to finish your book?' Joan asked, her head tilted inquiringly. She was still wearing her purple hat, as though she hadn't decided yet if she was staying.

'No, because I'd come to the natural end of the narrative. The road trip was over and that's where I ended it.'

'In the middle of the story when Marco comes back to see her the second time, she says she's tamed him,' Kathryn said. 'I liked that.'

'*Tamed* him?' Joan said sharply. 'What on earth's that supposed to mean?'

'I meant it in a jokey way,' I said. 'It was irony. Let's go back to—'

'Excuse me, that's not how I read it,' Kathryn interrupted, holding her red coat defensively around her throat. 'I thought it was because, when they're bonding in a domestic environment, men in love have lower testosterone levels.'

Eh?

'Nonsense,' Joan said. 'What makes you think that?'

'If anything, living together makes those levels go up,' Arthur declared, jutting out his beard shamelessly.

Joan turned her head to look at him and a strange smirk crossed her face so briefly I wondered if I'd imagined it.

'These testosterone levels,' she said, tapping her pen on her notes. 'I can't see how nature would benefit a man to have lower levels once he has a wife.'

'It stops him straying,' Kathryn said.

'If that were true, there would be no children,' Joan observed.

'And no affairs,' Neveen added suddenly.

There was no disputing that. We all fell silent, considering the implications.

Kathryn shrugged and poked a finger through a dark braid to scratch her head. 'Sorry. That's how I perceived it. It's something I read.'

'Okay!' I'd completely lost my thread. It was like stage fright: the actor's version of writer's block. I scanned my notes quickly. Perseverance! That was it. I had five tips on how they could persevere with their writing but they didn't really seem relevant any more. No one seemed to suffer from lack of perseverance, apart from me, since other than doing an outline I hadn't even got started on my sequel. We'd pretty much covered the subject, I felt. I looked up at the wall. What? The red clock had stopped.

I chewed the end of my pen gloomily. I felt cheated. I'd imagined my class of students listening to me intently and taking notes. My whole 'we're all in it together' speech was meant to show how modest and approachable I was. I hadn't imagined them disagreeing with me and dissing my book.

'Kathryn,' I said, 'tell us a little about your hero.'

She looked startled and reared away as much as it was possible in a grey plastic chair.

'It's a woman,' she said.

'Ah! Good!'

'She kills the abusive partners of women who come to her refuge.'

Whaddaya know? I would have put money on the fact she was writing magic realism. I didn't realise that under that red velvet coat with the twinkling mirrors throbbed the heart of an imaginary killer. What was she doing in a Romantic Prose class, anyway?

'Would you like to read some of your work to us?'

'No, thanks,' she said quickly.

'This course is not about me, it's about you.' Ha! 'Does *anyone* have anything they would like to read out to us?'

'Not yet,' Arthur said.

Joan shook her head.

Neveen doodled on her notepad.

If this was what being a teacher was like then it wasn't surprising my mother was the way she was; all prickly.

Arthur cleared his throat. 'So now that we know we have to keep writing until we get to the end, could you tell us how to get started on a story?' he asked. 'After all, that's the hardest part, isn't it? Deciding on the right place to begin.'

'True. You need an inciting incident,' I said. 'Something that provokes the action, acts as a catalyst.'

'But some authors start off with normal life and then bring the inciting incident in later so that you can contrast it with how life used to be,' Arthur pointed out.

'Well, that works too,' I agreed. 'It depends, really.'

'On what?' Joan asked. 'Because I don't have an inciting incident in my story at all.'

Just then, there was a tap on the door and Carol Burrows popped her head round. 'Sorry to disturb you, Lana, but I have some learning outcome forms for the students to fill in.'

I hurried over to get them.

'Everything going well?' she asked eagerly as she handed them over.

'Oh yes!' I lied.

'Good, good! I'll leave you to it.'

I handed out the forms, deep in thought. I knew what the problem was. Taking a class diminished me. Successful writers haven't got the time to give classes; they are a publisher's production line, going from one book to the next, sticking to a schedule. I didn't expect to give these students all the answers but I assumed I'd have a few for them, at least. I had wanted to give them the impression I was one of them and they'd sussed me and realised even before I had what I really was. No one had asked what I was working on and Joan, for one, hadn't read *Love Crazy*.

When they handed the forms back to me I glanced at the clock and saw to my relief that the lesson was over.

My four students scraped their chairs back and put on their coats and picked up their bags and said their goodbyes.

I put on my jacket, warm from the radiator. Obviously I waited until they'd left before I read the forms. In answer to the: *I feel this is the right course for me* question, out of the four categories to be ticked, I got one *completely agree*, one *agree*, a *disagree*, and a *completely disagree*.

I dropped them in at the office. The forms were anonymous but I was sure the one who completely disagreed was Joan.

CHAPTER ELEVEN

The Science of Attraction

The streets were glossed with rain as I called Jack on my way home that night. I wanted to hear a friendly voice.

I told him that I'd watched his YouTube video and he laughed.

'I liked the "How to Be a Hero" comment,' I said, shouting above the roar of the traffic. 'It's a great title.' An ambulance sped by, sirens on.

'Where are you?' he asked.

I stuck my finger in my off-side ear to drown out the noise. 'On my way home from the London Literary Society. I tutor there now. Tonight was my first night.'

'Well done! Do you have to get home or have you got time for a drink?'

The answer to my prayers. 'Definitely a drink,' I said. 'Edinboro Castle?'

'What time can you get there?'

'Ooh – twenty minutes?'

'See you there.'

In contrast with the damp night, the Edinboro Castle was warm, yeasty with the smell of craft beer, and sparkling with white fairy lights. Jack was at the bar when I arrived, looking out for me, and he grinned when he saw me.

'Got you a sauvignon blanc,' he said, 'and a bowl of fries.'

Wine and fries and good company in a warm pub on a cold night . . . I cheered up instantly.

'Thanks, Jack.'

I followed him to a corner table which the twinkling lights warmed with their silver glow. Jack took his overcoat and scarf off. He was wearing a red T-shirt. Next to my red suit we looked like two extras from a Virgin advert.

'So, you liked the video,' he said.

'I did. It made me laugh. That's quite a big deal for me these days,' I said.

'Job done. So I'm now officially your new fictional hero?' he asked.

'Totally. How to Be a Hero,' I said, but what I was thinking of was the way he said 'fictional', giving it a little more emphasis than it needed. Of course, fictional.

'Let me guess. Love, and it goes wrong, but they get back together, happy ending,' he said, grinning.

'You got it. Jack, why do you want to be a fictional hero?'

'I get to date you without the admin,' he said, gazing at me with that lovely, open untroubled expression.

'Admin?'

'You know, without all the whole emotional mess of it,' he said. 'The crazy bit.'

'Ah.' I nodded. We were back to that again.

'Do you know that the dopamine you get when you're in love is as addictive as cocaine? And that getting over a broken heart has the same physical reaction as cocaine withdrawal?'

'I did not know that,' I said, 'but I'm not the slightest bit surprised.'

'And did you know that a heart can literally break when a

relationship ends, due to stress cardiomyopathy? It's known as broken heart syndrome. That's what my mother had.'

He spoke with authority, as if he knew what he was talking about. He probably did.

I thought about my own mother going to live in Italy because my father's girlfriend was pregnant. That wasn't a broken heart but it was definitely an extreme reaction, a major flounce.

I thought about the unpublishable book I'd written under the influence of a broken heart. Jack was right. Love was a serious chemical imbalance.

Bloody admin.

This way we got friendship, date nights without any expectations and hopefully I'd get a book out of it. 'Broken heart syndrome, cocaine withdrawal . . . that's enough to put anyone off.'

'It's a pleasure to share.' We chinked glasses in mutual understanding. Considering the subject matter, the conversation gave us both a lift.

We looked up as a girl brought the fries to the table.

Dipping one in mayo, I asked, 'How's Nancy?'

'She's got a social worker, now. Caroline Carter. She's nice, actually. Late forties, plenty of experience. She's putting in a care package. And CCTV in the hall.' He sprinkled salt on his fries. 'Nancy has agreed to it, so she's compliant, and social services have addressed the problem and they can tick her off their list. It's all good. Compliance. That's the answer.'

I twirled the stem of my glass. 'Any idea what she's writing?'

'Nah. Not a clue. She writes phrases on scraps of paper and kind of bundles them together.'

'Really? And then what?'

'She'll look at them all and rearrange them to make a story.'

I wondered if it would work for me. 'What kind of phrases, for instance?'

'I don't know – they sound quite good, though. The one I remember is: "He was a man of sorrows and acquainted with grief."'

'And who's that? Her hero?'

'I don't know. Maybe.'

I chuckled to myself. To me, that would have been like finding a jewel in a cornfield. How beautiful, how poignant. I wanted to keep the phrase for myself. Steal it.

I almost asked him if the phrase referred to his father but then I would have to explain that I knew about him through looking at Wikipedia. From my journalist days I knew that it was better to pretend to be completely ignorant about a story. That way people want to talk about it. Everyone had a defining story in their lives, I'd found, and if we hung out long enough Jack would tell me it in his own way, in his own time.

'Has she always written like that?'

'Possibly; I don't know. She always used to work in her study but now she's living alone she's got the whole place to herself. Writing keeps her focused.'

'Even though she's got dementia?'

Jack shrugged. 'Look at Terry Pratchett. He was diagnosed with Alzheimer's in 2007 and he carried on writing until he died in 2015.'

'*The Shepherd's Crown*,' I said. 'I loved that book.'

Some writers plot and plan, some, like Stephen King, excavate it from their subconscious, some make it up as they go along. Me, I'd been ruined by journalism. I had to write from life. Which is fine when life is interesting but not so helpful when it's going badly. But even in *Love Crazy* I'd never come up with a line as good as 'a man of sorrows and acquainted with grief'. It takes the mind of a poet to come up with something like that.

'So,' Jack said, finishing his drink, 'for our next date I've got the loan of a two-seater kayak from a mate. Are you interested?'

'I might be. Go on.'

'You and me on the Thames, going past the Tower of London at dawn. Is that heroic enough for your book?'

'It sounds like fun and very adventurous.'

'Good. I'll check the tide tables.'

'Tide tables is just the phrase a hero would use.'

Jack grinned. 'I hoped you'd say that.' He put his coat on and wrapped his scarf around his neck. 'Are you catching the C2 back?'

'I am.' The bus stop was a ten-minute walk away.

Jack walked with me, for the fresh air, he said.

While I was waiting for the bus I told him the story about Louis and the pink curtain and the bed in the alcove, for comedy effect.

He was giving the story a lot more attention than it had a right to, and he grinned at my description. 'Why do you want to move house?'

'The rent's a bit steep where I am now,' I said, realising that I had well and truly demolished the image he'd first had of me. But I was going to get found out sooner or later so I tried to be philosophical about it.

The bus pulled up. 'I'll give you a call about the kayaking,' he said.

'Okay!' I said brightly. I sat by the window to wave, but he didn't look back.

He tucked his hands into his pockets, like a guy who didn't believe in love, and walked off into the night.

CHAPTER TWELVE

Defining Stories

My father called me shortly after I got home to explain in detail why giving Conte a red card showed gross misjudgement and an anti-Chelsea bias.

I was trying to unpick the piece of tinsel from the bedroom ceiling with one hand. I almost fell off the bed and my smile faded momentarily.

'Good old Conte,' I said, to prove to my father that I was still listening.

'Quite,' he said.

'How's Jo-Ann?'

'Oh, you know. Mood swings. Physical discomfort. I'll say one thing for your mother, she sailed through her pregnancy. Don't quote me.'

'Wouldn't dare,' I said.

As we spoke, I started wondering about my own defining story. It was being left. My father left and my mother left and then Mark Bridges left. But maybe I'd started it all by leaving home to go to university.

I was determined to be independent. I'd chosen it myself, I'd been to see it by myself and I drove myself there. The car park was full of tearful parents with empty cars and I felt slightly superior, slightly scornful.

I was on the road trip when my mother went to Italy. Sure, I was living with Mark when he left but I was also out a lot, pursuing my own agenda during that time.

How much did I contribute to their leaving?

And I thought about Jack, the cynical hero of my novel-to-be.

What if I liked him because I didn't want to be close to somebody? What if, deep down, I just wanted to be left alone?

This led to gloomier musings.

What if love really was nothing but a series of chemical changes and hormonal surges? What if love faded for the simple reason that our bodies didn't like being out of kilter and strove to correct the balance?

It would change the whole world of song writing, for a start.

Nancy Ellis Hall must have felt totally content to be on her own with her ideas of liberation and finding her fulfilment in her writing, until *whumph!* that day in Foyles in Charing Cross Road when she fell madly in love with Richard Buchanan. She knew he was married because he was there with his wife. What did he see in her? She was almost twice his age, a feminist and a spinster. I couldn't work it out.

After a lot of thought I was forced to agree with Jack.

That wasn't love. It was insanity.

It was still dark when I was awoken by my phone vibrating under my pillow. I pulled out my earplugs.

'I'm outside,' Jack said. 'Wear something waterproof.'

Jolted into full consciousness, I sat up in bed, trying to process it. I looked at the time. It was five in the morning. What? The kayaking was today?

'Give me a minute.' That's how easy it is to misjudge a person. I thought the kayak idea was going the same way as the pedalo, but no! It had actually gone the same way as the paragliding.

I must have fallen asleep momentarily, because my phone fell on my face and startled me awake again.

I rolled off the bed and buckled the blinds to see out. An estate car was idling in the middle of the road with a huge red kayak strapped to its roof.

Uh-oh. Wear something waterproof. Didn't like the sound of that. It meant he thought we were going to get wet.

I didn't possess anything waterproof; I did have my parka to keep me warm (and possibly drag me under if we capsized), but I really liked that parka. If I was going to drown, I didn't want to lose the parka as well. I pulled on my black cashmere, the one with moth holes in the sleeve, and put on my trainers.

I brushed my teeth, wore waterproof mascara for obvious reasons and grabbed a baseball cap on my way out.

The street was empty and silent in the early morning chill. Jack leant across and opened the passenger door. The red leather seat was very cold. I fastened my seat belt and Jack handed me an *A to Z*.

'We're heading east,' he said.

'Fine, but we don't need an *A to Z*, I've got satnav.' I got my phone out. 'Where exactly are we going?'

'Don't know. Somewhere quiet to park, that has easy access to the river.'

I opened the *A to Z* and shone my phone at it.

It was ages since I'd used an *A to Z*. So here was the river, and there was the bend just like in *EastEnders*. Pages 52 to 54. I looked up at the road and wondered which page we were on now; the starting point being a vital part of navigation. I found the page but I had no idea where we were on it.

'Holloway Road,' Jack said.

I wiped the window with my wrist. I didn't recognise

anything. *Pete's Plaice. House of Bamboo.* The shops were bright with neon. *Are your wheels loud enough?*

The streets were quiet. The city was alien. We were lost. I directed him down a cul-de-sac and a one-way street, and for a short while we drove a couple of times around an industrial estate. Jack was very forgiving about it.

'Find the Thames on the map around Canary Wharf and tell me the roads that go right up to it,' he said once we joined the dual carriageway again.

There was a red streak in the black sky, and I saw, between some modern buildings, the glint of red on the river.

'There it is!' I said. A metal gate shut off the alleyway and Jack pulled up.

'See if that gate's open.'

I jumped out and it was open, and he parked in a residents' parking bay which came into force at 8.30 am.

I helped him unhook many bungees and untie multiple straps and we lifted the kayak off the roof of the car. Despite being designed to float, it was incredibly heavy. With Jack shouting instructions such as 'Lift and lower' and 'Bloody hell don't drop it', we lifted it down the steps.

By the time we reached the river my muscles were trembling and I was steaming hot.

We lowered the kayak onto a dark shingle beach, garnished with the pale glow of polystyrene cups. In the river, plastic bags pulsed like jellyfish on the tide. I climbed into the front seat and Jack pushed me out into the water and jumped in behind me.

We were incredibly low down, almost at the waterline. The dawn's streak had broadened but the water was deep and black, splashing on the side of the small craft. Behind us was the O2 Centre and ahead of us was the broad sweep of feature-less river, flanked by illuminated buildings and bent-necked cranes with flashing red lights beaming from their apexes. We clattered purposefully through the water, avoiding driftwood and other debris, and slowly the black river faded to silver grey and then to rose gold as the sun breached the darkness. The kayak was so low that it felt as if we belonged in the water, gilded figures on a golden craft.

We propelled ourselves to the rhythmic sloshing of the Thames. Tower Bridge was ahead of us, ancient and unmistakable, and we floated towards the Tower of London, edging by Traitors' Gate, which was still in shadow as we drifted past.

My arms were trembling with the effort, and I wiped my forehead and turned and looked at Jack over my shoulder. He was taking a rest, so I stopped too, and as we bobbed in the silent beauty of the morning he grinned, his face dappled golden in the river's reflected light. I grinned back at him, feeling surprisingly and utterly happy, and for a moment we held each other's gaze.

Suddenly it was all action again.

'Shit,' he said urgently. 'River police! Quick! Get out of sight!'

We paddled like crazy into the shadow of HMS *Belfast* and watched the police boat motor past. The wake rocked us violently and the icy river water sloshed around our feet.

'Bloody hell, Jack! Why are we hiding?'

'I think we might need a licence or something.'

'You *think*?'

Now that the danger had passed we started to laugh helplessly. It was a few minutes before we got enough strength to carry on with our trip, mesmerically ploughing through the water until the buildings ahead of us began to look familiar and in the distance we could see the alien spacecraft that is the O2 Centre.

We found our starting point and lifted the kayak out of the water. A condom was stuck on one of the floats. This early in the morning I felt everything sharply and acutely. We carried the kayak back to the car, then heaved the craft onto the roof and strapped it down.

'That police launch,' Jack said and we started to laugh again.

Jack took off his damp sweatshirt and reached for a T-shirt from the back seat. The sun's weak beams outlined his bare skin in gold; his smooth forehead, his straight nose, his soft lips, his clavicle, his pecs, his flat stomach. He pulled on the T-shirt and looked at me. All I could see of his clear eyes was a small glow, like a crystal holding the light.

Around us the day was starting in earnest. All the quiet apartments were shedding their people who were hurrying for trains, getting into cars, putting up market stalls, all before the sun had been hoisted in the sky.

Jack drove me home with his iPod on loud. I leant back against the headrest, humming along happily, amazed and proud to have done so much before breakfast.

I imagined beginning my life afresh from now on, getting up before dawn and stepping out into that empty, echoey early morning when I had the world to myself. I always think things like that and imagine new beginnings. Sometimes I even give it a go but then it rains, or I've been out the night before and miss the alarm, and by default I go back to my old ways until something happens to inspire me again.

Jack pulled up outside the flats and we got out of the car, leaving the engine running.

We stood facing each other for a moment. It had been intensely beautiful on the river and I was still prickling with adrenaline from the unaccustomed early-morning exertion.

'That was amazing.'

He smiled. 'Wasn't it?'

For a moment it seemed as if he was going to say something more but he must have had second thoughts because he got back into the car and with a brief wave drove away.

CHAPTER THIRTEEN

The Way Forward

I was following Nancy's advice of words, words, words, without any of the technicalities like motivation and plot trajectory. That morning I tried to write up the story of Jack and me so far; Jack who wanted a relationship without the admin and me the bitter heroine who didn't believe in love.

Mid-morning, after a bacon roll, I had a call from the letting agent who said that the new tenants wanted to come for a final look before they moved in the following Friday.

I asked him if I could have my deposit back in cash, to save it going into my bank account and being swallowed up by my overdraft, but he refused for administrative reasons.

So I rang Josie at the Caring Share. 'Hello, it's Lana Green. I wondered if anything has turned up for me yet?'

'Unfortunately we don't have a placement at the moment,' she said, 'but things will pick up towards the end of October when the clocks change.'

I tried not to panic. That was a month and a half away. 'Seriously?' I asked sceptically. 'What difference will that make?'

She cleared her throat. 'Sundowning,' she said cryptically, lowering her voice.

Sundowning: yes, I could see it now; coyotes howling as the wagon train circles for the night. I lowered my voice too.

'What does that mean?'

'When it gets dark, the elderly start to wander. We get a lot of calls in the winter from relatives about wandering.'

As an ex-journalist, I was quite surprised I've never heard of this phenomenon of sundowning and wandering old people. But there again, how would I know the difference between an old person wandering and a pensioner going out to buy milk and a bottle of Scotch?

'What's the reason for that?'

'Nobody knows.' Her voice went back to normal. 'As soon as I get someone, you'll be the first person I call. You're top of the list.'

'Okay,' I said reluctantly. I gave my pillow a shake to get rid of my frustration and get comfortable again and sat back on the bed. Trouble was, I had no assets, I thought, gazing at the bike.

Well – apart from the bike, that was.

I unhooked the clothes off it. It really was magnificent. It was built for speed. It deserved to be ridden. The black and red paintwork was shiny and as unmarked as the day I bought it. For an inanimate object, I'd always felt deeply attached to it, but now I looked at it speculatively with fresh eyes, much like hungry Old Mother Hubbard when she turns from the empty cupboard and suddenly views her dog in a different light.

Twenty minutes later I left the house, wheeling the bike up Arlington Road and through Camden Lock to the bike shop in Chalk Farm where I bought it from, feeling as treacherous as if taking my beloved old pet to the vet for the last time.

I like the smell of bike shops – a purposeful mix of rubber and oil. I like the rows of bikes and the racks of neon reflective jackets and functional padded shorts. I like the intensity of the men who work there – it's almost always men. I like the focus they give the conversation, even when it means there's a queue building up, and I like the way nobody minds queueing because they know that their turn will come and at that moment all the focus will be directed at them.

So I stood protectively with the bike at my side until it was my turn.

My guy was the one in the red bandanna.

'I bought this a year ago and it's hardly been used and I wondered if you would buy it back from me,' I said, flashing him the wide smile I normally keep for group photographs. 'I've got the receipt here,' I added, handing it over.

He looked at the receipt and then he looked at the bike, checking the tyre tread and rotating the pedals. 'So what you've got is an ultra-lightweight Trek, OCLV carbon, eleven speed.'

'That's what I thought,' I said, mindful of the queue behind me.

'I can give you three hundred for it,' he said.

In books, people often reel with shock. I've never really understood what this was until that moment, when I reeled into the queue of people behind me.

'But it's almost new,' I said hoarsely.

'Trek don't do this model any more; they've got a new one out. It's lighter.'

'Why would you need lighter bike than this? I can pick it up with my little finger. Look!'

The guy and all the other people in the queue watched me try to pick it up.

'I've got short fingers,' I explained. 'Honestly, it's hardly been ridden.'

'I can see that,' he said. 'But this is what you have to take into account. I have to make money from it. Trust me, no one's going to pay any more than that because it's last year's model. You'd be better off selling it privately. There's a website called Gumtree—'

'I know Gumtree,' I said irritably, 'I've already sold all my stuff on that.'

'That's your answer,' he said. He gave me my receipt back and he looked over my shoulder at the man behind me.

I wanted to continue the argument but I'd had my allotted share of attention so I kicked up the bike stand and wheeled it out onto Chalk Farm Road feeling extremely discontented.

A combination of stress and the saltiness of a bacon roll had made my mouth dry. But I couldn't get a drink because I hadn't brought a bike lock with me. I couldn't leave the bike without one because it wouldn't last five minutes without being stolen. Even with a lock on, bikes get stolen every day in London. What you need is a couple of D-locks and to always fasten them through the back wheel and the frame. Otherwise you will come back to the bike rack to find all that's left of your chosen mode of transport is the lonesome front wheel. And I couldn't take it into Sainsbury's because it had 'No Bikes!' written on the door.

My phone rang; it was Jack. I could hear the undulating wail of a police car in the background.

'Have you read the *Camden Journal*?' he asked abruptly.

'No. I'm not at home at the moment, I'm in Camden. I've just been to the bike shop.'

'You're buying a bike?'

'No, I'm selling one. Where are you?'

'I'm in Costa in Camden Road having a sandwich. Can I get you anything?'

'Yes, please! I'll have a Pepsi Max!' I said, then realising that would be classed as rude, added quickly, 'Only joking. I won't be long.' I wheeled the bike past Sainsbury's and up towards the railway bridge.

Costa Coffee is right next to the canal. I propped the bike against the railings – down below us on the still green water, a red narrowboat was moored up and a black and white cat lay curled on its roof.

Jack came out with the drinks and the sandwiches. His yellow T-shirt accentuated his tan. He looked at me in that direct way of his.

'Take a look at this.' He flattened the freesheet out for me to read. The headline on the front page read: *Camden Pensioner in Sex Abuse Arrest.*

> *A forty-year-old sex offender was today arrested after breaking the conditions of his licence by taking an elderly Hampstead resident for a drink in the Rat and Parrot. The offender had recently been released from a twelve-year prison sentence for the rape of a ninety-three-year-old woman and the sexual assault of an eighty-seven-year-old.*
>
> *Tony Jackson, the manager, said that the pensioner was a regular customer who he'd had trouble with in the past. 'She often buys people a drink,' he said. 'People take advantage. This time, it could have got her into serious trouble.'*

The story was disgusting, appalling. 'They should have told you what he'd done at the time – their whole attitude would have made more sense if you'd known.' I sincerely hoped Nancy wouldn't read it.

'Hampstead pensioner.' Jack gave a dry laugh. 'She'll hate that.' He looked back at me, rubbing his hands wearily over his stubble. 'I've just had a meeting with Nancy's social worker. They've got a doll order against her.'

'Sounds cute.'

'Doesn't it? It's not,' he said, flushing. 'Turns out that it is a D-O-L order and that stands for deprivation of liberty. Who knew? You can deprive someone of their liberty as easily as that.'

I was shocked. 'That is the most awful thing I've ever heard,' I said heatedly. 'You can deprive someone of their liberty just because they're a bit eccentric?'

I suppose social workers must do a good job generally, but it did seem unfair.

The man vaping at the next table turned to look at us.

'It's because of that guy she had a drink with.'

'But why should Nancy be deprived of her liberty, when he broke the law?'

Jack looked weary. 'The way they see it, she hasn't got the capacity to judge whether a situation is good or bad. But they're wrong. What they don't realise – what they don't know, what they don't *want* to know – is that she's always been like that, sociable and impulsive. It's not the illness; it's how she is, it's her nature. Just because she's not like other old ladies doesn't mean she's not capable of looking after herself. Nancy is generally okay, she's still in the early stages, and I don't want them making it worse for her than it already is. I'm not in denial, Lana; I know it's going to progress. But I want to look back on these times as her good times, when things weren't too bad, when she just needed a bit of support.'

My heart went out to him. 'Does she have any other family that could help?'

He smiled faintly, shaking his head. 'It's just her and me.'

He looked so alone. I wanted to hug him, because I knew how that felt. I thought of the times that I'd stood behind someone and wanted to press my cheek against their back just for a moment, to feel close to another human being.

Instead, I got back to practicalities, which is what I'm good at.

'How are they going to deprive her of her liberty?'

'She's not allowed to go to the pub unsupervised.'

'But . . .' I could see a huge flaw in this. You didn't have to be with Nancy long to know how bad her memory was. 'Even if they told her not to go, she wouldn't remember, would she? And even if she did remember, she'd still want to go, DOL order or not.'

'That is perfectly correct.' Jack nodded. 'My job is all about problem-solving but I can't solve this one. There's no good answer. I can't give up my business to look after her and she won't have carers – they send different ones each time and she won't let them in when they call, which ironically shows good sense. Catch-22, right?'

He stood up and went to look over the railings.

I sat back and tried to see him objectively. In his yellow T-shirt he had the fanciable hard-bodied look that I'd caught a glimpse of by the river. Broad shoulders, slim waist. Really, he was fit, despite all his worries. Aw, Jack.

I understood for the first time the strain that he was under.

At the same time, there was something intriguing about illness, in a horrible sort of way. Three bestsellers popped into my mind: *Elizabeth Is Missing*, *The Memory Book* and *Iris*. Dementia is the new autism, as autism was the new AIDS. Illnesses are good subjects for books – where would Edgar Allen Poe be without consumption? How would *Love Story* work without leukaemia? (Seriously, that class thing was always an issue for Jenny and Oliver. If the heroine hadn't died they'd have been divorced by now for sure.) I suddenly had the beginning of an idea involving Nancy, but then I realised I was wandering dangerously into Jojo Moyes territory. Still; serendipity!

A black-headed gull swooped over us and rested on the narrowboat below.

'Jack, you should talk to Josie at the Caring Share,' I said. 'She'll find you someone to take a room in Nancy's house. That means there'll be somebody around to keep an eye on her and take her for a drink.'

I wasn't being disingenuous. I didn't necessarily mean me. Mrs Leadbetter would have suited me fine, but Nancy Ellis Hall was a different proposition altogether.

But.

Think about it.

Was it such a bad idea, in the circumstances; the circumstances being I was five days away from homeless?

The thing about writers is, we're always searching for the story. We are also aware of the signs of the times, the zeitgeist (as I knew from Kitty).

Jack had his phone out. 'Caring Share? Do you have a number for them?' he asked.

'I probably ought to tell you, though,' I said. 'If you do ring Josie, she's going to ring me because I'm at the top of the waiting list for a room.'

One thing I'll say about Jack, he catches on quickly.

'Is that so?' He narrowed his eyes against the sun, poised with his phone in his hand. 'When she calls you, what will you tell her?'

He watched me while I thought about it and I could see the combination of doubt and hope in his expression too, like a reflection of my own.

It could work.

Why shouldn't it?

'I'm happy to do it,' I decided. I lusted over that damask pink parlour with the photographs of Beryl Bainbridge and Molly Keane; the floor-to-ceiling books snug on mahogany shelves; the scraps of paper scattered around with verbal gems on them. And there was Nancy's simple insight into the writer's craft – *words, words, words* – which had got me writing again. 'I've met Nancy so it's not as if we're strangers. We've got a lot in common with the writing.'

'Are you sure? Nancy's not always an easy person to be around,' he warned, giving me a ready-made excuse.

But . . .

'Hey, you should meet my mother. I've had plenty of experience with bossy women.' I imagined telling her I was living with Nancy Ellis Hall . . . where better to move to than Nancy's? There is no doubt about it; the atmosphere of creativity makes you feel as powerful as God. 'How about this; I'll try it for a month. Don't bother going through the Caring Share – it will be less admin this way.'

And I didn't want to ruin my chances of another placement if it didn't work out.

Jack looked me in the eye with a certain interest. The warmth seemed to come back into him.

I'd always imagined relationships developing in a slow build-up, but the friendship between Jack and me was more like climbing uneven steps; uncertain and perilous. It felt as if either of us could lose our footing at any moment and go tumbling back to the start line.

He was studying me carefully, speculatively. 'But I don't understand why you would do that,' he said. 'You're a best-selling novelist with a book to write.'

'True. But I'm broke and I'm looking for a place to stay. And with the kayaking and you as hero and your novelist stepmother with Alzheimer's, I think I can probably make it work as a romantic novel.'

'So you liked the kayaking,' he said softly, his eyes clear beneath his straight dark eyebrows.

'Yes. The sunrise and the silence . . .' I looked from his eyes to his mouth and back to his eyes again.

'Obviously I'd organise the funding,' he said. 'You'd get Nancy's Attendance Allowance.'

I sat back, surprised at this business-like turn of events. Funding? I was going to get paid?

'I'll do it!' I said. I stuck my straw in the bottle, watching the brown foam rise, thinking of Nancy.

You know how it is when someone buys you a Christmas present and then you have to buy one for them because you don't want them to think you like them less than they like you, and you don't want to feel, to use one of my mother's favourite words, beholden?

I'm sure that's what happened, because Jack looked at the bike thoughtfully.

'Is that yours? Isn't it a man's bike?'

'Yes. It's an ultra-lightweight Trek, OCLV carbon, eleven speed.'

'I've been thinking of getting a bike,' he said. He swallowed the last of the sandwich, wiped his hands on his jeans and got to his feet. 'How much are you asking for it?'

'Three hundred,' I said apologetically.

Jack rubbed the edge of his jaw with the flat of his hand.

'It's like new. I bought it for someone. Mark, actually.'

Jack whistled appreciatively. 'Lucky guy.'

Lucky guy. A feeling of sadness bunched in my chest when he said that. *Lucky guy.*

I glanced at Jack.

That was what Mark was supposed to feel; that should have been his dialogue. If he'd taken the bike with him when he left me, even if he'd just left it at his parents' house, I honestly believe it wouldn't have hurt as deeply as it had. (I accept I could be wrong about that. It might have made me angrier that he took the bike and left me; I will never know, will I?)

'Yeah, well.' I shrugged.

I moved the black and red Trek bike away from the railings for him to see it in its full glory.

'It looks in good condition,' he said.

'It should be. It's a house bike. It's lived a pampered, indoor sort of a life. It's been in my hall for a year.'

To my delight, he laughed.

Jack lifted the bike with one hand, got down on his knees and felt the tyres, turned the bike over, rotated the pedals, straightened, rang the bell, tested the brakes and, finally, sat on it.

All serious man stuff.

Finally he came to a conclusion. 'Awesome,' he said. 'Mind if I test drive it?'

'Go for it,' I said happily and he took it onto the road. There was a breeze which chased the leaves along the pavement and into the gutter. Jack cycled across the road and down Royal College Street, out of sight.

The guy who was vaping on the next table squinted at me through vanilla-scented clouds. 'Where's he off to?'

'Test drive,' I said, holding my Pepsi.

We were both silent for a moment, looking across the small square of garden towards the traffic lights. A cat scurried past us and disappeared between parked cars.

'Be funny if he's nicked it,' he said.

I'd just been thinking exactly the same thing. 'I've got his phone number.'

'So?' He raised his eyebrows sceptically.

Unexpectedly I felt a low-level anxiety at the stranger's comment. It was true; I hardly knew Jack Buchanan at all.

Just then a cyclist turned the corner and came towards us, but it wasn't Jack.

'How long are you going to give him?' the guy asked,

breaking into my pondering, when suddenly there was a squeal of brakes from behind us and I clutched my drink in panic.

Jack laughed. 'Jump on, Lana,' he said, 'I'll take you for a spin.'

He moved over the crossbar and I sat precariously on the saddle and off we went, me clutching his hard, flat stomach under his T-shirt, my hair flying around my face and him pedalling fast in the bike lane along Royal College Street, avoiding parked cars, curving steeply around the bend by the pub and bumping up the kerb before finally looping back to Costa where our drinks were still waiting.

The vaping guy blew out a final cloud in our direction and shook his head at us like a disappointed father and went back inside to get warm.

Jack and I were laughing, both in high spirits as he lifted me off the bike. We were looking at each other eye to eye, and I got this feeling that was hard to describe. Obviously as a writer my job is to describe things that are hard to describe so I would say it was a blend of excitement, the butterflies-in-the-stomach sort, and the kind of relaxed feeling that you get when you are emotionally close to someone. Which is strange because it was impossible to be emotionally close to someone I hardly knew. Mainly I wanted to put my arms around him again, and keep them there.

'I'll take it,' Jack said, propping the bike against the table. 'I'll do a bank transfer, it will be in your account this afternoon.'

We broke our gaze; the deal was done and I patted the bike's handlebars fondly. It had been a good coat-stand and a good clothing rail and now it was off to fulfil its destiny as a bicycle.

'You'll need a strong lock for it,' I said anxiously. 'A D-lock would be good.'

'Don't worry,' he reassured me, 'it's going to a good home. And,' he added seriously, 'you can visit it any time you like.'

'Really?'

'Yes.' He folded up the *Camden Journal* and put it back into his pocket. 'When do you want to move into Nancy's?'

'How about Saturday lunchtime?' I said. The perfect relationship: no admin.

'Fine. I'll be there to meet you,' he said.

CHAPTER FOURTEEN

A Source of Inspiration

A couple of days later I packed up my meagre possessions, left the flat without a backward glance and caught the C11 bus to Nancy's house.

I rang the doorbell and heard voices arguing inside in the hallway.

'Let me answer it! It's *my* house and *my* doorbell,' Nancy was saying.

'Yes,' Jack replied, 'but it will be Lana Green.'

Silence. Then: 'Lana Green? Isn't that where I live?'

'No, that's South End Green.'

After a bit of scuffling, Nancy opened the door. She was wearing a poppy-patterned dress and a black cardigan buttoned up wrongly. A red light glowed in the CCTV sensor that was pointed at the door. The oil painting of Old Mother Hubbard hung on the wall and the chandelier above her head jingled in the breeze.

'Who are you?' she asked me, leaning forward to look at me closely.

'Lana Green.'

She looked at me with bright-eyed curiosity. 'Who told you that?'

I thought about it. 'My parents,' I said. I held my hand out and instead of a handshake she pinched the tips of my fingers.

'Come on in,' Jack said. 'Nancy, Lana is going to be boarding here for a while. Look, she's brought her luggage.'

'Where will she sleep?'

'In the green room, at the back,' Jack said.

Nancy looked at me suspiciously.

'Lana is a writer.'

She wasn't impressed. 'Anyone can write,' she said dismissively. 'Look!' She pointed her finger and wrote some cursive in the air.

Jack took me to my room. The window opened onto a garden dominated by birch trees. The leaves were just beginning to change colour and through the branches I could see the slopes of Parliament Hill Fields where a small dog was gamely chasing pigeons. We were right the other end of the Heath, so now I had lived both sides of it.

'It gets the morning sun,' Jack said.

'It's beautiful.' It was a calm room and I liked it. The carpet was deep green, with a small blue prayer rug by the door and a green one by the bed. On the bedside table was a green marbled lamp with a green shade, and most importantly there was a sturdy desk under the window. It had three books on it: an Oxford dictionary, a thesaurus and a reverse dictionary.

'Obviously, call me if there are any problems at all,' Jack said. 'One thing you should know, if there's a confrontation, don't try to talk Nancy out of it – just leave her be. Let her have her own way.'

'Okay.' I nodded, 'I'll do that.' I didn't know what he was worrying about. What could possibly go wrong?

'Who are you?' Nancy asked me as I let myself into the hall that evening. I'd been to Marks & Spencer's and on the way back I called in at the Shy Horse which was small and homely, and had a log fire in the grate – I was looking for an alternative to the Rat and Parrot.

I dropped my keys in my handbag. 'Hi, Nancy! It's me, Lana.'

She barred the way and looked at me with no warmth or recognition, as if she'd had a new hard drive fitted since I left.

I was looking at her suspiciously, too. I didn't know how to account for her hostility or her change of mood. When I left the house she'd seemed lively and buoyant. I wondered if she was responding to me and I tried smiling at her.

'There's nothing to laugh about,' she said sternly. 'Did you feed the dog?'

Oh, great. 'I didn't even know you had a dog.'

'Still, you're supposed to feed it,' she said, frowning. 'It's all skin and bone now.'

Considering I'd only been here a day, I couldn't take the blame for that.

I moved and she raised her hands into claws.

'Ka-choo!' she said as if pinning me to the door with an electric force from her fingers.

I remembered Jack's advice, and I stayed where I was, boxed in. From here I could look straight into the camera lens that was pointed at the door.

'Nancy, where is the dog now? Do you keep him in the garden?'

Her hostile eyes narrowed. 'He's in a thing like this,' she held her palms parallel and then horizontal. 'Layer by layer.'

113

'Right . . . okay. Have you got any dog food in the house?'

'You've got it,' she said. 'You know it. It's all in layers, one, two, three, four, funny.'

It was slightly alarming and Pythonesque.

Hanging above us was the painting of Old Mother Hubbard and the empty shelves and her skinny little dog. There was something unsettling about the painting and I had the feeling that I'd been dreaming about it, although I couldn't remember specifically what. I had a flash of insight.

'Is this the dog that's hungry?' I asked, pointing at it.

She looked at the painting, frowning as she studied it. 'I'm not keen on that *at all*,' she said after a moment. 'It's time for bed. Get up when you're ready.'

'Thanks. Goodnight.'

I followed her down the passageway and hurried upstairs, feeling my heart beating faster as though I'd had a lucky escape. I flopped down thankfully on the bed and groaned with happiness. My bed! Room to stretch out! Nancy was pretty eccentric, but she was appealing, too. Even better, she hadn't gone sundowning.

I could hear her talking to herself in her bedroom, and I wondered if she was working out her story aloud in front of a mirror, like Barbara Trapido.

I wondered if it would work for me.

I had an idea. Two stories being told in tandem in adjacent rooms; streams of words filling each room . . . like the Bloomsbury Group, but with just the two of us. But we could grow into something rich and memorable. She could come with me to the London Literary Society and our nurturing influence would predate our group's rise to fame . . .

And if I couldn't get a book out of living with an eccentric feminist ex-novelist, it was time to give up.

CHAPTER FIFTEEN

Rapport

Next morning I found Nancy in the kitchen. I was just about to put the kettle on when she shrieked loudly and jabbed a spoon at me.

'Who are you?'

'Lana Green,' I said, patting my heart to get it started again. 'Your guest.'

'How did you get in?'

'I stayed the night,' I said.

'Well why didn't you say so?' She put the spoon down and I made us both a cup of tea and we sat at the rectangular pine table.

Already I was getting used to her quirks. I wondered whether in time I too would start thinking oddly; whether my neurons would start taking diverse turns along unexplored pathways. In the *Evening Standard* there was a report about a Hampstead woman with a monkey who had conned people into thinking that she had the power to heal their lives. She asked them for money to take to Africa to pin on a money tree; crazy stuff, really. But the thing is, people believed her. She had created a complex fantasy world and persuaded them to buy into it too, bankrupting them, and causing great pain. The ability to buy into someone else's fantasy is what sells books, of course.

Writers have a very high rate of mental health problems, probably as a result of spending too much time wandering around inside their own heads. It can get very claustrophobic in there.

As I was pondering, I caught Nancy looking at me curiously.

'Now, that hair you've got,' she said, pointing at me and waving her finger. 'Those squiggles. What's my hair like?'

'Sort of – straighter. Do you have a mirror?' I suddenly realised that I hadn't seen a mirror in the house, not even in the bathroom. I had a small hand mirror in my make-up bag, so I went to fetch it for her. 'Here you are,' I said.

Nancy peered into the compact and smiled. Her smile turned to consternation.

'My teeth!' she yelped. 'What's happened to my teeth?' She turned to show me. 'Look! There are two missing! Show me yours.'

I bared my teeth back at her.

'They're nice. Are they mine?'

'No, these are ones that I have always had. If you want your teeth done, you could go to a dentist and have them fixed. I'll come with you if you like.'

'What's the point?' she asked energetically. 'Nobody ever looks at me!'

She slipped my compact mirror into her pocket. Every now and then during the morning she would find it in her pocket, take it out, smile into it and be astonished. So that afternoon, as my first outing with her, we went to her dentist to make an appointment. I'm not sure how we managed to get one there and then. At my own surgery I have to wait at least a month unless it's an emergency, but the dentist was willing to see Nancy right away. He was a young Indian guy, slight and delicately good-looking.

Nancy sat in the dentist chair and he began to recline it. She panicked immediately and insisted he put her upright again.

'I just want to look in your mouth,' he said. 'Shall I just tilt the chair a little?'

'Yes, but just a little.'

The dentist began to catalogue her teeth aloud to the dental assistant. She had three teeth missing altogether, but she was only bothered about the front ones, she told him.

The dentist began to discuss the options with her. Implants were an option, or a bridge was cheaper.

'I don't want anything complicated,' she said, getting energised. 'Just pop them back in, man! Look! I did that one myself!' She pointed to the back of her mouth.

The dentist paused for thought and said that he would have a look. He tilted the chair a little and let the light shine in.

He looked quite intently for long seconds and then raised the chair up again and seemed to come to a decision.

'Mrs Hall, your teeth look perfectly fine,' he said. 'If you get any pain or discomfort, come back to see me.'

Nancy was very pleased now that she had a clean bill of health, especially when she went to pay and the receptionist told her there was no charge. As we headed for the door, she looked at herself in the mirror, smiling broadly. Her smile dropped.

'My teeth are missing!' she said indignantly. 'Let me see yours.'

I showed her.

'Oh! Aren't those mine?' she said.

* * *

117

That evening, Nancy and I sat in the parlour in front of the fire with a glass of Harveys Bristol Cream sherry each. She was writing in her black leather notebook.

The sofa was like sitting on a cloud. The firelight glowed, the polished mahogany gleamed, the picture frames bounced rectangles of light on the rich rugs.

Nancy closed the notebook and put it in her handbag. She tapped my knee.

'If you write, you must write in hope,' she said.

I smiled. 'I'll remember that. How is your new book coming along?'

'Hard to quantify. You need to lose a layer of skin to be a writer,' she said. 'I may be too thick-skinned now, you know, to write anything decent.'

She ran her finger around the crystal of the glass until it rang out, a long, pure, haunting note, watching me out of the corner of her eye to see my reaction to this trick.

I laughed. When the note faded away I said, 'You could come to my writing class at the London Literary Society if you like. I'm tutoring it. It might help you with your ideas and it's only a small group, very intimate.'

'A writing class? The London Literary Society,' she repeated with a gap-toothed smile. 'Yes, I'll come.'

'Great!' I said.

She looked suddenly concerned. 'How old am I?'

'Eighty, I think.'

'Eighty?' she said in complete astonishment. 'That old?' She sat back against the cushions and pondered for a moment, watching the flames, her hands folded in her lap. 'Man would swallow me up. Thou tellest my wanderings. Put thou my tears into your bottle – are they not in the book?'

The warmth of the fire, the sweetness of the sherry, the beauty of the words. I felt delirious – and filled with strength.

It was like an out-of-body experience being with her. I wouldn't tell her wanderings or let any man swallow her up.

'And you, what are you writing?' she asked me.

'It's called *How to Be a Hero*. It's about Jack actually.'

'And what does being a hero mean?'

I sipped the sherry and reflected on the question. 'Well. A hero is a man who can fight for and win the heroine, isn't it?'

'Fighting and winning,' she said. 'Is that what you think? It's not about overcoming, you know. No. It's about what you give up for love. It's the sacrifice, not the power. You're seeing it entirely the wrong way around.'

'I don't understand.'

Nancy sat forward to look at me. When they look at you, most people's gaze meets yours and skims away again, but Nancy had a way of peering deeply into my eyes as if searching for something in particular.

It made me uncomfortable and after a moment I wanted to look away but I forced myself to sit still, looking back at her.

When she saw whatever she was looking for she sat back again. 'I'm going to tell you something. I know a man who gave up a great deal to be with me and I gave up a great deal to be with him.'

With a thrill of excitement I knew she was talking about Richard Buchanan. I nodded, honoured that she was confiding in me, but I didn't say anything because, as I've previously mentioned, you can find out more about people when you let them tell their own story their own way. She was concentrating on balancing her sherry glass on her knee and didn't seem inclined to carry on with the conversation so I said, 'You were saying you measure love by what you give up for it?'

'Yes.' She smiled sweetly, lost in thought. 'It was all worth

119

it,' she said softly. 'I would go through it all over again, all of it, the humiliation too. I would go through it all for the satisfaction of being with him again, just for one day. He was the first and only man I've ever loved.'

I understood. 'Do you think we each just have one person, one soulmate?'

'Oh yes, don't you?'

'But what if you lose him?'

She laughed. 'Ah! Then you are consoled by the joy of living your life without compromise.'

I waited for her to talk more about Jack's father, and even about the scandal from an insider's point of view, but she fell quiet, lost in thought. To prompt her, I picked up the silver-framed photograph of him from the mahogany wine table and held it out to her.

'This is him, Richard Buchanan, isn't it?'

She looked closely at the photograph, her brow furrowed.

'Is that his name?' She put it back on the table. 'I believe I knew his wife once,' she said.

CHAPTER SIXTEEN

Archetypes

The following day I phoned Carol Burrows. She sounded wary and a bit flat when I told her it was me, but she cheered up enormously when I said I was thinking of bringing Nancy Ellis Hall to the class. Yes, I was after the kudos, and I wasn't the only one.

'Well, I can tell you, it would be quite a fillip – Nancy Ellis Hall! *The Dent in the Pillow* changed my life!' Carol said gleefully.

I up-sold it, naturally. 'She wants a refresher course because she's starting writing again. It's about the married man she fell in love with.'

I waited for Carol to point out the obvious. That this wasn't the right class for her. She didn't need to learn about romantic prose. She knew more about writing than I ever would. What could I possibly tell her that she didn't already know? It'd be like teaching Shakespeare the fundamentals of playwriting.

But no.

'It's a wonderful boost for the college! And for your course,' she added quickly. 'I was surprised at the low uptake, actually. This group will be the first readers to hear her new book, see it take shape . . . It's been years since she was last published. Imagine!'

I hadn't thought of it that way. It did sound exciting to be in at the start of the new book by a writer like Nancy Ellis Hall. And she might acknowledge the Towards Publication: Romantic Prose class in the dedication. Or even me personally, if she found me inspiring enough as a tutor. But on the downside, she had once trapped me in the hallway with the invisible force of her fingers, which was something I needed to mention to Carol.

'I should tell you she has a social worker,' I confided. 'I think her behaviour can be a bit challenging sometimes.'

Carol Burrows gave a nonchalant puff into the phone. 'I think you'll find, as an institution, we have a policy of being inclusive. It was in the email I sent you. Paragraph 1c.'

'Okay then!' My conscience was clear.

On Tuesday evening, we were getting ready to go to the class at London Lit. I was prepared for all weathers. I had an umbrella, and I was wearing Compeed blister plasters in my leopard-print flats. Under my bed I'd found a full-length gilt-framed mirror which I'd propped up in the hall. As I zipped up my parka, Nancy jostled for space in front of the mirror to put her hat on – a yellow felt cloche hat, which matched her yellow cardigan and her yellow, grey and black skirt.

Satisfied with her appearance, she turned to me and her face fell. 'Where's your hat?' she asked me.

'I don't need a hat,' I said.

'You do need a hat. Look at mine! *I've* got a hat.'

'There's a hood on my jacket, look.' I demonstrated it to her by pulling it over my head.

'It's not a hat, is it,' she pointed out sharply. 'It's a cowl. I'll get you a hat.'

She went upstairs and came down with a shocking pink

felt trilby with a black ribbon and a feather attached. 'Here you are.'

I backed off. 'No, it's fine, Nancy,' I said. 'I've got my hood.'

'You can't go out without a hat,' she said sternly.

I was getting a bit edgy by now. All this hat business was taking time. I put the hat on. I'm not a hat person. You need a certain type of face to wear a hat well.

'How do I look?'

Nancy was biting her lower lip and looking at me intently in the mirror.

'Just a minute,' she said suddenly. 'That's my hat, isn't it?'

'Yes, do you want it back?'

She took the yellow hat off and we swapped. She looked at herself in the mirror and smiled. Then she looked at me and said crossly, 'Why have you always got the nicest hat?'

So we swapped again. I was getting stressed. 'We'd better go, Nancy. We're going to be late.'

'Where are we going?'

'To the London Literary Society,' I reminded her.

We walked quickly down the road and caught the bus from South End Green. Our hats caused amusement to two adolescent boys who were sitting behind us and Nancy had a lively conversation with them while I looked through the window.

We got off the bus and the night was cold and autumnal, with the faint smell of wood smoke tainting the air. I hurried her along Euston Road, my arm in hers, taking her like a trophy to the class.

We were late.

But as I walked into the blue classroom with Nancy, full of apologies and whipping off my pink trilby, Joan and Arthur murmured to each other and exchanged significant glances. Kathryn swivelled round in her chair. When they looked back at me I felt it was with renewed respect.

Nancy went to sit at the far end of the table, the CEO at a board meeting. She was still wearing the yellow hat, so bright she shone in the corner of my eye like sunshine coming in through a window.

I was laying out my pens and notepad when there was a tap on the door.

It was Carol Burrows, flushed and bright-eyed, dressed in purple.

'Lana! Sorry to disturb you! I just wondered how our newcomer was settling in. Ah!' She headed for the end of the table, hands outstretched. 'Miss Ellis Hall, welcome to the London Literary Society. I loved *The Dent in the Pillow* and I do hope you find inspiration here to continue your contribution to the literary world.'

Nancy pinched her fingers briefly. 'I'm sure I shall,' she said graciously, and began stirring the air with her hands as though wafting smoke. 'I can feel it around me already.'

'Excellent! May the creative force be with you,' Carol said, and blushed. Remembering Nancy wasn't alone, she added as an afterthought before she backed out of the door, 'And the rest of you, obviously.'

'Let's introduce ourselves,' I said.

Kathryn, Turo, Neveen, Joan and—

'I'm Lana Green,' Nancy announced brightly.

'Er – *I'm* Lana Green,' I said. 'You're Nancy Ellis Hall, aren't you.'

For the benefit of everyone, I explained that Nancy, after a long break from writing, was joining our class because she was now working on a new book.

My mother was going to be so impressed – even better than living with her, Nancy Ellis Hall was in my class!

'It's a love story.' Nancy smiled, showing the gaps in her teeth. She changed the atmosphere completely. It was true, it was a fillip to have her there. She made all the difference. She justified their choice of course, for a start. And she made me look good. There was a definite buzz in the air.

I cleared my throat and got to my feet to say my bit about heroes. I glanced at my notes.

'The role of the hero in romantic fiction takes many forms; for instance, the boy-next-door, the charmer, the Peter Pan character, the father figure. Each of these is an archetype and the benefit of using an archetype in fiction is that this character is instantly identifiable to readers.'

Turo put his hand up. 'In *Love Crazy*, which archetype was Marco?' he asked.

'Well, he was the – um – the charmer,' I said.

'Are there only four archetypes? Because my hero doesn't fit into any of those. My main character is Bob and he joined up at the start of the war to get out of going down the pit.'

I looked at my notes again. Oh yes. 'So—'

'Maybe he was the boy-next-door,' Joan suggested.

'Isn't the boy-next-door the dependable character who the heroine ultimately realises is the one she's meant to be with?' Kathryn asked.

'Ye-es,' I said warily, because I felt that Kathryn was probably going to have her own angle on this.

'I wouldn't call Bob *dependable*,' Turo said. 'If anything, he's a bit of a Jack the lad.'

'Then he's the charmer,' Neveen suggested.

I don't know what came over us. We were lively and animated; not just in our speaking but in our listening. Well actually I do know; it was because down the far end of the table was Nancy Ellis Hall, our audience.

Turo took his head. 'No, he's definitely not. Charmers are sophisticated. He's not the slightest bit sophisticated.'

'How would you define him, Turo?'

'I've just told you, he's a bit of a Jack the lad. Imagine that feeling of being seventeen and the excitement of going off with your mates to fight, leaving your girl behind with her tender-hearted sorrow. And they don't *have* to go, they *want* to. It's a big adventure, isn't it? They are getting out of their village. They think they will live forever. Why wouldn't they? When you're seventeen you can't imagine a world without your own self in it.'

Nancy got to her feet. 'You there with the beard' – waving her finger at him – 'it's a song, you know.' She put her hands behind her back and thrust out her chest. She sang: 'Swigging, gigging, kissing, drinking, fighting – Jack's the lad!'

'Is it? I didn't know that,' he said. 'You must write it down for me.'

'I can teach it to you.' She took her yellow hat off and put it on the table. 'Come on now! Swigging, gigging, kissing, drinking, fighting, Jack's the lad. Altogether! I'll keep time!'

Obediently, we all started singing. That was the effect she had on people.

'Swigging, gigging . . .'

Someone clip-clopped past the door and paused, enviously, I guessed.

Satisfied with our efforts, Nancy sat, and we settled down again, slightly breathless.

'You said that Marco was a charmer, but was he?' Joan asked doubtfully, tapping her gold-nibbed fountain pen on the table. 'I always imagine charmers to be sociable and gregarious. Marco can't be sociable and gregarious when there's a camera lens separating him from reality.'

'He's definitely gregarious,' I said.

'Charmers can be manipulative,' Turo said, stroking his beard. 'Shouldn't there be something noble about a hero?'

'Yes, but—'

126

'You also said Marco could be aloof. Charmers aren't aloof,' Joan said. 'They're the opposite of aloof. That's just my personal opinion.'

Kathryn gave a little hum of agreement. 'Is it possible to be gregarious and aloof? Don't they cancel each other out? Being aloof is all right in a novel but in real life it's not as attractive as friendliness. It's rude.'

I'd never thought about it before. Being aloof is something I'd taken for granted in a hero. It's the sign of an alpha male. He is not part of the pack. I was following in a sound literary tradition here. Take Mr Rochester for instance. I've never fancied Mr Rochester, personally. He seems a bit clumsy for a start, falling off his horse and that sort of thing. And he's deceitful – I definitely wouldn't have put up with the stuff Jane Eyre tolerated – I'd have gone for somebody more fun-loving myself. So Kathryn was right. Maybe Mark was just rude and the attraction of aloofness is confined to fiction.

'The point,' I said, copping out completely, 'is to identify the archetype for yourself. These are *your* characters. What you do with them is up to you, but having said that, there must be a reason why you have chosen to write about this particular person which means that they must be out of the ordinary to begin with.'

'Oh, I don't know. I like an ordinary man,' Joan said, 'one who isn't too full of himself. My husband was kind and self-effacing and I wouldn't have wanted him to be charming or a father figure or a Peter Pan.'

'Your husband sounds like an Englishman,' Neveen observed.

'Yes, he was. He called me Tiger,' she said and blushed.

'Are you putting that detail in your book?' Kathryn asked.

'Certainly not. My book is about Robin the Robber. If a robin were to call anyone a tiger, it would actually have to *be* a tiger.'

She caught Nancy's attention. 'Who is this Robin character?' she asked.

'A bird,' Joan said irritably.

'Why is he a bird?'

'Because it's a children's book and it's about birds.'

'It's not a romantic novel?' I asked. 'Not one of you is writing romance in this romantic prose group?'

The answer to that was no.

I sighed and sat back in my chair.

Undeterred, Joan passed round her sketchbook of water-colour bird illustrations that had given her the inspiration for her children's book featuring Robin the Robber.

'I understand,' Neveen said, 'that robins are naturally pugnacious and that they only sing to warn other robins off.'

'Perfectly true.'

Now the sketchbook was passed across to me. The drawings were charming; Joan had done something to the eyes of the birds so that they looked mischievous and engaging.

'These are lovely,' I said. I looked up at her, half smiling, expecting her to respond warmly to my praise as most people would. She adjusted the purple clip that was keeping her grey hair out of her eyes and looked disapproving.

I passed the book to Nancy and Joan watched her reaction, eyebrows lowered belligerently, and it seemed to me she was steeling herself against criticism.

Nancy looked at the book with great care, moving her chair so that she could see the pictures clearly under the light. The only sound in the room was the ticking of the red clock. As the minutes passed I realised we were all watching her; waiting for her verdict. Nancy was taking her time, giving the drawings her full attention. I glanced quickly at Joan and she was staring at Nancy as if frozen to the spot.

I had begun to realise that Nancy wasn't governed by ordinary rules.

It was impossible to predict what she was going to say.

I've been brought up to see courtesy as a sign of being civilised, so I wanted to reassure Joan that we all felt they were lovely drawings and break that frozen stare . . . but I held back.

'This boy,' Nancy began at last, tracing along the drawing with her finger, curving it over the head and along the short beak.

'The robin,' I corrected her but Joan looked at me sharply.

'No, not the bird, the boy, the boy in him . . .' Nancy was suddenly uncertain. She got up from the table and came round to give the sketchbook back to Joan, still open at the page that had intrigued her. 'Tell me – is he a bird or a thought?'

Joan was looking up at her, taking the book, and her face changed so very slightly; a crimping of the chin, fighting to hold back the tears.

Kathryn scraped her chair back and apologised for the noise, and Turo was gathering up his notes. I glanced at the clock. The class was over and we'd had such a good time trying to impress her that we hadn't asked Nancy about the intriguing contents of that little black leather book. But, I reassured myself, there was plenty of time for that.

When we got back home, Nancy let out a little shriek as she caught sight of herself in the mirror.

'Is this my yellow hat? Give me yours!'

When I went upstairs, I took the mirror and put it back under the bed.

CHAPTER SEVENTEEN

Antagonists

Memory loss. That's what it was called but a lot of the time Nancy's memories weren't so much lost as temporarily mislaid. For a good fifteen minutes, it was possible to talk to her and not realise for a moment that there was anything wrong with her. Longer than that and she would start to repeat herself; I hadn't realised before how tiring making conversation was for her, not just speaking but listening and trying to keep up with the thread.

Nancy and I went for a walk every day. She was well known in South End Green as a local character to most people and as a writer to some, and she talked to everyone, so the stroll around the village could take some time, especially if it was late afternoon when the children were coming home from school.

This meant she was happy to stay in in the evenings with the Harveys Bristol Cream, so since I'd been staying there the issue of her going to pubs hadn't come up.

I would sometimes go out by myself when she fell asleep in the late afternoon, just for the novelty of striding out alone on the Heath in the crisp autumn air.

I came back after one of these walks and let myself in.

131

I could hear her talking to someone and I tapped on the parlour door. 'Nancy, I'm home.'

There was a man on the sofa drinking tea, balancing the saucer on his knee. Thirties, clean-shaven, short hair, wearing a cream cable-knit sweater, no jacket. He looked like a nice guy. I wondered who he was.

Nancy looked up at me happily. 'Hello! Look who's here! This is – who are you?'

'Shane,' the guy said, smiling at me.

'Hi, Shane.' I was just about to leave the room again when suddenly I hesitated. There was something about the smile. It was a bit too wide, a bit too friendly. 'So how do you two know each other?'

'We're old friends,' he said. 'We go to the same church, don't we?'

I didn't know that Nancy went to church, so I asked curiously, 'Which church is that?'

He barely hesitated. 'I forget the name of it,' he said, still smiling.

One skill that writers soon learn is an ear for dialogue and this whole scenario seemed a bit off to me. Seriously? No one forgets the name of their church any more than they forget the name of their school. Added to that, he was still smiling despite my growing scepticism, and that was the strangest thing of all. If he was perfectly innocent and doing a good turn by visiting a fellow parishioner, my suspicious, hostile attitude would have been pretty rude.

And yet, Nancy, who wouldn't allow the carers in, seemed perfectly happy with this guy, this stranger – and not just happy, but excited that he was here.

He finished his tea and stood up, still holding the cup and saucer. 'I'll just take this to the kitchen,' he said.

'No, I'll do it,' I said, taking them from him in case he was

132

familiarising himself with the place or, as crime novelists call it, casing the joint.

His smile didn't falter. 'Goodbye Nancy,' he said. 'Thanks for the biscuits. I'll come back and see you again very soon. That's a promise.'

I followed him down the hall. As he opened the door I said, 'What did you say your name was?'

He half turned, glancing up at the CCTV.

'Shane,' he said, still smiling.

I closed the door behind him and went back into the parlour and put the cup and saucer down. I wondered if he'd taken anything.

'Have you got your handbag, Nancy?'

'Here it is,' she said, holding up a Burberry check bag that I didn't recognise. She was in high spirits.

'Is that it? You had a black one yesterday.'

Nancy opened it up curiously. She emptied out the contents – rosaries and holy medals in self-seal bags spilled out onto her skirt – and she held it out and looked up at me gleefully. 'Look!'

'Are you a Catholic?'

'No,' she said. 'Are you?'

'No.'

She laughed and scooped them back into the bag.

Had Shane brought them with him? Why hadn't he mentioned it?

'I've brought her a rosary and some holy medals,' he could have told me. Maybe I'd scared him off with my questions. The camera would have recorded him coming in and if I called the police they might know him.

I got as far as unlocking my phone to talk to John the police officer and then I thought of Jack saying that Nancy needed to keep under the radar. Was this going to go against her, that she'd let a stranger in?

133

'You're a writer, aren't you?' Nancy asked suddenly, tapping my knee.

Surprised, I put my phone back in my pocket. 'That's right.'

'So have you done many book signings?' she said, passing me the plate of biscuits.

I took one and smiled. 'A few,' I said.

'Have you done Foyles?' she asked eagerly.

'No. Have you?' I asked, knowing the answer but wanting her to continue.

'Oh yes. We should go there!' she said. 'It's where I met him. I like to fix on a couple of faces, the ones paying attention. I look at the ones who are listening. I'm not keen on the scribblers. A talk isn't meant to be read, it's meant to be heard.'

I laughed. 'That's true.'

'It's mostly women that come,' Nancy reflected, picking up a biscuit crumb on the tip of her finger and licking it off. 'Just a few odd men with their mothers, wanting me to go for drinks with them and tell them off. Richard came with his wife.'

'Richard Buchanan?'

'Yes, that's his name. Do you know him? Richard Buchanan.' Nancy sank back against the cushions, smiled and closed her eyes. 'I like to have a talk prepared, the same talk each time, so I don't find myself lost for words and so that the throb of my beating heart won't dictate their tempo; do you know the feeling I mean?'

I smiled. 'I do.'

'I was arguing against Simone's *Absolute and the Other* concept.' Her smile faded and she fell into thought. 'Jean-Paul Sartre had terrible breath, I think that's why she didn't marry him.' For a moment, she seemed to fall asleep.

I stroked her arm. 'Nancy! What about Richard Buchanan?'

She opened her eyes, startled, and gave me a half smile that lifted the corner of her mouth.

'Well you see, I fixed on him and as I was talking about liberation from stereotypes, independence, autonomy, the solitary writer, Richard winked at me as though I was telling a joke. He winked at me!' She chuckled softly. 'He was young and good-looking and of course he was there with his young and good-looking wife Penelope. They were well suited.' She ran her tongue over her weathered lips. 'Before Richard, I had never seen love, the divine, that source of deepest, richest joy and laughter. It wasn't a man/woman thing – I could have just as easily have seen it in a dog, if I'd looked. But I hadn't looked. The truth is I didn't know what I was looking for and so it evaded me.'

My heart jumped. 'And then?'

'I was fifty-eight. I understood him because I had been thirty-four once and I knew what it felt like. But he had never been fifty-eight, well-regarded, the top of his field, had he? He had a wife and child, and I had my good reputation. You take what you want out of life, and that's what I wanted. But then I did the worst thing that a feminist could be accused of – I put another woman down on the grounds she wasn't his intellectual equal. I would have done anything to be with him. I moved in with them, for inspiration, to write. Penelope was all for it because there's nothing quite as intoxicating as being a muse, is there? The little boy moved into their room and I moved into his. I slept in his cabin bed; I had to climb a ladder to get into it.'

'Bloody hell, Nancy,' I said.

'It *was* hell. I couldn't write.' She bumped her forehead with her fist. 'I was agitated, I couldn't concentrate. I was obsessed with him. I stayed there for a month and then I gave it up and went to Paris, to Le Meurice, do you know it?'

I shook my head.

She giggled. 'Richard came to join me.'

Infidelity is as old as love, I suppose.

But it was hard to see it as love, which should surely be pure and untarnished, when the by-product was to cause pain to others.

Insanity, Jack had called it, and I could see why.

The bigger the force, the greater the destruction.

I was familiar with that destruction and I glanced at Nancy with a little less respect.

She saw the change in me and she flinched as though I'd hurt her, and tears rolled down her cheeks.

'I don't *care*,' she said defiantly, plucking a length of peach toilet tissue out of her sleeve to wipe them. 'I would go through it all again, just for the satisfaction of being with him.'

I couldn't think of anything helpful to say. She'd loved him, and she'd lost him and, although I wanted to, I couldn't say that she deserved that grief. I ate my biscuit and it seemed to take all the moisture out of my mouth, like an unripe banana. Finally I swallowed it down and Nancy was still watching me warily.

'Have you ever written about it?' I asked her.

'Yes.' She looked around her and waved her hand towards the Jiffy bags that lay about. 'It's all here, in these envelopes.'

'And in your notebook? The black leather one?'

'Yes. It's all here.' She nodded. 'I'm dammed when I'm not writing. I can feel the force of the words building up under the pressure, waiting to burst.'

She was still holding the length of peach toilet roll and she draped it over her face and blew. It lifted up like an elephant's trunk.

It was so ridiculous that, despite everything, I started to laugh. Her comic timing was perfect. She let the toilet paper fall, and when I stopped laughing, she blew it again. It floated in mid-air and from underneath it I could see her looking at me intently, joyfully, into the peep-hole of my eyes, finding something good in there.

CHAPTER EIGHTEEN

Barriers

Jack came round to Nancy's after work, bringing the Trek bike into the hall. He was wearing a pink cycle helmet and hi-vis jacket so bright it made my eyes ache. The bike had two new additions; a black D-lock attached to the frame and a black water bottle.

'Where's Nancy?' he asked cheerfully, unclipping his helmet and hanging it on the handlebars. 'I've got her *Times Literary Supplement*.'

'She's sleeping on the sofa.'

I told him about Nancy's visitor in the cream cable-knit sweater.

He frowned. 'Okay,' he said, 'let's take a look at him.' He looked at the camera, reached up and pulled it off the wall.

'What are you doing?'

'Checking the memory card,' he said, showing me. I followed him into the kitchen where he opened his phone, took out the memory card and swapped it for the one in the camera. 'Let's see what we've got here.'

We sat at the table and watched the recording. He fast-forwarded it: Nancy coming in the house and going out of the house, Jack going into the house and leaving the house, Jack and Nancy by the door and letting me in, all of us leaving the house.

'Stop! There he is.'

Jack paused the film. Shane was smiling straight up at the camera. Hand on heart, I've never seen anyone look so innocent.

'Do you know him?'

'Nope.' Jack shook his head. 'Never seen him before.'

'What should we do?'

Jack swapped the memory cards and put the camera back. 'I'll give John a call. See if he recognises him.' Suddenly his phone buzzed. He checked the screen. 'I've got to go.' He went back into the hall and put his cycling helmet back on.

I had a bit of a pang – I wished he was staying. 'One more thing – is she a Catholic?'

'No. Why?'

I showed him the Burberry bag with the rosaries and medals.

He frowned when he saw the contents. 'You think the guy left it?'

'Yes. What's the alternative? I haven't seen this bag here before.'

He wheeled the bike to the door. 'Lana?'

'What?'

'Which is your favourite season?'

I love this kind of game. 'Winter,' I said. 'Especially when there's snow, and it settles. The buses can't get up the hill. The schools close. People go sledging down Kite Hill. That's in Highgate, of course. You walk into Kentish Town and there's nothing but grey slush.'

Jack laughed.

'What's yours?' I asked him.

'Spring,' he said. 'It's the most hopeful month. The first catkins. Green shoots poking through the ground. Rising sap.'

'Interesting. I thought you'd say summer.'

'I thought you'd say summer too. You look summery. Okay. Winter it is. What are you doing tomorrow?'

'Is this another date?'

Jack grinned. 'It is. I'll pick you up at six.'

The following day, Jack picked me up at six in an Uber. He was wearing a navy jacket with a turquoise T-shirt underneath.

We pulled up outside the Icebar in Heddon Street.

Geared up in silver reflective parkas and thermal gloves, we entered the Arctic chill. With his fleece-lined hood, his clear, grey eyes and his dark stubble, Jack looked like an explorer as he tapped his ice glass of champagne against mine. I giggled with happiness because it was fun and somehow exciting to find myself in this completely different place, like an instant holiday, our breath mingling and clouding in the cold. And something else was different – this was the first time I'd ever seen Jack in subdued colours.

He looked darker, edgy, as he found a place in a corner on a bench carved out of ice and an ice table to put our drinks on. Our warm lips melted their own shape into our ice glasses, and when we put the glasses down they froze to the table. The lights changed constantly like the northern lights and I shivered with the sudden thrill of being alive and happy.

When we left, the early autumn air was warm and muggy. The taxi was waiting for us and we climbed in and we were now driving along Piccadilly, past Hyde Park Corner, down the Brompton Road.

I didn't ask where we were going, so it was a surprise when we pulled up outside an Alpine chalet with 'Herman's Schloss' carved over the door. There were oak panels, red gingham curtains, old wooden skis propped up in bundles, sledges, and through a window, a surprising view of a Poma lift taking skiers up the slopes.

A guy in lederhosen greeted us and took us to our table.

'Fondue?' Jack asked me, grinning as he took off his jacket.

'Yes, please.' This was the most fun I'd had in a long time. Dipping the warm Swiss bread into the melted Vacherin cheese, I told him that Nancy had been talking about how she was writing about falling in love with his father.

He raised his eyebrows.

'Yes, I know: in other words, insanity,' I said before he could say it.

He laughed and pronged a chunk of frankfurter. 'It was. I always wanted to ask him about it, what he saw in her, but it's not the kind of question you can ask your dad. My mother was gentle, not like Nancy. Nancy is volatile, she would argue just for the pleasure of it. She was a perfectionist. Both my father and I fell short of her high standards.'

'And you never talked about it?'

'Hell, no.' He shook his head. '*Way* too weird.'

'Yes, I suppose it is. Well, the whole world's going to be able to read about it eventually. It'll be a big deal, her life story.'

Jack didn't have the same enthusiasm as I did over the idea. 'I don't know. It's an old story. Infidelity, betrayal. Lives messed up and for what? Who's going to want to read about it?'

'I've been hoping she'll read it out in class, it would be such a fillip.'

'A Philip?'

'An inspiration. To be in on it and maybe even advise her . . .' I realised I was being insensitive. This wasn't fiction, it was his family. I took another mouthful of wine and looked at him over the glass. 'The good thing is it will probably give you some answers, at least. You could come along with us, and if you're not happy with what she's writing you'll be able to tell her so.'

'And you think she'll listen?' He crumbled the bread in his fingers. 'Well, you never know. She was kind when I moved in with them – when my mother died I was relieved that they actually wanted me – but once I was living there of course I didn't want anything to do with them. I hated them both. So pretty much for the first couple of months I stayed in my room. Nancy never came in, never asked me how I was feeling, not that I would have told them anyway, it was too hard to articulate. But at mealtimes and through the day I'd hear this one tap on my door. She'd leave a mug of hot chocolate with whipped cream in a little dish. A tray of food on the stool, with a napkin and a miniature salt-and-pepper and ketchup in a dish. Or soup and a warm roll wrapped in linen.'

He laughed. 'Totally pointless really; I was twelve. But it gave me the feeling of being looked after, I suppose.' His eyes gleamed. 'And it allowed me to stay angry.' His clear grey eyes met mine. 'It's a weird thing to be grateful for, I know. What about your parents?'

I told Jack the story – all memories become a story in time. 'Their separation was totally unexpected. I was heading to uni in the car my father had given me the year before on my seventeenth birthday, even before I could drive. It was a lovely little yellow Fiat and the insurance premiums were through the roof. My parents were busy people and they encouraged me to be independent.'

When you're eighteen a car makes you very popular and I thought it might make me some friends.

'My father helped me to pack my things into the car, fitting suitcases, bedding, lamps, crockery in neatly; in other words, he was behaving perfectly normally, like my perfectly ordinary

141

father. Hand on heart, and I've gone over this many times in eight years, he was the same that morning as he'd always been; upbeat, methodical and reliable. He had showered and shaved and there was not a single sign that anything was wrong, or that he was going to have left home himself by the end of the day – no clues, no words of wisdom.' I looked at Jack ruefully. 'Nothing in the least significant. We had a last meal together of scrambled eggs on toast, during which my mother got snappy about the butter being salted. But that was perfectly normal, too.

'And when at last I was ready to go, they both came out on the road and hugged me, and told me to call once I got there, and my father patted the roof of the yellow car and by the time I parked up on campus a couple of hours later and rang them, my dad had taken his house keys from his key ring, pulled his wedding ring off and left. Couldn't get out of there fast enough, my mother told me bitterly.'

I took a bite of pretzel, looking at the little wooden shutters with their pretty carved hearts, thinking about the similarities in the way they both left, the two men in my life, both of them leaving their keys and Mark leaving pretty much everything else.

'Just clearing off, basically. It still makes me angry. It's such a cowardly way to do it, not having the guts to wait around for the reaction, not giving the other person the chance to understand, plead, hit out, demand an explanation.

'Despite the whole keys and wedding ring thing, we expected him to come back "with his tail between his legs", as my mother so bitterly put it. But he didn't. And then one weekend, he came to see me at uni and he brought his girlfriend along. Jo-Ann was tall and dark-haired. Anyway; I met them. It had obviously been my father's idea to spring this lunch, because Jo-Ann wasn't the least bit interested in meeting me. She kept her hand on my father's knee possessively and as he left he gave me a handshake. Actually it was a fifty-pound note. You can do a lot of partying with fifty pounds when you're a student.'

I said it in a more light-hearted way than it sounds – distance lends a certain irony to pain.

Jack rubbed his jaw. 'Dopamine,' he said gloomily. 'It's got a lot to answer for.'

As a response, it was so unexpected that I laughed. 'Love, eh?'

'Yeah, love.'

We had chocolate fondue for pudding, plus some herbal yellow liqueur in shot glasses.

'How's your story going? Have you found a barrier to overcome?'

I dunked a chunk of warm waffle. 'Having a hero and heroine who don't believe in love is quite a sturdy barrier,' I said truthfully.

He thought about this for a moment. 'I've got an idea. How about if I wore a suit?'

It was such a random statement that I laughed. 'Jack, have you ever read a romantic novel?'

'Yes. Yours.'

'Did suits play an integral part in it?'

'Maybe I'm not thinking of novels. Maybe I'm thinking of a romantic film.' He pointed his fork at me. 'I know! *Ivanhoe*. It's very romantic.'

'It had *suits*?'

'Suits of armour. And jousting. They were knee-deep in jousting in *Ivanhoe*.'

'That explains a lot about your idea of dating,' I said, and I couldn't hold the laughter in any more.

That look came on his face as if he was on the brink of a smile. I loved his smile.

And then I started to wonder . . . Actors are notorious for confusing their roles with real life. Look at Angelina Jolie and Brad Pitt. Acted as if they fell in love and lo! The result was one shattered marriage lying in ruins on the floor of the set. I didn't know if it happens with writers; if authors fall in love with their heroes, but I suspected they could.

So far, like me, my heroine was viewing the would-be hero's attempts to be the protagonist with a certain detachment. The paragliding had been funny. The kayaking on the Thames was exciting. But this homage to my love of winter was romantic, no getting away from it. We'd looked into each other's eyes and found that deep interest about each other; the urge to know more about each other's experiences, who we really were. We both had our baggage, and even though it wasn't actually matching, it was definitely the same brand.

'You're smiling,' he said.

'I like being with you. We understand each other.' My gaze drifted to his turquoise T-shirt. He suited turquoise.

'By the way, I can't do a fake date next Saturday because it's my mate's wedding,' he said, as if it was something he'd only just remembered.

I looked at him hopefully. 'Are you taking a plus one?'

'It's a very small wedding,' he said, then quickly added: 'You know something? I've lost him now. We used to go to Cornwall every year for a weekend and he brought her along last year but she didn't like it much. It used to be our test – did they like Cornwall? And he's marrying her anyway.'

'Jack, you do make me laugh.'

That was my official line on the whole business, but I'd been drinking all evening and suddenly, despite the fun we'd had, I realised I wasn't really a part of his life at all. And as I smiled I felt my mood sink into the tender featherbed of melancholy.

CHAPTER NINETEEN

The Shape of the Hole in the Hero's World

Jack unexpectedly turned up at the next writing class. Nancy and I had got there early, and she was sitting at the head of the table, under the red clock, and she greeted him with some surprise. When she saw him in his pink cycling helmet, her face lit up.

She said, 'Oh! It's you! Who are you?'

'Jack Buchanan,' he said.

'And why, exactly, are you Jack Buchanan?' she asked him with the same bright-eyed curiosity.

He thought about it. 'For identification purposes,' he said. 'And who am I?'

'Nancy Ellis Hall.'

'There you are, you see?' she said to me with great satisfaction, as though she'd proved a point in a debate. She turned back to Jack. 'I haven't the vaguest idea why I'm called that. It doesn't sound like me at all. I would have liked to have been called Anaemia. Anaemia is such a pretty name, don't you think?' She turned to Jack. 'And what are you to me?'

'I'm your stepson.'

'Are you?' She looked at him sceptically. 'How old am I?'

'Eighty,' he said.

'Eighty? Or am I eight?'

Footsteps sounded in the corridor and a sudden burst of laughter which trailed off as they went past. Seriously, I needed to find out what they were doing in that end room.

Turo came in wearing his leather jacket. The rain had made the jacket squeaky and he sat down sighing and protesting about the weather.

Kathryn came in next in her red velvet coat with mirrors and swinging a laptop bag.

Joan came in wearing her purple hat. When she took it off I saw that she had a purple hair slide holding her long fringe out of her eyes.

They all looked at Jack, the newcomer. I glanced at the clock and watched the hand jerk to the hour.

Once again, we all introduced ourselves for Jack's benefit.

Jack told them that he was Nancy's stepson and he was thinking of writing something but he didn't have any concrete ideas at the moment.

Hopefully this was just his cover story – I had enough competition as it was.

My topic of the day was: *What Shape Is the Hole in your Hero's World?* Bearing in mind this was no longer just a class for romantic novelists, I had planned the session so that it covered fiction in general. I stood up to deliver the inspirational opening argument that I'd been planning all week.

'Perfection doesn't make a good story. If things are perfect then there is no motivation for change. Change is what drives a novel and what makes us change is the search for something different, something better, more beautiful, more fulfilling, more exciting, more comfortable. Our characters are searching for the all-important missing part. The missing part is different for each of us. Married people want freedom. Single people want marriage. The unemployed want a job. The settled want adventure. Today we're going to find out what is missing from our heroes' worlds.'

'I will tell you what is missing from my hero's world. Liberty,' Neveen announced, pointing at the ceiling. 'That's what he wants.'

'See if you can find the hole in mine,' Joan said, as she volunteered to read. She read the story of Robin, who had his head turned by a beautiful emerald-green parakeet called Pandora and who put himself in danger from the church kestrels by being dressed in some of Pandora's feathers and becoming a brightly coloured small bird.

Neveen argued that Robin was being aspirational. 'Because he feels inferior.'

Kathryn disagreed. 'He's obviously transgender.'

Joan was aghast at these inaccurate interpretations. 'You're both wrong. He is simply showing off. Vanity gets you nowhere is the core of the story,' she explained sharply, 'and I wanted children to know that Robin's personality suits brown and red, and when you are small and defenceless it's a good idea not to stand out.'

'But your hero hasn't got a hole,' Neveen said, pointing at her.

Joan frowned. 'Of course he has! It's the need for love. Everyone's hole is the need for love.'

'I disagree,' Kathryn said heatedly, 'because the hole in my hero's life is the desire for revenge.'

The atmosphere was getting lively. I thought of the hole in my own life, the one that Mark Bridges punched through my heart.

'First that which is natural, then that which is spiritual,'

Nancy declared from the end of the table. She had the kind of authoritative voice that carried and we all suddenly sat up and paid attention to this wisdom, without, in my case, necessarily understanding the context.

I glanced at Jack. He was sitting back in his chair with his hands behind his head. He caught my eye and a faint smile flickered on his face that said – *wait for it.*

I was desperate for Nancy to read, for his sake. I was beginning to see what Carol Burrows meant; she did add excitement to the class.

'Would you like to read to us an extract from your new book?' I asked her hopefully.

'Yes indeed.' Nancy opened her handbag and produced several things from there – a navy beret that she unfolded to display a handful of pens, a wooden pastry brush, some of the holy medals and rosaries from the mysterious Burberry bag and finally she took out the small black leather notebook with gilt-edged pages and got to her feet.

One thing's for sure, she had presence. Against the navy walls, her electric-blue dress created a halo of light. She began in a strong voice, rocking from the balls of her feet to the heels.

'Remember me is all I ask. And yet, if the remembrance be a task . . . Forget.' She turned the page. 'Remember me is all I ask and yet, if the remembrance be a task, forget! Remember me is all I ask and yet if the remembrance be a task, capitals, FORGET. "Remember me" is all I ask' – she looked up at us – 'that's underlined. But, if the remembrance be a task, and this bit is in capitals, you understand? FORGET.' She frowned and hesitated disapprovingly. 'That's not written very neatly at all.'

She picked up one of the pens and made a note. Then she closed the book with a self-satisfied slap and put it back in her handbag.

Wow! It was so interesting to listen to her – to understand the mechanics of her writing. We sat in silence for a few moments, still watching her, absorbing it. I glanced at Jack. He raised an eyebrow sceptically.

I was suddenly uncertain. Was it the mechanics of her writing, or was it gibberish?

'The repetition makes it really powerful,' Neveen said, resting her chin in her hand.

It did. It took guts to repeat a poem that many times, but I suppose that's what people expect from Nancy Ellis Hall – literary courage.

'Nancy, would you like to tell us the inspiration for that opening chapter?'

Nancy thought for a moment. 'It's like this,' she said, gracefully plucking imaginary wisps out of the air with both hands.

'Can you identify a hole in your character's life at this early stage of your novel?' Kathryn asked her.

'Oh – I can see the hole, of course I can. It's very black,' she said. 'It's there and it's not there.'

'Does the hole have to be one big hole?' Turo asked, clearing his throat. 'My character Bob has had his wages docked following his gambling and I'm undecided what the hole in his life is. It's not a need for freedom and it's not, like Joan's Robin, a need to blend in. I feel that his needs are smaller than that and somehow more immediate; the need for a smoke, the need to be warm and dry, living from one transitory satisfaction to the next, just something small to keep you going, just to make you believe that life is worth living another day for.'

There was a wistfulness in his tone.

Joan turned her head as if she was going to say something to him and her purple hair slide dropped onto the table and rocked and dithered to a halt. Her hair slid over one eye and she brushed it back with her fingers, the gesture so distinctly feminine that Turo gaped.

'Joan? You were about to comment?' I prompted her.

'I agree with you,' she said softly, looking at him. 'You learn to live with the big holes in your life but the small ones, yes, they matter just as much in their way.'

'Didn't William Percy French write that?' Kathryn asked timidly, looking at me.

'Yes, I think he did, didn't he,' I said brightly. I had no idea whether William Percy French had written about holes or not.

'I suppose it's out of copyright now, is it?'

'What is?'

'"Remember Me Is all I Ask". William Percy French wrote it.'

We stared at her in silence. That Kathryn, she knew everything.

'Yes, I believe it will be out of copyright by now,' I said, hoping it was true and hiding my disappointment that it wasn't Nancy's own work. 'How about your main character? Would you like to tell us a bit about her?' There's always room for a homicidal maniac in a writing class, that's my opinion.

Kathryn delicately bit the edge of her thumbnail. 'Okay. My heroine, Shelley, manages a women's refuge, a calm, sunlit house with fruit trees and a herb garden, but the refuge is compromised when a social worker gives an abusive partner the address.'

Her nervous eyes flick towards me and away. 'Yes, there is a hole in her life. She has learnt to hide her fear by building a defensive wall around her emotions. As a character defect, it's not such a bad one. It enables her to hear the women's stories calmly, and to advise them with wisdom and clarity. But she doesn't handle anxiety well when it breaches her defences and at first she tries to carry on as before after

Ryan turns up looking for Donna. Shelley persuades him that Donna isn't staying there any more, but she knows men like Ryan don't give up on a woman and she decides to kill him.'

Turo chuckled. 'Now that's what I call role reversal. How far have you got with it?'

'Six chapters, about fifteen thousand words.'

'How does she kill him?' Jack asked.

Kathryn turned to look at him and she seemed to see him for the first time and reared back. 'With a corkscrew,' she said in a small voice.

'Interesting,' Jack said.

Was it my imagination or was his voice suddenly deeper, more seductive?

'Doesn't violence breed violence?' Joan asked.

'Kill or be killed,' Kathryn said.

Neveen agreed. 'We don't know how far we'll go until we are tested.'

Kathryn sat forward again. 'Thank you.'

Just then, I looked at the clock and to my surprise our time was up. I collected my pens and closed my notebook, vaguely wondering whether it was still raining.

After the chorus of goodnights I was putting my notebook away, watching Jack and Nancy heading out with Neveen and Joan.

Not bad, I thought to myself, putting my coat on and straightening the chairs before I left.

Jack was in the corridor, waiting outside the ladies' toilets. He smiled. 'Remember me is all I ask.'

There was the whoosh of the hand dryer and the door of the ladies' cloakroom opened and Nancy came out, swinging her umbrella, suddenly startled and surprised to see us.

'Gosh! When did you two get here?' She tilted her head as

if listening to the echo of her own words. 'I've been saying gosh a lot lately.'

'Come on,' I said, taking her arm. 'Let's go home.'

The night was misty and cold. It had stopped raining but the streets were still slick and bright, cars spraying puddles as they pulled up by the lights. Jack headed for the bike rack and unlocked his bike.

He kissed Nancy on the cheek and turned to me.

'I'll call you.'

'Yes, sure.' Ahead of us was Euston station, dazzling in the gloom.

He switched the lights on and cycled away.

We watched him until we couldn't see the flashing red light any more.

'Who was that?' Nancy asked.

'Jack, your stepson.'

'My stepson? How old am I?' she asked as we walked to the bus stop.

CHAPTER TWENTY

Return of the Antagonist

I was making lunch when I heard the doorbell. I took the pasta sauce off the heat and heard Nancy talking animatedly to a woman.

As I came to the dining room I saw the woman push past her roughly and go into the parlour.

Protesting with indignation, Nancy followed her, grabbed her by her jacket and was trying to pull her out of the room.

The struggling woman was in her twenties, fair hair in a high ponytail, smudged eyeshadow, a backpack slung over one shoulder.

She struggled free and as she saw me, she swore.

'She's got my money,' she spat, pointing at Nancy. 'She was keeping it for me and now she won't give it me back.'

Nancy lashed out at her with a tight fist and the girl ducked out of reach.

'It was in that bag there!' The girl was pointing at the Burberry bag with the holy medals and rosaries. 'She's been keeping it for me!'

'Keeping it for you?' Nancy said scornfully, trying to duck under the barrier of my arm. 'Get out!'

I grabbed Nancy's house phone and waved it at the girl. 'I'm calling the police.'

'Good, call them, because she stole the money she was keeping for me, two hundred quid.'

I didn't believe her, but just the same, I didn't make the call.

What if she *had* left money with Nancy? No, I didn't believe her.

'It's all up there on film,' she said, going into the hall and stabbing her finger at the camera. 'You assaulting me and stealing my money, you crazy old bag!'

I opened the front door, letting the daylight stream in, and as soon as Nancy had pushed her outside I slammed it shut.

There was a loud thud as she gave the door a kick and it all went quiet.

My heart was beating wildly and I was shaking with adrenaline. 'Are you all right, Nancy?'

'Oh, yes,' she said, thoroughly energised by the encounter. She smiled sweetly at me and once again I didn't notice the teeth that were there, but the ones that were missing.

I could smell the pasta sauce and I went back to the kitchen to finish making lunch.

Nancy followed me, suddenly anxious as she looked up at my face to read my expression.

'You're quiet. Are you cross? What's happening?'

'We're going to have lunch in a minute.' I smiled, and forced myself to relax. 'Spaghetti Bolognese.'

'But what's happening? Are you vexed?'

'No, not at all.' She followed me as I laid the table using fresh table linen and put the napkins into silver napkin rings. To change the subject I said, 'Do you remember, you used to do this for Jack when he was twelve? You used to serve him food and drinks at regular intervals to nourish and sustain him.'

'Yes I do! Where is the boy now?' she asked.

'He's a man, and he's at work.' I put the food on the table and we sat down. I spread my napkin across my knee. 'How did you feel when Jack came to live with you after Penelope died? Was it nice to have a child in the house?'

When I looked up she had her veined hand pressed against her mouth. She whimpered softly.

'I'm sorry, Nancy, I shouldn't have asked.'

She shook her head despairingly, her eyes reddening. 'That little boy,' she said. 'There was absolutely nothing that we could put right for him. All hope was gone.'

'The hope of his parents getting back together again, you mean?'

She nodded.

I couldn't think of anything to say to cheer her up so we ate in silence.

My thoughts kept coming back to Jack, and I wasn't sure what to do about our latest visitor.

How much of a coincidence was it that Shane had turned up while I was out and the girl while I was in the kitchen? Were they keeping an eye on the place? Yes, paranoia was setting in.

She's vulnerable.

While these gloomy thoughts were going through my mind, Nancy's mood had cleared like mist in the sunshine.

'Dig in,' she encouraged me happily through a mouthful of pasta, 'before it gets cold.'

CHAPTER TWENTY-ONE

Heroines

On Tuesday evening I was looking at the big red clock as it ticked calmly and the hand inched past the hour. Nancy had gone to her usual seat at the head of the table, wearing a flame-red cardigan with pearl buttons and a grey skirt, and she was holding her black leather book up as if it was a Bible she was swearing an oath on. Joan was right opposite me, Kathryn was sitting next to Jack, Neveen was next to Joan.

We listened to the people going to the class at the bottom of the corridor, waiting for Turo. He was never usually late so, despite my rule about starting on time, I decided to give it a little longer before my motivational speech.

It was ten past when Turo hurried in apologetically. Instead of wearing the black leather jacket he was wearing a tweed overcoat with elbow patches.

That was the first thing I noticed.

The second thing I noticed about him was that he had a black eye. The bruise looked quite fresh, blue with red undertones, and his eyelid was beginning to swell shut.

'Sorry I'm late,' he said as he sat in his usual chair, rubbing his hands to warm them and he took a bottle of water out of his bag, then his notebook, and lined them up.

'Good *evening*,' Joan said to him pointedly. Suddenly she noticed his swollen eye and her voice softened. 'Whatever's happened to you?'

'Nothing much,' he said, smoothing his beard. After a moment's silence he added, 'From now on I want you to call me Arthur.'

Ah.

There it was; the whole story told in a sentence.

Joan didn't pursue it, although her eyebrows were still raised in a query.

She'd never liked calling him Turo. She always used it archly, as if the word was faintly ridiculous.

I began with my theme of the day, which was heroines.

'There's a temptation to make the heroine of a novel the feeble kind of person that needs to be rescued,' I began.

That was as far as I got because Kathryn interrupted me breathlessly.

'I have a question about that,' she said. 'My heroine is both the protagonist and antagonist. Killing Ryan sets up a whole new set of problems for her and each solution seems to make things worse for all of them rather than better. I don't know what to do about an ending.'

'She's quite obviously a psychopath,' Joan said. 'At the end she gets locked up – I can't see that you have any other alternative.'

'Or she could get away with it,' Neveen pointed out.

'Get away with murder?'

'Er, women very rarely get away with it,' Kathryn said. 'They're usually judged more harshly than men in court because their actions are premeditated – they have to be because how could a woman win in a fair fight?'

'It depends on the size of her,' Neveen said.

We all looked at Turo; sorry, Arthur. He was a tall man. We were forced to re-evaluate our mental picture of his ex.

'Donna might be grateful that he is dead.'

'It's a huge burden to carry,' Kathryn said. 'Always knowing you could have handled things differently.'

Joan looked at me. 'Lana, your heroine was weak,' she said. 'I've been wondering why you didn't have a companion for her in *Love Crazy* because she doesn't seem the kind of girl who would set off travelling by herself. She doesn't like the countryside, so it all seemed a bit improbable to me, if you don't mind me saying. She's even scared of cows.'

'Lots of people get killed by cows,' I said. 'You might think it's improbable – or is she actually brave?' I asked hopefully. It obviously hadn't occurred to them that, like me, my heroine had no one in her life to travel with. 'And she's not weak, she's independent. She's always had to stand on her own two feet, that's the point, so it wasn't at all out of character.'

'It seems unlikely, that's all I'm saying. Anyway, I was just wondering why you took that route in your novel, seeing as we are on the subject of weak heroines.'

'It's true she seems more of a home bird than an adventurer,' Arthur said.

Neveen was interested in this comment. 'Is home bird an actual breed?' she asked, taking notes.

'Home bird!' I laughed cheerfully to disguise the fact that I was crushed to the core by the criticism. But it's a bit off-putting, laughing by yourself, so I added, 'The point is, my heroine was living outside her comfort zone, which is what made it into an adventure. She'd always been used to routine. If it was the kind of thing she'd always done there would be no inner conflict, would there?'

'But she was lonely and had to be rescued by Marco.'

'He didn't *rescue* her,' I said. 'He joined her on a few legs of the journey, which is a different thing altogether.'

'She was scared of a dog, too. The dog she was scared of, what type of dog was that?' Neveen asked.

'Springer spaniel.'

'In my opinion' – Jack leant back in his chair, took a deep breath and stared at the ceiling to consider these criticisms – 'if Lana's heroine was travelling *with* someone, it would be a different sort of story. If you're with another person, you have to take them into account,' he said. 'The whole point of her going on that road trip was to do something different, to write about her experiences and please herself for a change.'

'Exactly!' I could have kissed him.

'And she changes a lot by the end,' he added.

It was true, I did change a lot. I'm still scared of sheep, cows, horses and any dog that isn't kept in a handbag, but during the course of the journey and therefore during the course of the novel, I went from the misery of loneliness to the ecstasy of being in love; from being a blogger to being a novelist. That was huge.

I decided to drop the subject of the feeble heroine and I asked who wanted to read.

To my surprise, Kathryn said that she wanted to read first. She twisted a coil of hair around her finger. Her voice was intimate and breathy, like a voice on radio at night.

'Ryan was lying next to Donna, his breathing gradually coming back to normal. He propped himself up on the pillow. He was like a dragon, breathing fire. If he were to kiss her again her saliva would be cool, her tongue playful and her mouth a shady oasis.

'"I had my coil out yesterday," she told him, her mouth breathing out words against his arm.

'Bitter anger surged through him and there was no room

for anything else. Let it go, he thought fiercely. Oh, it wasn't the big betrayal that broke a relationship, he thought, it was all the little ones eating it away. For a moment he almost heard the crunching.

"'Ryan, I'd booked it," she said, her voice steady with justification, sweeping her hair across his chest. "What's the big deal? Kids are sweet, baby!"

'Her words were hot on his face.

'He jerks that elbow back, feels bone on teeth – whoops! And then says, the reason steady and justified in his voice as he wipes the blood from his elbow: "You deserved it."' Kathryn put her pages down and looked up at us. She added in her normal, quiet voice, 'And that's why she's got false teeth.'

Nobody spoke for a moment. Personally, I was speechless. You can't judge a book by its author.

Neveen asked, 'Why did you write it from Ryan's point of view? Doesn't it make him more sympathetic?'

'No one could ever feel sympathy for a man like that,' Arthur commented brusquely.

Kathryn looked at Jack, but as usual Jack was sitting back in his chair, arms folded, hair ruffled. He felt the intensity of her eyes on him and let the front legs of his seat drop to the ground.

'I'd read your book,' he said.

'Thanks.'

'I can see she's tricking him into pregnancy,' Neveen said, 'but why would she even want a baby with Ryan? He's vile!'

Kathryn said. 'That's what Donna wants. Every human likes his own way.'

'She may not get pregnant.'

Kathryn smiled. 'That's right.'

'Because his testosterone levels might have dropped,' Neveen said, which made us laugh.

'I notice you changed the tense at the end,' Joan said.

161

'For immediacy.'

Throughout all this, Arthur was quiet, weaving his pen through his large fingers, one blue eye distant, the other swollen shut. The bruise was spreading downwards, almost meeting his cheekbone.

Four weeks into the course and we didn't know much about each other. Kathryn had created an opening for Arthur to talk, but that was as far as it went. The phrase 'Every human likes his own way' hung in the air, it seemed, even though no one commented on it.

'I would like to tell my story to you,' Neveen said, breaking the silence. 'Like Joan's and Kathryn's, this is not a traditional story of romantic prose. I was married to Monir, an Episcopalian and a prison chaplain. He was diabetic. He ate too much, always the wrong things.' She took a deep breath and sighed. 'When he died I prayed for a reason to carry on. Bala asked me to visit him. His full name is Ratnam Balendrarajah. He was arrested in a drugs sweep at Cairo International airport when he was twenty years old, escaping from the civil war in Sri Lanka. He has been in Zamalek prison for twenty years now. This is the subject of my book. This prisoner.'

Nancy had been watching her intently. 'Ha!' she said, pouncing, suddenly coming to life. 'You love him.'

Neveen blushed.

'I have a love story, too. Would you like to hear it?' Nancy got to her feet and opened the little leather notebook carefully.

The tension was electric.

This was it; this was what we'd been waiting for, Nancy's story.

I glanced at Jack. His face was tight and wary, one foot tapping against the table leg, waiting for the inside story on why Nancy had destroyed his family. Suddenly it seemed a really bad idea, but Nancy began to speak with gusto.

'Chapter One,' she began. 'Ham, toilet rolls, tomatoes, sugar, soap. Bisoprolol fumarate, warfarin, levothyroxine, white, brown, blue. The man upstairs. Banged at nine thirty, nine thirty-two, nine thirty-seven, nine forty-one. Banged at ten oh three. Bang bang bang to the bathroom. Bang bang bang to the bedroom. Loud voices, arguing and suddenly' – she pointed a dramatic finger at the ceiling – 'silence.'

We listened in wonderment to that Joycean stream of consciousness. It was thrilling, seeing a good writer at work. It had a drama and an immediacy about it that made you want to read on. But . . . I was slightly puzzled, too.

I glanced uneasily at Arthur who was frowning, at Joan smiling faintly, at Kathryn looking confused, at Neveen nodding and tapping her pen on her pad.

Jack had a thousand-yard stare, his face expressionless, his jaw tense.

He relaxed as Nancy closed the notebook and put it back into her bag.

I tried to think of an appropriate comment. I looked at the others hopefully.

'Amazing,' I said in the end.

This is the drawback with writing classes. They're frustrating. Each week you get a small bit of the story and the overall book is as difficult to judge as buying a dress online. It takes a long time to read a book aloud, which was why I preferred to read to myself. The other problem is that books are not meant to be read aloud. Nancy's extract from her first chapter had meaning because she read it out as she meant us to read it. To the untrained eye it would have about as much meaning as a random list.

Or . . .

. . . it actually *was* a random list.

Before she left, Kathryn patted Arthur's shoulder and told

him that acupuncture would get rid of the swelling and bruising.

Joan pulled her purple knitted hat over her fine grey hair and waited for Arthur.

And Jack came over to me. 'That was fun,' he said, smiling faintly, eyebrows raised.

Nancy came over to us slightly querulously. 'Now, you,' she said, pointing at me, 'where have I seen you before?'

'I'm Lana.'

She came close up to me and put her hand on my cheek, looking at me quizzically but kindly.

'Are you my mother?' she asked.

CHAPTER TWENTY-TWO

The Wrong Turning

Jack had decided, against his better judgement, to show the video of Shane to John, the police officer I'd met before. He brought Claudia the CPSO with him and we sat in the dining room, where Nancy told Claudia that she was very beautiful, and John that he looked big and strong. They asked her about her visitors – Shane and the girl who said she'd got her money.

I've noticed that any attempt to tell Nancy to correct her behaviour went down badly. So it didn't start well.

'I've always helped people,' she told them, and she turned to me for confirmation.

'True,' I said. I asked them, 'Do you know this guy?'

Claudia and John looked at each other in that expressionless way that police officers adopt.

'Yes,' Claudia said.

I was discovering that a conversation with a police officer is not really a conversation at all, it's a one-way source of information. 'So?'

'I'm sorry, we're not saying anything else, except that this is not the kind of man you want in your house.'

'Has he done this kind of thing before?'

'I'm sorry. Can't say.'

I showed them the Burberry bag; it seemed quite light because Nancy had redistributed the medals and rosaries, which were turning up all over the place, and I told them about the money that the girl had said Nancy was keeping for her.

Again I saw that little flicker of interest. 'Was her attitude intimidating?'

'Yes.'

'Did she intimidate Nancy?'

I knew from past experience that the correct answer was yes, but the truthful answer was no. From the film it probably looked as if Nancy was intimidating her, rather than the other way around. I searched around for a compromise.

'Possibly,' I said.

Claudia looked at me. 'They'll start targeting her now. They'll make a mark on the house to let other people know there's a vulnerable adult living here.'

'What kind of mark?' I asked sceptically. I was pretty sure I would have noticed a mark if there was one.

The four of us went outside to have a look. To my surprise there was a mark just to the right of the door, in chalk. It looked like an open book.

'Yeah, that's it,' John said grimly. 'Vulnerable person.'

'That's a *book*,' I said indignantly. 'It's probably because she's an author.'

He looked at me pityingly. 'Trust me, we've seen these before.'

I fetched a wet sponge to wash it off and after dabbing the wall and erasing all trace, we went back into the parlour.

'Let me get this straight,' I said, 'you know he's a criminal and you suspect that they were working together to get money from Nancy; you know where they live, you know about the signs they chalk on people's houses, so why is it our fault? How come you're not arresting them?'

'On what grounds? What have they done, exactly? Nancy let them in, and there was no intimidation involved, she was obviously happy to see them.' He shrugged. 'You've got a bag that the girl said was hers – maybe there *was* two hundred pounds in it, who's to argue?'

I couldn't believe what I was hearing. 'Let me get this straight. You're blaming us for letting them in?'

'I'm just telling you to be aware. People don't realise how clever they are. They know this game off by heart. It's how they make a living.'

I groaned in despair and his attitude softened slightly.

'This is what you need to do. You should get a safety chain for the door. Maybe consider having a camera by the back door too. Don't let anyone in and, if you speak to someone on the doorstep, don't engage with them. And for your infor-mation, turn away the guys who say they're just out of prison and turning their lives around by selling household goods, because they leave their marks too – they mark out the suckers. They'll rob you blind.'

'Anyone who pays a pound for a single yellow duster has already been robbed,' Claudia said, and they laughed.

Police humour, hilarious. I'd bought dusters from those guys. They always seem to choose a cold wet night to come round, dripping wet and with that jail-house pallor. I'd always felt I was playing a crucial part in their rehabilitation and now I'd just found out I was as gullible as Nancy.

'So you want us to get CCTV cameras, door sensors, a security chain . . .'

'You could consider sensors along the perimeter of the garden too,' he said.

'How about a couple of guard dogs,' I said sarcastically.

John ignored me.

'Basically you're telling us to lock ourselves in to protect us from people out there that you know for a fact are preying on vulnerable people? Shouldn't you be locking them up, instead of us?'

'We're not telling you,' Claudia said. 'We're advising you.'

They both got to their feet. I wasn't sure how much of this Nancy had followed, but she wasn't her usual buoyant self and I didn't blame her. It's no fun being put in the wrong for being friendly.

Claudia had a last final look at the video. 'Is she often this aggressive?' she asked, replaying the scene in the hallway with me holding the door open and Nancy pushing the girl outside.

Once more I was stuck for the right answer. Isn't it a good thing to be aggressive when the circumstances warrant it?

John put the camera back up on the wall. 'Tell Jack that we called,' he said.

'We will.'

Once they'd left, I asked Nancy if she wanted to go for a walk. I didn't have any particular route in mind, but I wanted to get out of the house.

It took a while to get ready. A visit to the bathroom, a search for her handbag, then finding the yellow hat and the gloves, and a scarf that didn't itch. We headed for Daunt Books, her favourite destination.

Once she stepped inside the shop she took a deep breath. 'Smell those words,' she said happily.

'Good afternoon, Miss Ellis Hall,' the girl behind the counter said.

'Now, do you know my sister? She's also a novelist.' Nancy turned and looked up at me. 'That's correct, isn't it?'

'Yes – I mean, I'm a friend, really, aren't I.'

'You're part of the sisterhood, aren't you?' she pointed out.

'Definitely,' I agreed.

'What name do you write under?' the girl asked.

'Lana Green.'

'Oh – you wrote *Love Crazy*. I love that book! My dream is to travel in a camper van! I'd tour Europe and then maybe head for Eastern Europe, Croatia's beautiful. When's your next book out?'

'Next year or the year after,' I lied confidently.

'We'd love it if you had an event here, a book signing maybe. We do a lot of them – let your PR department know.'

'Thank you, I will!' My mood lifted immediately and I turned round to look for Nancy. I did a circuit of the shop and came back to the counter, giving the girl an awkward smile because we'd already said our goodbyes. 'Where did she go?'

She nodded towards the door and I went back out onto the pavement, looking for Nancy's familiar pink coat and yellow cloche hat. Across the road was Hampstead Heath station, the route home. To the left of it, if you followed the path, was the car park, the lower part of Hampstead Heath and the pond. To the right were the shops, the bus terminus, Marks & Spencer's and the hospital.

Where had she gone?

I felt suddenly anxious. She could have gone in any direction to any of those places. We hadn't come out with any particular plan; the idea was to get into the fresh air; the *fresh* air as she put it. I couldn't understand how she'd disappeared so quickly. Although Nancy could walk fast when she wanted to, she generally didn't. She was fascinated by children and she would always stop to compliment them on their liveliness or their hair or anything about them that took her fancy. She liked to talk to beggars too, usually asking them where they came from and offering them her gloves if she thought they were cold, or her hat, which so far had been refused.

169

I was angry with myself. I was supposed to be keeping an eye on her.

I expected to see her at any moment, willing her to appear. I worked my way down from the bookshop, anxiously looking into each shop as I passed it and trying not to panic because it wasn't as if I'd been talking to the woman that long.

A tall, white-haired man tapped me on the arm. 'I'm Harry Hegarty, your neighbour,' he said.

'Oh yes!' We'd said hello a couple of times as we put the recycling out on a Friday.

'I've just bumped into Mrs Ellis Hall in the charity shop.'

'Great!' I could have kissed him. 'Where's that exactly?'

He pointed, and just then I saw her coming out with a doll nestled in the crook of her arm. Nancy's face brightened as she saw me.

'Look what I've got!' The doll had long dark braided hair and a red and white dress that looked handstitched.

'Nancy! Why didn't you tell me you were going?'

Her face fell in confusion and I felt really bad. Maybe she hadn't liked to disturb me while I was talking. Maybe she'd forgotten I was even there.

'But,' I said, changing my tone, 'it's fine because we've found each other! And you've got a doll!'

'Yes! Look at her eyes.'

They were a startling blue, the kind that open and close, framed with long dark eyelashes.

I laughed.

'Isn't she lovely?' Her voice softened maternally. 'My baby.'

I nodded. It wasn't a baby doll but I agreed. 'What will you call her?' I asked, getting into the spirit of it.

'Oh, it hasn't got a name, it's just a doll,' Nancy said, suddenly enthralled by a dark-haired boy riding high on his father's shoulders. 'Look! There's the boy!'

170

A few years ago I bought a non-fiction book about difficult mothers.

It was like a manual, really. I've always been the kind of person who reads the instructions, not because I'm diligent but because I'm lazy. I like knowing that someone else has already gone through the trial and error stage for me so that I can take the short cut.

The book covered all manner of mothers but what I liked best about it was the conclusion that children of difficult mothers were often patient and understanding as well as a few other good qualities that appealed to me. These skills were coming in useful for dealing with Nancy.

I held out my elbow and she gripped it and we went to Marks & Spencer's to get food for supper.

When we eventually got back to the house we stood outside for a few moments while I looked at the wall to check whether there were any new marks on it. There weren't.

What the police should do is tell us which marks are a warning and then chalk them on people's walls to keep them away.

When Jack turned up that evening in the bright orange Nike sweatshirt, I confessed that Nancy and I had lost each other in South End Green.

He didn't look surprised, or disappointed in me. 'She's easily distracted,' he said, taking his trainers off in the hall.

'True.' It made me feel slightly better.

'Lana – when I first met you in the Edinboro Castle,' he went on, 'you were wearing a red jacket and skirt. That's a good jacket to wear when you're out with Nancy. Bright colours catch her eye.'

I looked at his sweatshirt and laughed. 'Ahhhh, that explains it. I thought it was for cycling. Is that why Nancy wears bright colours too? So that you can find her easily?'

'It helps,' he said, smiling back at me suddenly. He had a lovely smile.

'So, the red jacket, you think?' I could go shopping for bright colours because I was now solvent again. I could go to Uniqlo. I liked that he'd remembered the suit.

We had a strange relationship. Honestly, I'm blonde and not bad-looking when I make an effort. I'd expected him to at least be slightly flirty by now but, despite our deep conversations, our shared concern about Nancy and our fake dates, there was still a barrier between us, a line that he would not cross.

He looked into the parlour where Nancy had fallen asleep with the doll on her lap.

'Coffee?' I asked him as we went into the kitchen.

I switched the kettle on.

If he was really committed to not committing, one day we could get married and live in separate houses and use each other as excuses for our hermit-like states.

'What are you thinking?' he asked curiously, leaning on the wooden table.

'I was thinking about us. How ideal we are for each other. We're both quite solitary.' I was testing him, seeing how he'd respond.

He straightened up, putting distance between us.

'I'm not solitary. Where did you get that idea from?'

'It's just – you never talk about your friends or anything.'

'Why would I? You don't know them.'

'I suppose. What I mean is, we're both bitter in our own way.'

He smiled faintly. 'You think I'm bitter?'

'Yes.'

For a few moments he didn't say anything and then he tilted his head. 'Or maybe I'm just sensible,' he said.

CHAPTER TWENTY-THREE

Conflict

It was a strangely muggy night considering it was the middle of October. When Nancy and I got out of the bus at Warren Street the blood-red sky was turning the yellow of a bruise and it grew ominously dark as we headed to the writing class with Nancy gripping onto my arm.

I'd taken Jack's advice. Not only had I been to Superdry and bought a yellow box quilt jacket but I'd also found a colour-phasing Twilight umbrella with twinkling lights inside and out which was impossible to miss in the dark.

We arrived at London Lit and passed the office. Carol Burrows greeted us enthusiastically.

'How is your new book coming along?' she asked Nancy.

Nancy's notebook was still in her handbag from the previous week. Although I was hoping to read it, she had been very secretive about its contents.

'Marvellously,' Nancy told her.

In the classroom, she sat in her usual spot at the end of the table, wearing her salivary-gland-stimulating lime-green dress, and smiled cheerfully as the others drifted in.

Jack came in with Kathryn – she was telling him something that involved a lot of hand movements.

I felt an unexpected pang at their closeness, but then he looked my way, and when he saw I was watching him he winked at me, setting off a rush of warmth right through me.

My speech to the class that day was about the Power of Description. I'd planned it all week and practised it with authority and I put a lot of emphasis on the all-important reader's reaction to elements of the story written for dramatic effect, making it obvious that this was A Good Thing.

'So,' I concluded my introduction, 'let's think about that today.'

Jack listened to this with his arms folded and his grey eyes on mine.

'Who wants to read?' I went on. 'Neveen?'

'Yes . . .' She opened her laptop. 'So if you remember, Bala is coming to the end of his sentence after twenty years. Okay. This is a letter he sent. "Dear Sister in Christ. About the beadwork you told me there is a Market, Thank God. Please try to keep with you beads money. When I need I will write you because next year my freedom. Now have thirteen months to get freedom so I'm very happy I'm going see my family. We have completed sentence after twenty years. Really I don't know how I'm finish my sentence. We have fine problem and ticket problem, pocket money. Really I am doing fine, thanking you for your prayers. You say that the bags are very beautiful. If you get any order let me know. I am sorry for the terrible Bombings in Europe. Also we prayed in our Prayer Group and our fellowship with all our brothers and we pray for Europe for peace. Thank God for the Police, Doctors, and Churches. God Bless You and may God will give you peace, joy and happiness for ever. Thanks and God bless you. Your Brother in Christ. Bala."'

Neveen looked up from her laptop and bit her plump lip.

'What's the fine problem?' Arthur asked.

'They have to pay a fine after twenty years or stay in prison for another five years. It's a thousand pounds each.'

'Better than another five years in prison, I suppose,' Arthur said. 'How near is he to finding it?'

Neveen shook her head and turned towards the window to steady herself. When she turned back she said, 'He's raised three hundred at the moment.'

I knew what it was like to be broke. I thought of this guy and his optimistic faith – what else did he have to keep him going? And I wondered what we could do to help him.

'This beadwork,' Joan said doubtfully. 'What do you mean by *bead*work? What exactly does he make?'

'Yes,' I said, bringing the conversation around to my subject for the day, 'let's have some description of this beadwork so that we can have a visual des—'

'All sorts of things,' Neveen said to Joan. 'Bags, pens, necklaces, bracelets. The beads are bright and sparkling, mostly glass. It's good for them to make them. In prison it provides colour' – she swallowed – 'and beauty.'

'Why don't you bring some in for us to see? It's coming up to Christmas and I always think that if you buy a gift in a good cause you're giving twice,' Arthur said.

Neveen looked startled, and then she looked at me.

I was all for it. 'Yes! Of course! Bring some beadwork in!' It seemed highly unlikely that the seven of us would buy seven hundred pounds' worth of beadwork between us, but it's good to be optimistic.

Neveen nodded, pressing her lips together. 'Thank you.'

'Now, about the description,' I began again.

'Neveen, I like the reference to events outside of that prison,' Kathryn said, 'like the bombings in Europe. We can see life going on around them while they are stuck in that one place for all that time. Despite their isolation, we get the sense that they still belong to the wider world.'

'They are still very much of their time,' Arthur agreed.

There was a low rumble that vibrated the windowpane and we all fell still and turned to look.

Lightning stabbed through the black clouds and the wind began gusting. Rain was hitting the window like gravel.

'Hang onto your hats,' Arthur said drily. The deafening din of thunder rattled the windows.

Nancy jumped to her feet in agitation. 'What's that noise?'

'It's just the storm,' Kathryn said.

'It's *far* too loud,' Nancy said crossly, hurrying into the corridor to sort the thunder out.

We thought she'd be back at any moment, so we waited, but after a couple of minutes Jack went out into the corridor to look for her.

When Nancy started shouting, we followed him out.

Down the end of the corridor near the reception desk, Nancy was yelling at Carol Burrows who was trying to stop Nancy from leaving the building by barring her way, arms outstretched.

'It's okay,' Jack called, 'you can let her go!'

But Carol was mindful of the fact that this was a famous author, in her building, agitated by the storm. She did the worst thing possible. She got hold of her shoulders, intending, I think, to turn her around and steer her back towards us.

'Don't worry, I've got her!'

For a moment it looked as if they were not struggling but dancing.

It wouldn't have seemed a difficult thing to do, to restrain her. Nancy was small and old. But Nancy didn't want to turn round, because she wanted to put a stop to the thunder. Feeling

176

threatened, she retaliated by biting down hard on the hand that was gripping her.

Carol screamed. Those corridors really carry noise.

I have never heard a person scream like that before.

And I'm not sure it was the right response in the circumstances because Nancy was already panicked by the thunder and adding noise to noise wasn't going to make it better.

'Let her go, Nancy,' Jack was saying, but what eventually worked was the tin of mints that Arthur had in his pocket which he offered to Nancy.

'Here, Nancy, have one of these,' he said, rattling the tin. 'They're Extra Strong.'

The distraction worked. Nancy let Carol go and chose a mint. 'I'll take three,' she said, putting a handful in her pocket.

Carol was nursing her hand in weepy distress and the thunder boomed and echoed overhead as if the sky was falling in.

Nancy was clicking the mint against her teeth, eyes widening. 'That noise,' she said to me. 'Switch it off.'

'Don't worry, it's thunder, that's all.'

Neveen sat Carol down behind the desk and looked closely at her hand and the indentations left by Nancy's remaining teeth.

'You might have a bit of a bruise,' she said. She apologised to Nancy. 'I don't wish to be rude.'

Nancy agreed with her wholeheartedly. 'Not at all. Nobody does. That's the beauty of it.'

'I had no idea she was *this* bad,' Carol said, looking up at Nancy warily with the desk between them. 'I'm going to have to record it as a works injury. And I'm sorry, Lana, I can't allow her to come here again. What if she'd bitten another student? I've given her a fair chance – you can attest to that.'

There wasn't a lot to argue with so we drifted back into the classroom while Neveen repacked the first-aid kit.

So much for paragraph 1c.

I glanced at the red clock, and then at Jack, sitting with his elbows on the grey table, avoiding our eyes.

He looked despondent, lost in thought.

The storm had passed and Nancy had recovered. As we settled down again, she opened her handbag and flicked through her little leather book. At last! She held it up high over her head and it cast a shadow on her face.

'Cereal, milk, bread, ham,' she recited.

Jack's mood darkened. He stood up, startling us. 'Shut up, Nancy! It's all rubbish,' he said fiercely. 'What's the point?' He stood up and knocked his chair off balance; it juddered and righted itself again. He grabbed his jacket and walked out.

I got up to follow him.

Arthur waved me back. 'Leave him be, Lana. He needs a break. He's got a lot on his plate and we've all had a crisis of confidence at times.'

'It's tough on him,' Kathryn said.

'He is a man who is powered by his feelings,' Neveen added.

'Here I am!' Nancy announced, realising she'd lost our attention. Her voice was loud and clear, overriding us as she looked towards the open door. A small, fierce woman, she was undeterred. She carried on reading from her place at the head of the table, but this piece she knew by heart, and she pressed the book against her chest. 'And I will not be a burden, because I do not want what is yours but you; for children ought not to lay up for their parents, but parents for their children. I will most gladly spend and be spent for you. If I love you more, am I to be loved less?' It was a small, clear lens of clarity focusing on a blurred world.

The question hung in the air and we looked at her in the silence. Her insight moved us all; it sounded like a quote and she addressed it towards the door, not saying it to us but to Jack.

'I recognise that as a Bible quotation,' Neveen said.

We heard the faint beep of the key pad as Jack left the building.

Arthur closed his notepad decisively, too. He scraped his chair back from the table. 'We can't follow that, Nancy. I don't know how everyone else feels, but I suggest we go to the pub.'

I helped Nancy into her coat and we, the little band of writers, went back down the corridor. The office lights were off.

Outside it was drizzling steadily. I held out my elbow and Nancy tucked her arm into mine and we stood under the twinkling lights of the umbrella. In the pattering of the rain I fretted about Carol's threat and Jack walking out and decided I would have a brandy.

The pub that Arthur took us to was called the Queen's Men. 'A good, real ale pub,' he assured us.

However, as we gathered outside it, a wooden sign barred our way. 'Private Function' it read in gilt lettering.

'Private Function,' Nancy told us excitedly as we listened to men's laughter and the music inside.

A stocky bouncer came out, tapping a cigarette out of a packet. 'Sorry, girls,' he said. 'Stags only tonight.'

'Let's find somewhere else,' Neveen said.

'Come on,' Nancy said, ignoring him and tugging my sleeve, 'let's go in.'

'It's just for men,' I said.

'Don't be ridiculous,' Nancy said sternly. 'You can't have a party just for men. I've been a feminist all my life.'

Joan laughed. 'We like the argument, Nancy, but . . .'

'We can easily find somewhere else,' Neveen repeated calmly as the bouncer went round the corner to light up.

'Follow me. Look! It's easy.' Nancy pushed the sign to one side and marched on in.

Oh, great. I am a law-abiding person with a teacher for a

mother, but I knew that once she was inside she wouldn't remember how to get out, so I closed the wet umbrella and went in after her, pushing through the crowd. The music blared and as I looked around for her I heard above it a wave of laughter which swiftly turned into cheering. My heart sank.

I found Nancy dancing by the bar, kicking her legs with gusto and ending with a twirl which almost made her lose her balance. Somehow she recovered and held onto a stool, swaying as they stood in a semicircle, filming her on their phones.

The bouncer came through the crowd and grabbed her, twisting her arm behind her back and pushing her towards the door. 'I told you to stay out.'

'Let her go,' I yelled at him, dropping my umbrella and trying to prise his fingers off her arm to loosen his grip.

'Get her out of here and don't come back, she's a bloody liability,' he said, giving us both a final shove back into the dark, tripping over the umbrella and then throwing it out after us.

Arthur picked it up from the puddle. The lights had broken. It looked like a dead bat.

Nancy looked up at the sky in astonishment, her arms raised in bafflement by the sudden transition from one scene to the next, from the cheerful heat of the crowd to the cold wet of the night. She rubbed her shoulder.

'He hurt me,' she said in a small voice.

Neveen rubbed it gently.

'I'll get you a taxi,' Joan said to her.

'I'm so sorry, Nancy,' I told her, putting the bent umbrella over her head again.

'Who *are* you?' she asked from under the dark canopy, her face dim and uncomprehending.

'Lana Green.'

'Take me home with you.'

Our little group walked back to Euston in the driving rain.

CHAPTER TWENTY-FOUR

Consequences

The next morning Nancy was her old self again. She took me into her shady book-lined study, pointing out a book she'd written, pulling it from the shelf.

'When was it published?' I asked her, sitting on the edge of her chair.

The image on the book jacket looked like some kind of obscure fertility symbol and the whole cover was in shades of purple. She showed me the flyleaf and looked at me, slightly startled.

'Last week, was it? It's all here,' she said.

I started to read it aloud with her behind me, resting her chin on my shoulder. 'Tell me that bit again,' she said. The fresh thinking and boundless enthusiasm for feminism were purely her.

When she got tired of listening she took it from me and put it back on the shelf.

'Why did you have a break from writing?' I asked her – I'd wondered about that a lot.

She frowned. 'I didn't have the authority to carry on with it,' she said.

181

'In what way?'

To divert me, she handed me a black and white photograph of Rosamunde Pilcher from her desk.

'This is my mother, I think. And this boy' – she smiled and looked at it closely – 'I know him well.'

'Yes, you do.'

It was Jack, aged about thirteen, facing into the sun and half shielding his eyes, wincing with embarrassment at having his photograph taken.

My phone vibrated in my pocket and it was Jack. We hadn't spoken since he'd walked out of class. I went on to the landing to talk to him.

'Morning,' he said. He sounded weary. 'How's Nancy today?'

'Fine. Why?'

He let out a long sigh. 'Carol Burrows,' he said.

My heart sank as I realised what he was talking about. 'Oh. She called you?'

He paused. 'Worse than that. She called social services. They've assigned her a new social worker, fresh out of uni, talking about care homes again,' he said. 'Ranya feels that she shouldn't stay in her own home and she's got others to back up her argument. They're having a "Best Interests" meeting tomorrow.'

'Why can't she have Caroline Carter back as her social worker?'

'Yeah. Doesn't work like that, apparently. Once they signed off on a case, that's it. It's back to square one.'

Suddenly all my energy was back. 'You know Nancy will hate being made to feel bad!' I lowered my voice. 'And things are working out fine here, generally.'

'You can tell them that at the meeting tomorrow if you want to come?'

'Yes, I do.'

His voice softened. 'Thanks, Lana. We'll give it our best shot.'

I glanced inside the study. Nancy was still looking at the photographs and I went into the hall to continue the conversation out of earshot.

'Jack, how can social services and the doctors have the right to make decisions about a person they barely know? It's a travesty.'

'Yeah; you don't have to tell me. We'll see how it goes.'

'Okay.'

I put my phone in my pocket and went back into the study. Nancy was holding a picture of Richard Buchanan. 'Que sera, sera! Sing it!'

'Que sera, sera! Whatever will be, will be!' We were both on surer ground, but I felt my chest tighten. 'We're going to Wembley!' I sang.

'That's not it,' she said.

We went to the best interests meeting, which was held in a social services office, a bleak, concrete building. We got there on time but we had to wait in the dull entrance hall for over half an hour and Nancy began to get irritable and restless, which didn't help.

Eventually we were taken to the small meeting room. To my dismay, Claudia, the PCSO with the short dark hair, was there, with a district nurse called Jan and a young geriatric consultant called Tom Broadhurst. Ranya, the new blonde social worker, was sitting with Nancy's GP, an Irish woman with red hair.

Tom Broadhurst had a baby face and an officious attitude to offset it. He started by asking Nancy her date of birth.

We willed her to give the right answers, feeling like anxious parents at an entrance exam.

Nancy stood up to answer. '1910,' she said. And then added with aplomb, '1938.'

'And your full name?'

'Nancy May Ellis Hall, no hyphen.'

'What day is it?' he asked her.

She frowned at him irritably. 'If you're so clever, you tell me.'

'But I want *you* to answer,' he told her. 'I want to hear what you've got to say.'

'It's one of the days of the week, obviously,' she said.

'And what's the date today?'

'Ten!'

Broadhurst made a note and went on to his next question. 'What is the name of our current Prime Minister?'

Never short of confidence, Nancy answered this with great authority. 'Lloyd Brown.' And this was how the meeting progressed. Nancy employed a lot of creativity. She didn't remember having a husband, and she wasn't sure Tom Broadhurst was suitable to be asking her questions because his face was too young. She told Ranya she was fat. She berated Claudia for not smiling. As for the seasons, they were very variable, sometimes cold, and sometimes warm, 'Like this – like this – like this!' she said, demonstrating the nature of the weather with her hands.

Tom Broadhurst pressed his lips together and glanced at Jack. 'You say she has a live-in companion?'

'Yes, Lana.'

I raised my hand.

'This is not a job for one person,' he said, 'or even a couple of you.' He looked at his notes. 'Her behaviour can be challenging.' He turned to me. 'How do you deal with that, Lana?'

'I try not to frustrate her,' I said. 'I think about the way I speak to her. I used to be quite abrasive but she responds really well to kindness and we enjoy each other's company.'

184

'But that doesn't always work, does it?'

'It mostly does.'

He looked at his notes again. 'We understand that she occasionally resorts to physical aggression. There was an incident in the college, and a woman she was recently in close contact with had to have medical treatment. She's also presenting with memory problems.'

Nancy's GP took over and said that she had anterograde and retrograde memory loss, she was vague about whether she'd ever been married and her last scans showed higher executive frontal lobe problems.

Claudia the CPSO said that Nancy tended to habitually engage with young people in the community.

'And what's wrong with that?' Jack asked sharply.

'It makes her vulnerable.'

Jack shook his head in despair.

The consultant turned his attention onto him. 'And you're in full-time employment?'

Jack nodded. 'Yes,' he said. 'I've got my own business.'

'And there aren't enough days in the week,' the consultant said sympathetically.

Jack avoided the trap. 'She's been a lot happier since Lana moved in. She's calmer and she's stopped going to pubs.'

'And yet you still can't manage to control her behaviour at times.'

I glanced anxiously at Jack – he was keeping his cool although they seemed determined to catch him out.

Nancy was suddenly aware of the change of atmosphere and that our attention had drifted away from her. 'Who's dead?' she asked brightly. She pointed at Jack. 'Tell me!'

It seemed quite a broad remit.

'Do you mean who in our family?' Jack asked her.

'How about Jesus?'

And while our attention was completely back on her she cheerfully raised her skirt and showed Tom Broadhurst her legs for him to admire.

I had never loved her so much as I did then, when my heart was breaking. She looked at me and saw the tears in my eyes.

'Don't be so ridiculous,' she said to me sternly. 'You are ruining the moment, look at me. You can do this!' She wiggled her fingers up and down in front of the doctor's impassive face.

And that settled it.

Tom Broadhurst reached a conclusion. 'I am recommending the considerable benefits to Nancy of residential care. She will be in a safe environment, and she will be given occupational therapy to keep her engaged and stimulated.'

And so the best interests meeting was concluded. Nancy needed to go into a care home to live out the rest of her days.

The next day we went to look at a place nearby called Greenacres Lodge. We drove there with Nancy. It was a large, detached house in Belsize Park, on the hill, only about a mile from her own home, and from the front it really did look like a hotel except for the banner reading 'Greenacres Lodge Nursing Home', advertising for staff.

We had to ring a bell. A smiling woman named Virginia let us in. She was wearing a white coat, which looked authoritarian and vaguely medical. She glanced at Nancy, but spoke to us.

'It's a closed facility,' she said, leading us down the passageway, 'especially for dementia patients. We give them a good quality of life here. This is the bar where we serve non-alcoholic drinks.'

'Non-alcoholic drinks?' Nancy asked. 'I like to have Harveys Bristol Cream in the evenings.'

'I think we have some of that,' Virginia said with a wink.

'Why are you winking?' Nancy asked her.

'She's a sharp one!'

'Don't talk to her, talk to me,' Nancy said.

I could imagine her sitting at the bar complaining that the fake drinks weren't strong enough, and getting into a fight as a result.

'And this is the bus stop.' Virginia showed us the wooden bus stop in the main hallway, with a wooden bench next to it. 'When residents want to go home, we tell them to come here and wait for a bus. After a while they forget all about it and wander off again.'

'Fools,' Nancy said disapprovingly.

Really, it was heartbreaking because Nancy was nowhere near that bad. I could imagine her demanding to be let out so that she could put the bus stop sign on the street where it belonged.

'And here,' Virginia said, 'we have the cuddle room.' It was a small room with sofas pressed up against the walls and soft toys propped up, glassy-eyed. 'And this is the communal lounge where residents are free to take up any pastimes that they like, or to play bingo or snap in the afternoons.'

None of the residents was playing bingo or snap. I have never seen people so ill, yet still alive. They all stared into their own bit of space, as glassy-eyed as the toys.

I thought about the spin that the doctors, the consultant geriatrician, the social workers and the community health nurses had put on the wonders of a care home; pushing us into a decision that we didn't believe was right for Nancy but that we desperately hoped we were wrong about.

We trudged after Virginia as she showed us the bedroom that was available. It was big, with an ensuite bathroom.

'You can bring Nancy's furniture with her. And make a

187

book about her life so that we can talk to her about things she might remember from her past, like pets. We can play music that she likes. And if you have photographs, they're always helpful too.'

The window opened onto a large garden. Birdfeeders hung from the trees and a magpie flew off as we walked across the lawn, casting hour-long thin shadows as far as the flower beds.

Virginia smiled at us. 'Once she's settled, she'll be happy here,' she said. 'She won't want to leave. Take your time and look around again.'

I waited until she'd left, and I looked up at Jack. 'She's going to hate it,' I said. 'How are we going to tell her?'

'If we had a choice it would be different, but we don't. What's the answer, except for a miracle?'

He was a good guy, was Jack.

It was impossible to shake off the guilt.

If we were better people, if we'd fought harder at the meeting, if Nancy had been calmer, maybe things could have gone on for longer as they were. So yes, as we looked out at the empty chairs and the swinging birdfeeders, we felt sick at heart. We weren't just letting her down, we were betraying her. It was impossible to get away from.

Virginia came back a few minutes later and reminded us that Greenacres Lodge had a waiting list and if Nancy wasn't moving in then they would contact the next person.

Just then, Nancy reappeared, full of excitement. 'Come into my parlour! Follow me!'

She beckoned us down the long carpeted corridor and opened the door into a large bathroom with a plastic seat, grab bars and a hoist.

'Lovely,' Jack said.

Satisfied, Nancy turned around and led us back to the office where she showed us the late book, took a certificate off the wall and tucked it under her arm, and answered the phone most charmingly.

Back home she and I stood in the green bedroom looking out of the window.

'That,' she explained, waving a hand at the sky, 'that blue up there and you see, it's got those bits on it.' She had seen a lot of that lately, all that, and the bits. And after marvelling at the clouds she told me that the trees on the Heath needed cutting.

I agreed that they did and I said I would organise it.

I had learnt by now how flexible I could be with the truth.

After years of believing in the importance of honesty, living with Nancy I saw things differently. The truth wasn't important. How could it be; it was always subjective. If Nancy's truth was that there were five cats on the roof, what difference did it make that they were pigeons? What did I gain from arguing about it? She saw pigeons and said cats, and I knew what she meant. Language is just a means of communication, and she could communicate and I could understand her.

Nancy went downstairs and I stayed in my room a little longer. I loved this place. This was Nancy's house, where she belonged. This furniture, these photographs, the little rugs so beautifully chosen to match the colour scheme.

I reminded myself that even if she left this house, she hadn't died. She was still here and lots of people sell their homes and move somewhere smaller, newer, more manageable, and they keep the things that they like and create a new home in a new environment.

It was downsizing.

It was a change, that's what it was.

I sat on the bed and found myself listening to Nancy and Jack talking in the kitchen. And I was thinking of the leather, gilt-edged notebook she brought to the class which so

189

intrigued me. I wondered exactly how she'd go about putting a story together out of the snippets that she'd read out in the class. I wondered if there even was a story.

This might be my last chance to find out, and I went into her bedroom.

I'm not proud of it. I was full of nervous excitement. There is something strange about looking in a person's bedroom when they're not there. It's like looking into a part of them that you wouldn't normally see and you never know what you might find.

Nancy's room was neat. The bed was made and apart from the baskets of papers in the window the surfaces were clear. There were a couple of oil paintings on the wall; a hunting scene and an apple orchard.

Generally I am an honest person with an averagely robust conscience. What I'd imagined was that the little leather book would be next to her bed and I could have a quick look and put it back. Having to actually search for it was a completely different proposition.

I pulled my sleeve over my shaking hand to open her bedside drawer – personally I think this is the kind of knowledge that gives crime novels their educational value. It contained paper napkins, some loose change in a shower cap, and a large quantity of knee-high socks.

I went over to the wardrobe and opened it. Her pink coat was on the hanger and I patted it down, fingers closing over what could have been a wallet, but which could also be the book I was looking for. And it was. My heart was thumping. It was the little black leather notebook with the gilt-edged pages; quite possibly literature's Holy Grail.

I opened the book. It wasn't a book, it was a diary – an old one.

I flicked through it. The poem was in it, just as she'd read it: *remember me is all I ask*, repeated over and over with various underlinings. There were shopping lists and the complaint about an imaginary man making a noise upstairs. Quotes from the Bible with verse numbers – the same quotes that I'd thought were hers – Neveen had been right. I was forced to comprehend the obvious.

There was no story, no biographical notes, no insights into why she'd ruined a marriage.

I had a familiar feeling, like one of those nightmares where you get chased and chased but you still keep running even though you know that eventually the thing that is chasing you is going to catch up with you and get you.

It's not a fear of death, it's a fear of there being no redemption, and whatever comes after that is a different worry.

The following day Jack came in the early afternoon and we packed a suitcase and the rugs, her books and some photographs and we drove up to Greenacres Lodge and the staff came out to welcome her.

Nancy wasn't happy. She kicked the bus stop in the hall with great irritation and we carried her suitcase to her room and added her possessions to it feeling very subdued.

Nancy had some lively ideas about how we could all get out of there and her embroidery scissors were moments later swiftly confiscated by the manager.

She was upset when we stood up to go. 'Don't leave me,' she said plaintively. 'I haven't done anything wrong.'

So we stayed a bit longer and left about an hour later when her food was brought to her room, distracting her.

Jack and I didn't talk on the drive back. There wasn't much to say and no consolation we could offer each other. Jack dropped me off and I let myself in the house under Old Mother Hubbard's hungry glare.

I sat in the parlour with my head in my hands. The empty silence was total. The guilt pressed against my chest, making it hard to breathe. All I could see in my mind's eye was Nancy's face. All I could hear was her voice: *I haven't done anything wrong.* I couldn't bear the thought of her being in an unfamiliar place, without us.

At six o'clock, Jack turned up at the house again. 'Hey.' He looked terrible. 'Can we talk?'

'Of course,' I said but my heart sank at that early warning signal – *Can we talk*. I held the door open for him to come in. 'You want me to leave,' I said, to make it easier for him.

'What?' He looked confused. 'No, it's not that.' Under the glittering chandelier, his eyes burned into mine. 'It's not right, is it? What are we saving her from, Lana? What are we saving her *for*? So that she can live a long old age locked up in a place that's not her own? That's not what she needs. She needs to be accepted and involved. Nancy's always taken her chances in life.'

'I know.' I nodded although I still wasn't sure what he meant. I stared back at him, confused.

'So tell me, what's your opinion?' His eyes searched mine. 'Did leaving her there feel *right* to you?'

'God, no.'

'Okay, then. I need to know what you think because you see her more than I do and this depends on you agreeing to it. I know it's a lot to ask but I want to bring her home again. When the time comes and there's no other choice, we'll take her back there, but it's not now, is it?'

Hope flared up in me. 'No, it's not now. But I thought we didn't have any choice?'

'They'll have to apply to the Court of Protection for a full deprivation of liberty order and that's going to take a while. Until then, she can come back here where she belongs. Agreed?'

'Definitely.'

'Right. I wish I'd never taken her there. I'm going to fetch her. You coming with me?' he asked.

The weight lifted off me and I grabbed my jacket.

And that's how we made the decision.

When we got to Greenacres Lodge, Nancy was sitting in the porch wearing her coat and yellow hat. She had tied the net curtains into a knot so that she could see out. It was hard to know how long she'd been there but she got to her feet eagerly when she saw us.

'There you are! I've been waiting for you,' she said.

A woman started screaming wildly in another room. Nancy said, wide-eyed, 'It's quite an exciting place, don't you think so?'

'Very.'

Our decision to take her home didn't go down very well and Jack had to pay a month's fees to cover it, but we packed her belongings while the staff looked on, much to Nancy's indignation. She couldn't stop talking.

'The people here are wordying all the time,' she said. 'I'm not going to be seventy any more, I'm going to be sixty-seven. It's half-past six. Which world would it be? Our decision.'

We brought her home again.

Home.

She was happy to be back, dancing in the parlour in her yellow hat while Jack and I sipped Harveys Bristol Cream in front of the fire.

He caught my eye and touched my glass with his, giving me the faintest trace of a smile.

And suddenly it came to me in an epiphany. We'd been pursuing the hero thing all wrong.

He already was one; I just hadn't recognised it before now.

CHAPTER TWENTY-FIVE

Departures and Reunions

On Tuesday I went to the writing class without Nancy. I hadn't seen Jack since Friday, and I knew that there wasn't any reason for him to turn up.

I was sitting at my usual seat in the middle of the grey table with my Smythson bag front of me, and my notebook and Berol pens lined up nicely, listening to the lazy, persistent, hollow tick of the red clock as the minute hand hitched past the hour. I checked the time on my phone. Strange. Where was everyone?

Was it because Nancy wasn't coming any more?

Had they got bored and staged a mass mutiny?

Or had they all been struck down by some new animalistic flu and I was the only survivor? If I was absolutely the only survivor then I was heading for the canteen to eat myself to death.

This is probably how most apocalypse books get written. The author, sitting in the solemn isolation of his thoughts, suddenly surfaces into the real world and wonders if life is still going on outside his head.

Not that I'm paranoid, but it was quite a relief to hear

footsteps in the corridor. Jack came in through the door, took his jacket and his cycling helmet off, sat down opposite me and folded his arms. He was wearing a brown T-shirt and he seemed impervious to the cold.

He raised his eyebrows. 'Where is everybody? What did you do to them, Lana?'

It was good to see him.

I told him my apocalypse theories, but he wasn't convinced.

'I didn't see anything out of the ordinary and I'm reasonably sure I would recognise a zombie invasion if I saw one,' he said, so we agreed to be patient and wait a bit longer.

It was almost ten past when we heard the clatter in the corridor of people approaching, and the four other members of the class came in and dragged out the chairs they always sat in. They brought with them into the room a quiet seriousness. Something was up.

'Right,' I said cheerfully, to lift the atmosphere, 'let's get started.'

But Arthur got to his feet and smoothed his paisley cravat. 'Before we begin, there's a subject that needs to be aired. It's about Nancy. We've discussed it and we really don't want to carry on the class without her.'

My heart skipped a beat. Mass resignation!

'Is that so?' Jack asked mildly.

Arthur frowned. 'We are a writing group. We're more than a group; we are a society.'

'A literary society,' Joan corrected him.

'And Nancy's part of our group,' Neveen said. 'We don't want to lose her.'

'I suppose I could ask Carol Burrows to reconsider,' I said doubtfully.

'Actually, we wondered if we could meet somewhere else instead,' Kathryn said.

My heart leapt with joy at this simple solution, but as tutor my job was to be practical. I tapped my pen on the table, thinking it through.

'The problem is, if we do that you'll lose your course fees,' I said, 'and you won't get your CAT credits at the end.' Also I would lose my job and not get paid.

'We don't write for CAT credits,' Kathryn said. 'We write to be writers.'

'Fair point,' I conceded. That's the kind of reasoning I understand.

Jack looked just as he had when we first met in the beer garden; amiably happy with his dark hair ruffled and his face smooth and untroubled.

'We could meet at her place,' he suggested.

I wanted him to stay looking like that. 'All right, leave it to me. I'll explain to Carol how we feel,' I said, smoothing my skirt, straightening my collar and generally preparing to be a tutor again. I glanced at my notes, hastily prepared this morning. 'Right, let's get started. Today we're going to talk about overcoming obstacles to love.' It was a subject close to my heart. 'Who wants to start?'

Kathryn read an extract in which Shelley and her best friend are digging a grave behind the shed to bury Ryan who she killed with a corkscrew, and it's blisteringly tough, digging through London clay, so they are wearing oven gloves.

Arthur's hero is sent back to the front to join a different regiment as his own has been decimated in his absence. Robin has discovered that Pandora is shrill and self-centred. (Moral of the story, don't be taken in by showiness.) Neveen's prisoners are celebrating Christmas with a feast of food and soft drinks and Bala invites the Muslim guards and inmates to join them.

None of these readings had anything to do with obstacles

to love but, despite that, it was a very constructive session. At the end of the class, Jack waited for me to gather my pens together and I walked out with him into the cold night. The sky was clear, the wind was chill and the lights of Euston Road looked bright and festive.

I was feeling good – exhilarated even – after all we'd been through. We'd put Nancy in a care home, and taken her out again; both actions had been a bonding experience. And Jack had no need to come to the class without Nancy. The fact that he'd turned up anyway gave me a warm and optimistic feeling.

As we approached the bike racks I took my chance. 'Jack, I've got a problem with my story,' I said recklessly.

'Oh? What's that then, Lana?'

'There's an obstacle to love.'

'What's the obstacle?'

'It needs more passion in it.'

He stopped walking and looked at me, his eyes glinting under his straight dark eyebrows. He kept his hands in his pockets and studied my face.

'Is that so? If there's anything I can do, just let me know.'

My hair was blowing in the breeze and I held it down to look at him clearly. 'That's what I'm doing. Letting you know.'

I could hardly see his expression in the dark but the air around us changed suddenly, charged with sexual tension. I was intensely aware of him.

'My place, then?' he asked softly. 'You want a lift?'

'Yes, please.' I smiled, remembering that first wild ride with my arms tight around him.

I zipped up my jacket as he bent to unlock his bike. He stopped, mid-motion. 'Hey . . .'

'What?'

'Look at this!' He rattled a huge heavy-duty chain with a

brass padlock the size of my fist that was hooked through both wheels. 'This isn't mine.'

Confused, we looked around at the other bikes propped up around us, half convinced that we'd gone to the wrong one, but no. I'd recognise that red and black Trek bike anywhere.

'I don't understand it,' he said, straightening, throwing his shadow over me. 'Why would someone put a lock on my bike?'

The pedestrian crossing beeped and I looked distractedly towards the sound as the green man glowed. People crossed, phone-watching with bowed heads and illuminated faces.

And then I saw Mark Bridges. I recognised his cocky walk. His fair hair was longer, bright in the street lights. He was wearing a tan overcoat and holding a coffee which he was drinking through the lid.

The shock hit me so hard that I couldn't move; heavy as stone I watched him come towards the bike racks and suddenly he saw me and our eyes locked and his frown eased instantly from his face as he gave me that generous, warm-hearted grin that had made me love him and he lobbed his coffee into the bin.

'Lana!' he called, hurrying towards me against the glittering backdrop of traffic. 'I've been looking all over for you!'

This is what a reunion of two lovers reads like – running into each other's arms, hair floating in the breeze, a joyful gaze, laughter, the joy of being together again . . . This is how I would have written it.

The flaw is that in this scene, all the logical and psychological aspects are ignored.

I've read that it was only possible to feel one strong emotion at a time. It isn't true. Excitement and anger, that's what I felt at that moment and both feelings were equally intense and pure.

'Who's this?' Jack asked, and I jumped in alarm – I'd forgotten all about him.

Mark smiled confidently at Jack. 'Hello! I'm Mark Bridges.'

'Jack Buchanan.'

Mark looked at the cycling helmet in Jack's hand. He looked at the bike. And then he looked at me.

Putting the facts together.

His smile faded and he looked hurt. 'You gave him my bike, Lana?'

'She didn't *give* it to me. I bought it from her,' Jack said.

Mark tucked his hands into his coat pockets and hunched his shoulders against the cold. 'Ah.' It came out like a sigh. He seemed to be considering his response, and after a moment, he took the keys to the bike lock out of his pocket with a crooked smile. 'In that case I suppose you'd better have these, then,' he said.

Jack unlocked the bike and let the chain rattle to the floor and he straightened to look at me, his expression unreadable.

'What do you want to do, Lana?'

My heart was racing.

I'd been *that* close to going home with him and now, just a few minutes later, it was unthinkable.

'I'm sorry – I'll call you, okay?' I said, in a rush, willing him to understand.

He nodded, wheeled the bike round, bumped off the pavement and rode away.

Mark took my arm. 'Let's go for a drink,' he said. 'We need to talk.'

'Yes.' We were standing close now, close enough for me to smell his aftershave. I was now feeling completely unreal but somehow cleansed, the feeling you get when the pain has stopped. 'Yes, let's do that.'

'We've got a lot of catching up to do,' he said, without any irony at all.

We went to a champagne bar in St Pancras International station. The banquettes stretched along the platform. I switched on the heater under the seat and as Mark pressed the little button by the table to buzz for champagne, a train pulled in alongside us and behind the glass the travellers spilled out and I watched them, feeling invisible in my different world.

The waiter came to our table and did a double-take. Mark Bridges was beautiful by any standards. Falling in love is personal but attraction is a different thing altogether. Attraction is universal, or at the very least international.

You know the way you go into a bar and have a quick look at who's there, your gaze sliding across faces and coming back to one in particular? That's what happens with Mark Bridges. In the same way that your eyes will linger on a sunset or a celebrity, you just keep looking at him. I've watched it happening with men and women, old and young; I've watched them looking at him because he is so nice to look at.

The waiter poured our drinks and the bubbles rose and crowded the rims of our glasses.

Mark took off his coat and pushed up the sleeves of his caramel cashmere sweater. His blond hair was longer, like a surfer's, and his arms were deeply tanned, hairs bleached gold by the Honduras sunshine. He leant forward on the table, studied my face and smiled.

'It's good to be back.'

'Is it?' I raked my tangled hair out of my eyes. He was making it seem so easy and it wasn't. My anger was bunched up tight behind my ribs as I thought about the pain he'd put me through. 'There's nothing to come back to. I had to give up the flat. I couldn't afford the rent by myself.'

His eyes didn't waver from mine.

'What happened with the writing?' he asked softly.

'They didn't like the second book. It was about heartache,' I said. 'Write what you know.'

He frowned. 'I'm sorry I put you through all that. Your mother told me you'd got a job now.'

I felt a fresh new flare of resentment. 'When did you talk to my mother?'

'About five minutes after I got home, put my key in the lock and found some strange woman peering back at me over the safety chain. I wanted to surprise you. The surprise was on me, I guess.' He rubbed a line through the condensation on his glass and looked up at me.

'Yeah,' I said, thinking of my nightmare wait at the airport. 'I hate ruined surprises. And she told you I was at London Lit.'

'Yes. The security guy wouldn't let me in without a pass. Then I saw the bike and I got a lock from the bike shop in Euston in case you cycled away when I wasn't looking.'

I'd got tunnel vision. Adrenaline does that. My peripheral vision had closed down and all I could see were the words coming out of his beautiful mouth. I wondered what had happened to Helga the free-diver. Maybe she'd dumped him.

Ah well, stiff upper lip and all that. Whatever happened, I wasn't going to mention her. I had my pride.

'What went on with you and Helga?'

'What went *on*?' he repeated, looking into my face as though he didn't understand the question.

I fumbled in my bag for my phone and held it up for him to look at. 'See this, Mark? This is for communicating with. You've spoken to me twice in ten months. What was I meant to think?'

I slammed it down, swallowed the last of my champagne

and hit the buzzer above the table. The waiter came back with the champagne bottle. As if mesmerised, I watched him pour, saw the foam rise and settle and waited for him to leave before continuing.

'Well,' Mark said, 'I did try to call you but your phone's dead. As for Helga' – he shrugged – 'she seems to be doing okay.'

'Oh, good,' I said sarcastically, back in my rude default mode. 'As long as Helga's fine.' But I noticed his expression shifted a little, the way he'd said it. 'Why, what happened?'

'She had an embolism on her third dive. She came up too fast and got the bends. It caused a blood clot and paralysed her down one side.' He looked slightly hurt. 'You didn't know? It made the headlines in Europe. My photographs were syndicated worldwide.'

That's what happens when you give up social networking. You don't have the foggiest what's going on in the world. I gazed out at the distant blue arc of night beyond the Gothic building.

Mark took my hands in his, tugging my attention back to him. 'The free-diving community, it's close, it's got the vibe, healthy eating, holistic healing, the kind of intensity you get with extreme sports; this deep appreciation of life because death is potentially so close, you know? She's getting a lot of support.' His voice held a faint transatlantic twang, and he spoke in a monotone, a story with the feelings taken out because that's the only way he could tell it.

I nodded. He thought I'd understand. I *did* understand.

He'd talked about guys he knew coming back from war zones and their girlfriends leaving them because they couldn't sleep with the light off and I'd thought, that's awful, that lack of empathy, that's not me. But I couldn't help thinking of all those wasted months, all the crying I'd done, the heartache, the bad writing, giving up the flat.

'It was lucrative,' he said philosophically. 'I got some powerful images. My next assignment is in California; you'll love it. Let's go there together. You can write a book anywhere, can't you?'

It seemed hopeless. We'd come full circle. I moved my hand from the warmth of his and rested it on top of my glass, feeling the bubbles burst against my palm. I sipped it, and the brittle glass was cold on my lips; the champagne prickled my tongue.

'I've got responsibilities now. I'm a live-in carer for Jack's stepmother. And there's the job at London Lit.'

He laughed. 'You're always so diligent, aren't you? You haven't changed a bit.'

'Not true.' But the champagne was smudging the memories, taking the sharpness out of them. And the miracle was, he was here, wasn't he? His same old beautiful self in this most romantic of settings, a railway station; a place of departures and reunions. I dunked an olive in my drink and watched it fizz.

I looked up at him. 'What's going to happen to us now?'

He ran his thumb along his lower lip. 'I'll tell you what I want to happen. I want us to take up where we left off and get another place together.' He raised his eyebrows. 'The question is, Lana, what do you want?'

'I don't know. I want us to be like we were,' I said desperately. I could feel my emotions shifting again.

He leant towards me and put his hands on my forearms, tucking them under my sleeve, skin on skin. I shivered.

'Come home with me,' he said. 'The folks will be glad to see you.'

'I can't,' I said regretfully, shaking my head. 'I've got to get back to Nancy.'

'Just for a couple of hours? I'll get you a cab home.'

He turned my hands over and stroked my wrists.

I seriously thought about it. She'd probably be in bed by now. What difference would a couple of hours make?

'Ask her son to call in on her.'

'Stepson,' I corrected him. 'I can't, because looking after her is my job.'

'How about if I come back to yours, then?'

He could come back with me to my lovely green room and my big soft bed. It would probably be fine. Nancy liked men, especially good-looking ones. If she was awake it would make her day to meet Mark. She'd probably flirt outrageously with him and show her legs.

But.

'No. Not tonight. I can't. I've been out all evening.' The truth was, I didn't know how I felt about him any more. I didn't really know how he felt about me.

I was expecting him to try talking me into it, but instead he nodded.

'Okay. I understand. What are you doing tomorrow?'

'Nothing much. You?'

'I'll tell you what I'm doing. I'm going to have breakfast with the woman I love,' he said. 'Are you up for that?'

I watched the express train on the other side of the glass pull out of the station.

'Maybe,' I said.

CHAPTER TWENTY-SIX

Reliving the Dream

Nancy greeted me with buoyant delight as I came into the hall that night. She looked at me carefully and frowned.

'That face,' she said, waving her hand at me and almost poking me in the eye. 'What's different about it?'

'Nothing.'

'Yes there is.'

I smiled at her.

'That's better,' she said with relief. 'Come into the parlour.' The fire flickered in the hearth and the crystal sherry glasses threw rainbow reflections on the gilded tray. Nancy plumped the cushions. 'Sit there. Sherry?'

'Yes, please.'

She poured it carefully and measured it against her own, adding a drop each time in scrupulous fairness until the two glasses were full and quivering at the brim. She studied them critically, bent down and sipped a bit from both to lower the level before handing one to me. We clinked glasses.

'Cheers. Nancy, I had a surprise this evening,' I said when she sat down. 'The man I wrote about in my book, Marco Ferrari, he's back.'

'Oh! Is he your sweetheart?'

'Yes.'

Her expression became avid. She lowered her voice. 'Do I know him?'

'No, this one is my man. He's been away for a long while and now he's back again.'

Nancy nodded encouragingly.

'The thing is, my life is more complicated now and I don't want to jump into getting back with him again because . . .' I felt a shiver of anxiety.

Because how will you manage without me, Nancy?

We were leaning towards each other and Nancy's expressions were mirroring my own – eyebrows raised, eyes wide, one cheek flushed from the heat of the fire. She seemed to understand my dilemma.

'Because you're not sure how strong your feelings for him are.'

I nodded gratefully. 'I was sure once, but after he left, it all changed, and now he's back I don't know if I can trust him.'

She gave a gentle smile. 'Whether you trust him or not is your choice, and nothing to do with him.'

'But what if I'm wrong to?'

She didn't answer immediately, and I stared at the fire, thinking she'd lost her train of thought.

After some minutes had passed, she said, 'The question is, what will you give up for love?' Her eyes searched mine.

She'd asked me that before and I frowned because it gave me a jolt. 'Well, I don't know, I suppose we could work things out somehow . . .'

'Your pride? Your hurt feelings?'

'Oh, that sort of thing.' Safe in the feather cushions of Nancy's sofa, my mouth sweetened with Harveys Bristol Cream, my defining negative emotions didn't seem that hard to give up. Actually, I'd be glad to get rid of them. 'I suppose I could try.'

'You can work on it,' she said.

I groaned; I've never liked the idea that you have to work at a relationship. My parents were always working at their relationship, having counselling, group therapy, that sort of thing. It didn't change anything. In my opinion, if being together is that hard, it's probably not the right person.

'But I was so sure of him before, though. I had no doubts about us; it was literally as if we shared the same emotions and then suddenly, bang! He went off to cover a story and just left me to get on with things and I didn't know where I was for all that time.'

'And?' Her eyes widened and she rested her chin on her fists.

'And – I thought it was all over. I thought I'd lost him forever. I've been trying to get over him ever since and now he's back,' I said.

She took the words from me. 'You thought you'd lost him forever. And now he's back,' she repeated happily.

'Yeah, he's back.'

'No,' she said impatiently, 'not like that, that's not how you're supposed to say it. Say it as I'm saying it. *He's back!*'

I nodded. 'He's back!' I said, copying her joy. 'He's back!'

'Yes!' she said, as pleased as if she'd delivered him to me herself. She lifted her chin up and opened her arms wide. 'Look at me. Do it like this. He's back!'

He's back! My doubts fell away. That was the core of it, the nub, the truth, the bottom line. I felt a surge of excitement and relief and I found I was crying. Covering my mouth I thought: *He's back! Oh, he's come back to me, after all this time.*

Lying in bed that night, I was happy. But I couldn't sleep.

With my duvet tight around me it wasn't Mark's face that

I saw when I closed my eyes, it was Jack's. I'd forgotten to ring him. That look that he gave me before he rode off – I knew what that look was. Validation. The look of someone who'd had his worst suspicions confirmed.

I buried my face in the pillow. I'd so nearly gone to his place. It was like looking back on some mad, drunk night – I was mortified at the thought.

While I visualised Jack, I felt the presence of Mark. In terms of narrative, the punctuation following *He's back* should have been a full stop, but I liked the fact it was an exclamation mark. I was too excited to sleep. I wanted to talk to him. I went over our conversation word for word. I rehearsed witty sentences for when I saw him next.

I'd get comfortable to the point of sleepiness for a short while, ten minutes maybe if I was lucky, and then I'd have to turn over, hugging the pillow again. Each new position would seem luxuriously blissful, briefly, but my muscles would stiffen and the awkwardness of the angle made it difficult to sustain and soon I would dangle my legs out of the bed and drape my arms above my head until that became intolerable. It was a long night. Finally I lay on my back, unmoving, and stared at the moon through the blinds until the alarm went off and woke me from my brief sleep.

I got up and looked out of the window and to my surprise it had started to rain. I'd been expecting blue skies. Pathetic fallacy, that's what Thomas Hardy called it, the idea that the weather could match your mood, but then, Hardy only wrote novels to pay the gas bill; I've always liked him more, knowing that.

I was watching the raindrops sliding down the window when my phone buzzed and it was Mark.

CHAPTER TWENTY-SEVEN

Viewpoints

Mark wanted me to have breakfast with him at Le Pain Quotidien. It was still raining; I was going to look wet, with red cheeks. However, I consoled myself with the knowledge it wasn't the worst he'd ever seen me.

I put on my yellow jacket and hurried out of the house and when I was almost there I stood under an awning and checked my mascara in my rain-spotted mirror. Although waterproof mascara doesn't run, it does smudge.

I was excited about seeing him again but it was in a highly nervous way, as if I'd caught a stomach bug. I rooted around in my handbag for gum. It was a bit soft but it was better than nothing in the event he greeted me with a kiss.

My heart was pumping fast, as if I was about to go on stage and do a reading.

Ting-tong! And there inside the cafe was Mark, warming himself against the radiator, feeling the cold after coming back from sunshine. His hair was pushed back from his eyes, he was wearing that tan coat and holding a tan felt trilby that was speckled with rain. The wooden floor in front of him was speckled with rain too, as if he had shaken himself after he'd come in. Only Mark could carry off a hat like that. I whimpered softly. He was like a salted caramel ice cream.

I just stood there and looked at him. I looked at him the same way that he'd looked at me the night before – taking in his blondness, his tan, reacquainting myself with the sight of him.

'Lana,' he said. 'You're very bright these days, I've never seen you in yellow. It suits you.'

He's back! He's back!

'Hi, Mark.' I smiled and then I couldn't stop smiling. I hung my jacket up next to his coat and sat opposite him at the big scrubbed pine table. I ordered a double espresso and he ordered a chamomile tea.

'And this – what colour is this?' He stroked my sleeve. 'Purple. Remember your Zuma Jay T-shirt?'

I knew what he was doing; he was re-establishing our connections. Like writers, photographers notice everything. That was something else we had in common.

'Change of plan about the flat-hunting,' he said. 'I'll tell you why in a minute.'

The relief!

We both chose eggs Benedict and as the waiter took the order to the kitchen, Mark stroked my fingers one by one, looking deep into my eyes.

'Remind me to pick up my suits from yours today. I *really* need to have them back.'

My stomach lurched. Oh, great. I'd forgotten about the suits.

I curled my damp hair around my ear. 'Mark . . .' Sounding whiny was probably one of the negative things I was supposed to be giving up for love. Start again, bolshie this time: 'Actually, I've given them to charity,' I said.

'My suits? Why?'

'Because . . .' I waved my arms, letting the gesture finish the sentence for me. I wasn't going through all those reasons again.

He pinched the bridge of his nose and screwed up his eyes as if in pain. 'Which charity did you give them to?'

'Oxfam.'

'Okay, Oxfam,' he repeated, getting out his phone. 'Oxfam, Oxfam . . . Oxfam . . .'

'What are you doing?'

'I'm going to get them back. Which shop did you take them to?'

'I dropped them in the clothing bank in Kentish Town. Mark – it was ages ago. I don't think there's much hope of finding them now.'

He stared at me with the anguish of someone who had just witnessed his brand new car being crushed. Then he came back to life, put his phone back in his pocket and said philosophically, 'You know something? Those suits are really going to make someone's day.'

Seeing it from his point of view, he'd gone away on an extended assignment, had the space he craved, and when he was ready he'd flown back from Deadman's Cay and then Miami, all ready to surprise me and seeing in the camera lens of his imagination his old life hanging in the gallery of his mind, illuminated by the mellow beam of spotlights. He'd probably imagined his bike waiting in the hall, the lemon velvet sofa with its wide and generous arms to fall into, his pristine suits lined up in the wardrobe ready to be worn, everything the way he'd left it. Instead: no flat, no suits, no bike. If you look at it that way, he was taking it really well.

We tucked into breakfast. I watched him stir his tea. That was new. He never used to drink herbal tea. He used to be a coffee drinker, like me.

Halfway through eating, he slowed down, mellowed by carbs, and looked up at me. 'Tell me about your housemate,' he said softly, reaching out to take my hand. He stroked the back of it with one finger, his eyes half closed with desire. 'Will she still be asleep?'

'I doubt it. She gets up quite early. I'd like you to meet her, though. She has a lot of regard for true love. She's a writer – Nancy Ellis Hall.'

'Never heard of her,' he said decisively.

I told him a bit about her, leaving out the dementia in case it put him off.

'What is it, a literary house share?' he asked. 'Bouncing ideas off each other?'

'Kind of.'

'Is she helping you with your heartbreak book?'

'It's irredeemable.' I dabbed my mouth with my napkin. 'I wrote about' – *our break-up* – 'what life was like without you and it was too bitter to be published. The bitterness burned through the pages and they fell to bits when handled. Kitty locked the whole typescript in a lead box to save contamination,' I said, trying to sound ironic.

'Aww. Poor Lana.'

'Yes, it was hideous.'

'You missed me.'

'Of course I missed you. The worst bit was not knowing what was happening, not being able to get in touch with you.'

'I should have realised. It hit you hard because of how your father left,' he said. He spread his hands ruefully: *there you have it.* 'You've got to start trusting people. You can't judge all men by your father's behaviour,' he said gently.

Can't I? He was right, though.

It was all about viewpoints and it would make a good subject for our next writing class.

His viewpoint was that our relationship could tolerate neglect.

I knew what mine was.

On the other hand, it was true that we had been living our own lives when he left. I was promoting my novel, and when publicity arranges signings and an interview on *Good Morning* you don't tell them you're going along with your partner on his assignment instead. Ha! I hate that kind of dependence.

I've seen women bringing their reluctant husbands along to readings, as if they had to be together at all costs. Look how that worked out for Richard and Penelope Buchanan – that's a cautionary tale to learn from, right there. Give the guy a break, that's what I wanted to tell them.

'I'm shelving the flat-hunting this week because I've got an exhibition on in Covent Garden.' He folded his napkin so meticulously it was like watching him do origami. 'I want you to come and see it. I want you to understand what it was like out there, to see a person broken for her sport. It was hard to leave because we were all tight-knit, being together day after day, trying to heal her with our concern and support. And do you want to know why? Because we had one common bond. That's all it takes to make a relationship, you know? One common bond.'

'I'd really like to see it.'

I didn't feel as if I'd moved towards him but suddenly we were leaning across the table, very close to each other. He smelled damp in a nice way, organic and warm. I was instantly turned on.

We were taking up where we left off and editing out my heartbreak in the middle, which wasn't even real heartbreak, just a temporary break-up.

No, hang on, delete that. Trust me, it *was* real.

215

Anyway, this was a love story and I now gave myself permission to forgive him and love him again.

We kissed as passionately as we could get away with in Le Pain Quotidien in the early morning. Mark's eyelids grew heavy with lust, hiding the amber glow of his eyes.

'Get ready to start work on the sequel.'

That was the nicest thing he could have said to me.

'I will,' I promised, locking onto his gaze.

CHAPTER TWENTY-EIGHT

Equanimity

I met Mark by Covent Garden tube the next day.

'Morning!' he said cheerfully, taking my hand in his.

The gallery was closed for installation – his installation. A middle-aged Italian man, Franco, opened up for us. Mark's prints were leaning against the walls in groups.

'Come and see,' he said, steering me around a stepladder and towards the Digital Nomad section. 'Here it is. This is how I remember you when we first met.'

I wasn't that interested in the pictures of me because I'd seen them all before, but I admired the print, currently propped up against the wall, which was big enough to make it seem as if I was looking at myself through a window.

He had taken it early in the morning in a layby outside Telford. I was too hungover to smile, and that pensive look as I was sitting in the doorway of the camper was me wondering whether I was going to be sick.

Mark had cropped out the overflowing rubbish bin and a shredded truck tyre. The camper van and I were in the shade, monotone. My blonde hair looked dark, and as visual proof that the camera does lie, my pale skin was flawless, my lips plumped up and slightly parted in contemplation. Behind us the sky was an outstanding red and gold, the glory of the dawn as the backdrop.

'It's beautiful,' I said. I was happy that he had Photoshopped out the rubbish bin and the tyre; after all, it was only fair because I'd edited them out of *Love Crazy*, too. I looked so perfect that I could easily have fallen in love with myself. Ha! Take that, Helga!

Then I remembered about the stroke and felt bad for her.

Mark patted me on the shoulder and left me to admire myself while he went to talk to the Italian guy. I studied the other photographs in the Digital Nomad series. The guy in Bali was on the beach being watched by a few skinny stray cats in the bushes. The girl in Tuscany was leaning against an olive tree, looking at a laptop balanced on her khaki shorts. The guy in Alaska was in the doorway of a log cabin with a frost-etched beard.

I hung around them for a couple of minutes, and then, consumed by curiosity, I went to see what Mark had been up to in the time we'd been apart. The free-divers were in a section of their own entitled: 'Dean's Blue Hole'.

Free-diving is the art of sinking into the ocean as deep as you can on a single breath of air.

I didn't get it.

I don't actually get any activity that is potentially fatal. Free-diving looks like one of these ambitions that on the surface, literally in this case, the only aim is to achieve a record. The goal of a sports person is usually to be the best. But what if the goal is actually death? Because why else would a person keep plunging down into the ocean, or summiting in the death zone, or jumping off cliffs in a wing suit, if that wasn't the ultimate intention?

Helga looked like a friendly sort, but in these photographs

she seemed to be looking death in the face. She didn't quite look beautiful, but she did look determined, something to do with the angle of her chin. Sure, she had the grin, but she also had the wide-eyed stare. Obviously I was influenced by hindsight. There was a wide-angled shot of Helga in a group of people on a catamaran and yards away, in the shallow turquoise water, carefree families spectated happily. They were facing an indigo patch of water. This wasn't the normal, gradual colour shading of the sea. This was a hole in the ocean where the seabed turned from shallow to deep, so deep it was almost fathomless; a hole that you could easily just step into and drown.

Here was a photograph of the medic giving her the thumbs up. Of Helga talking to the judges. Of her adjusting her goggles and blowing a kiss. Plenty of people out on the ocean that day and then –

– one woman diving alone in the deep blue sea, her hair a long blonde plume, falling into the inky blackness, one shot after another like a flip book.

And the process reversed. The small figure increasing in size, approaching the surface, breaking water, head up to the air-rich sky and this dazed, drunken look on her face. Next shot she was sinking, her hair floating like seaweed. Being dragged out by many arms, bloody froth staining the water.

The last in the series was of Helga apparently alone on board a catamaran, wearing an azure blue swimsuit and throwing a garland of flowers towards the sea, blonde hair blazing gold against a blue sky. The stroke had ravaged her. She looked very thin and her teeth were big in her narrow mouth and her hand was twisted at the wrist. I studied her slack face closely. Her eyes were filled with sorrow and regret.

I stayed looking at her for a long time. A photograph is like a stare, a voyeuristic activity in which you can study someone with all the time in the world and make up a narrative about them.

I would never know what Mark really felt about Helga, or the circumstances that kept him away for so long – for two reasons: firstly, he might tell me a truth I didn't want to hear; secondly, he might tell me a lie I didn't believe. So I wasn't going to ask him.

And it really didn't matter, because although the photograph looked as if it was taken with love, Mark was now in London with me, and we were together, which proves that a picture is *not* worth a thousand words; I'd say it's worth a hundred at best. Let's face it, if a picture was the equivalent of a short story, we would have stuck with picture books.

I started thinking about my new sequel. Marco returns after a long absence and they fall into each other's arms and begin the new period of getting to know each other again. *One cold night, Marco found Lauren in the busy street ... 'I've been looking for you all over,' he said.*

Mark was still discussing the installation with Franco.

His phone rang and he looked at the screen before he replied. 'Hello! Yes ... yes ... yes ... I'm at the gallery ... Yes, she's with me right now ... Yes, will do. Speak soon.' He tucked the phone back in his pocket and ruffled my hair. 'The folks send their love.'

'Aw, really?' The folks. Judy and Stephen. They were ideal parents – friendly and admiring. I felt a warm and sentimental glow.

'They said they'll see you at the opening, darling,' he added, tilting my chin up and kissing me.

Out of the corner of my eye I could see the print of Helga.

'I can't wait,' I said.

CHAPTER TWENTY-NINE

Regrouping

As promised, I met his parents again at the private viewing a couple of nights later and found myself once more buffed and polished by their easy charm.

Unlike my own parents', their marriage was solid and they lived a happy and tolerant life together. This is a definite plus, because children of divorced parents know that they have options and are likely to go for them during the hard times, whereas the child of a happy marriage understands the power of perseverance and the cyclical nature of discontent.

Judy had advised me one night when she was sitting outside having a sneaky cigarette on the patio that the secret to a good marriage was glossing over each other's faults. This came as news to me. I told her that glossing over faults was the kind of attitude that made my mother spit in disgust because she thought they should be pointed out to a person so that the person could address them and put them right.

Judy had lifted her face to the sky thoughtfully and blown out a white stream of smoke. 'I expect that's why they're divorced,' she'd said after a moment.

I'd done a circuit of the gallery carrying my champagne

glass. I recognised four of Mark's friends while I was loitering by my own picture; Freddie and Nicole and Nick and Charlotte. They didn't seem at all surprised to see I was back in Mark's life, and we talked about the exhibition and how Mark could absolutely capture the soul of a person, and I was happily heading for the waiter with the drinks tray when Judy and Stephen turned up, all warmth and hugs, as though they'd only seen me yesterday. Stephen was dressed in a black shirt and black trousers like a member of a film crew. His steel-grey hair was cropped. He had a nicely shaped head. Judy was wearing a black dress with floaty chiffon sleeves and her fair hair curled around her face. We got reacquainted through the medium of interrogation.

'When did you last see Mark?' I asked. (He's been terribly busy recently.)

'When is your next book out,' they asked. (Next couple of years, fingers crossed.)

'Have you ever visited the Bahamas?' (We went out there to see Mark on his birthday.)

'Is Mark the hero of your new novel?' (Who else?)

'What did you think of Helga?'

I sneaked that one in.

It was an essay question and if they'd had pens in their hands they would have frowned and chewed on them but, in my opinion, there was no point in being coy about it. I expected them to say she was sweet, because it was their cover-all metaphor for everyone.

'She's been awfully brave about the accident but . . .' Judy beckoned to me and bent forward, smelling of Joy, and she said softly and confidentially into my ear, 'she doesn't *read*.' She looked at me pointedly and nodded once, for emphasis.

'Disgraceful,' I said, feigning shock. It's so much easier to bond over negatives. And it was of course a bonus point to me. But I wanted to be fair. 'I suppose it's because she's sporty.'

'Sporty? I don't consider plunging into deep water a *sport*,' Stephen said. 'It's more a pastime, in my opinion. And, as has now been proven, a dangerous one at that.'

'True. If it were a sport,' I pointed out, 'it would be an Olympic discipline.'

'Exactly!'

And so, like Mark and I, we rebonded.

London is the most romantic city in the world. That evening, Mark and I walked along the wind-ruffled Thames, watching the slow roll of the London Eye, and I saw the city with new eyes – his eyes. He pointed out architectural details, reflections in puddles and anything else that caught his attention and would otherwise have escaped mine. He was so intensely visual that I was entirely caught up with seeing things his way.

Back at Nancy's that night, with the lingering sensation of Mark's arm around my shoulders, obtrusive as a phantom limb, I sat on the sofa next to her.

Nancy barely looked at me – she was watching television in a state of great excitement. It was the first time I'd seen it on for a while, because we kept losing the remote control, but there it was, in her hand. On the screen were three men, one of whom was Gary Lineker.

'Excuse me!' Nancy said, calling to him with great authority. 'You! You there!'

Gary Lineker's face filled the screen.

'You should give that other young man a chance to speak,' she told him sternly.

Gary Lineker ignored her and carried on talking and she looked at me and rolled her eyes.

'I don't know why you bring these men here,' she said, waving the remote at me. Her voice softened to a whisper. 'Which one's yours?' Just at that moment she accidentally changed to the Discovery Channel. 'Ooh!' she said, watching penguins shuffle along an ice shelf. 'Look at them! So brisk and purposeful!' She got out of the chair and looked intently at the screen. Suddenly there was a close-up of a chick; grey, downy feathers fluffed out and blowing in the breeze.

'Would you like it?' she asked eagerly, turning back to me.

When I laughed, she pinched the screen, trying to get hold of a fluffy feather.

Nancy's world – it was full of joyful surprises; the world through a child's eyes.

I thought of Mark's photographs in the gallery. How much of our behaviour is governed by our self-image? We are brought up with the idea that at our age, whatever age it is, we should act it. But an act is all it is; inside every adult, layered like the months of a calendar, all our other ages are stacked up, interwoven with sensations, ideas and fears. Nancy was all ages at once; an authoritarian, a child, a woman in love.

In the busy days following Mark's return, I'd put off calling Jack. But I wanted to see him before the next class to save any awkwardness in front of the others so I texted him suggesting we meet at the Edinboro Castle.

As part of the apology I got there early and bought the drinks. I sat at the table and looked at the candle burning in a glass jar. The white fairy lights twinkled magically under the high ceiling.

Jack came in and slid along the bench opposite me. He'd shaved and he smelled of cologne. The candle cut shadows under his cheekbones and made light dance across his face.

'Hello,' he said amiably.

'Hi!' I pushed his beer across the table, happy to see him. 'Thanks.'

'Listen, Jack.' I decided to get the apologies out of the way. 'About last week. I shouldn't have come on to you like that, and I'm really sorry. But—'

'Yeah, don't worry, I know what it was,' he said, 'it was just for the book.'

'I'm not *that* shallow!' I sipped my wine without tasting it. The fairy lights rippled on the surface. When I looked up, he was watching me, his face serious.

'You said it was research. That you needed more passion in it.' He shrugged and looked into his beer again. 'Forget it. No big deal.'

I wanted to carry on arguing but it was a get-out, though, wasn't it?

'Good. I'm glad we've sorted that out.'

He looked at me for a moment, and his eyes were shaded in dark. 'Okay. Me too.'

He dipped his finger into the melting wax of the candle, and peeled it off his fingertip. It looked like the Pope's cap sitting there on the table. If the Pope was very tiny.

Jack looked up at me, his dark hair shining in the string of lights.

'So he's back. The legendary Marco Ferrari. Do you still love him?'

Well that was direct! 'Er . . . yes,' I said. 'Of course I do.'

Jack nodded. 'He's still your perfect version of a hero, is he?'

I shrugged. Funnily enough, I'd been asking myself the same question. 'Nobody's *perfect*,' I said lightly, trying to make a joke of it. 'I mean, he did make me pretty miserable, if it's any consolation.'

'It's not, actually.' He frowned. 'Well, I gave it my best shot.'

'What do you mean?'

'You know, the hero thing, for the sake of literature.'

I sat back and sighed. I just wanted him to drop it now. Somehow we seemed to have got stuck in a groove, repeating an anecdote that had stopped being funny.

'Don't get me wrong, I enjoyed our fake dates, but for me, the best times we've had have been at Nancy's, sitting in front of the fire, talking about whatever comes into our heads,' I said.

'Really? How does that fit in with you being an independent adventurer?'

'I'm being serious, Jack.' I don't know why I was bothering because he seemed determined to misunderstand. And I wasn't going to let it bother me because I had Mark now, lovely, gorgeous Mark. Mark who always looked squeaky-clean and who wanted me in his life, whose parents admired me and whose friends actually liked me.

Jack pinched his lower lip thoughtfully, never taking his narrowed eyes off mine.

'You know something? This is what I don't understand. I only met the guy for five minutes and it's obvious he's an idiot. Seriously, he dumps you and now he's back you're welcoming him with open arms, as if nothing has happened. Don't give me any of this hero bullshit, he's an arrogant prick. What's that?' He cocked his head. 'Oh yeah, I forgot. You like your heroes arrogant.'

'He's not arrogant! If you got to know him you'd realise he gets on with everyone; he's a real people person. You can't judge him by a five-minute encounter in the street.'

'That's not what I'm judging him on. I'm judging him on his behaviour towards you.'

'Jack, that's not fair! I don't have to listen to this,' I said, so agitated that I knocked my glass of wine over.

I'd never seen this side of him before and I was humming with anger, burning with indignation. I could never forgive him for this. It was the end of a friendship, the end of a chapter, and it seemed to require some dramatic climax. An open-handed slap, skin smarting against skin, screaming followed by a vigorous wrestle which turns into a kiss.

Instead, I was facing a man who was ignoring the wine dripping on him and who seemed to be taking a particular interest in the foam that clung to the side of the glass.

As I stomped off I felt nothing but the undramatic down-pull of regret.

CHAPTER THIRTY

The Lonely Hearts Literary Society

On Tuesday night at seven o'clock, Nancy gleefully greeted the writing group as they turned up at her door. Our subject of the week was viewpoint.

She was delighted to see them and her face lit up. 'It's the Lonely Hearts Literary Society!' she cried, clapping her hands. She ushered them into the parlour and moved some of the Jiffy bags from the chairs. 'Come in,' she said with warmest bonhomie, 'and sign the visitors' book.'

The visitors' book was as heavy as a Bible, leather, gold-tooled and hadn't been used in years. The last person to sign it was Fay Weldon, in 1989.

Kathryn opened it politely, took the fountain pen that Nancy offered her, looked through the pages for inspiration and paused. She looked up at me in wide-eyed surprise.

'I *know*,' I said, because I'd felt the same amazement when I'd first opened it.

'We can't write in this, Nancy,' she said with a faint laugh.

'You're a writer, aren't you?' Nancy said, sounding hurt.

Kathryn was leafing through the pages. 'Yes, but – Betty Friedan's in here.'

'The *Feminine Mystique* is in the bookcase. Signed first edition,' I said, as proud as a librarian. It was on the middle shelf, next to *Love Crazy*, where I'd put it.

She had a look at Betty Friedan's book with the same excited reverence as I had. And then she took down the copy of *Love Crazy* and flicked through it.

'Lana, did you know it's a library book and it's overdue?' she asked me.

I pulled a face. 'Yes.'

'Fair enough.' She put it back on the shelf.

Joan had picked up the silver-framed photograph of Nancy and Beryl Bainbridge, soft-focused by cigarette smoke.

'I didn't realise they even knew each other,' she said. 'Fancy that!'

The thing is, it's hard to put writers in any sort of context. We know them through their books, their scandals and their deaths. Written on the wall of Oddbins in Kentish Town is a Karl Marx quote. Sure, everyone knows he's buried in Highgate cemetery and his last resting place is commemorated with a giant model of his head, and that seems perfectly fine. What's mind-boggling is that Karl Marx used to live in Kentish Town, the tattier, less cool version of Camden Town. Imagine that! Karl Marx, drinking with the locals, tormented by his skin condition, arguing cuttingly with biting satire in the pub.

'We should start our own movement,' Kathryn said, completing her signature with a flourish.

'I vote for adopting the name the Lonely Hearts Literary Society,' Arthur said cheerfully as she passed the book to him. 'Nancy can chair it.'

Nancy had gone to the kitchen to look for more sherry glasses. She came back with a large selection of containers including jars, vases and egg cups on a tray, and invited us to choose our receptacle. As we settled down to the session with our sherry, Jack bowled in, slightly breathless. I couldn't believe he'd come. He was wearing a floral multicoloured shirt with the cuffs undone, his dark hair flattened by the cycling helmet. Kathryn and Joan made a space for him on the sofa and he took his laptop out of his bag.

I tried to catch his eye, bearing in mind how we'd left things, but he seemed completely unaware of my existence. Annoying.

'Excuse me, you,' Nancy said, wagging her finger at me from the armchair. 'Yes, you. Why are you looking at him like that?'

'No reason,' I said innocently, feeling my treacherous face flush.

Jack opened the laptop, typing so fast that his fingers were a blur.

'Are you writing a book, Jack?' Kathryn asked him in that delicate voice. She was wearing a black full-skirted dress with an embroidered bodice. I would love to know where she got her clothes from. A chalet in Switzerland or somewhere, I expect; somewhere snow-capped and beautiful by day, but come the dusk, a place where wolves howl duets with the wind.

'I am, Kathryn,' Jack said warmly. 'I've got this story and I want to know how it ends.'

'Oh – *that* story,' Nancy said dismissively. 'You've told it to us already.'

Jack looked up from his screen. 'No I haven't.'

She frowned. 'Don't be ridiculous,' she said crossly. 'I know the one. It's about you and her,' she said, pointing at me again.

What?

Jack ignored her.

It was hard to believe he was writing a book – why hadn't he mentioned it before?

'How much of it have you written?' I asked suspiciously.

He cocked his head to look at me. 'Actually, I'm quite a way into it, Lana,' he said.

'Oh, really? What's it called?'

'*How to Be a Hero.*'

What??? Outrage! He'd pinched my story! Okay, it was his idea in the first place, but I'd actually written about thirty pages of it.

'It's about this guy who takes on challenges to win a woman, kind of like, you know . . .'

Me?

'Odysseus,' Joan said helpfully, adjusting her hair slide.

'Yeah, that's him! Odysseus. I'm just having a problem with the ending.'

'I have exactly the same problem, Jack,' Arthur said warmly. 'I'm never precisely sure how to decide on the resolution.'

Just a minute, I thought suspiciously, chewing the edge of my nail, if he really was writing a book, why hadn't he mentioned it before? Here he was, in a class full of writers and now, halfway through the term, he's allegedly been writing a book all along. I looked around to see if anybody else was sharing my scepticism. Seemed not. They were looking at him all agog, full of interest and admiration.

'And don't you find that writers often carry on writing after the true story is resolved?' Joan asked him earnestly.

Jack considered this and gave her a slow grin. 'Yeah, I do find that, Joan.'

Liar, I thought.

Neveen raised her hand. 'Lana, could you tell us, is this to meet a word count imposed by the publishers?'

'Eh?' I sat upright, remembering I was supposed to be working. 'Oh! Er, well, obviously word count is important, you can't have it too short, but really a book ends when the threat has been faced and overcome, ensuring the protagonists' survival and the restoration of order into their world,' I said, reeling it off.

'But some people,' Joan said, 'carry on even after that, I'm thinking of *The Poisonwood Bible* – oh, and *A Secret History*. They go on after the conflagration, don't they?'

'That's true,' I agreed. 'Sometimes, after the resolution, a writer will restore the balance of the narrative by showing us the aftermath. It's a type of downtime.' Come on – I didn't believe for a minute that he was writing a love story. He'd never mentioned being the slightest bit interested in writing.

'But you don't *have* to have downtime, do you?' Neveen asked.

'That's true, you don't. You can end with the resolution. It's your story and you can end it how you want.' I dropped the idea of talking about viewpoints. I looked at Jack, smiled and addressed him directly. 'Jack, why don't you start by reading some of your story to us?'

Yeah, buddy, I thought. Get yourself out of this one.

'Okay!' He cleared his throat and rotated his shoulders, as best he could, wedged in between Joan and Kathryn, putting on a real show of flexing his muscles as though the reading was physical. He clicked and tapped at high speed, leant back and settled himself before he started reading.

'This is how it starts.' His voice was deep and dreamy. 'This is the reason that the narrator wants to be a hero. It's because the heroine's eyes are as deep as the ocean, full of flecks like little fish. Her shoulders were speckled like a new laid hen's egg. Her nose was quite short and in silhouette it looked a little bit like a razor shell if you sort of hold the shell at an angle. Her hair is blonde and the strands all kind of separate in the rain like candy floss. She's quite hard to figure out.' Jack folded his arms. 'Then this other guy comes along and he's an archetypal antagonist, arrogant and selfish and full of himself. But perhaps they are a perfect match, destined to be together; that's the bit I don't know.'

Oh, sarcasm, very clever.

Arthur gathered his speckled beard in his fist. 'Jack, I like the fact that the similes are mostly aquatic.'

I snorted, couldn't help myself. But as they looked at me I realised I had to be professional about this. Generally I'm really careful about criticising new writers' work. Writing is hard enough without people putting you off before you've properly got going. *Encourage, Advise and Nurture* would be my motto, if I ever had to come up with one.

'That was very nice, Jack,' I said insincerely. 'It was – evocative and full of atmosphere.' I fake-smiled so hard that my cheeks hurt. 'Any other comments, anyone?'

'You're right, Arthur, they are mostly aquatic apart from the hen's egg,' Joan said. 'My feeling is, that jars, a little. Maybe you could find something speckled that relates to marine life?'

'Hmm, hmm,' Jack said thoughtfully, wagging his foot and staring at the ceiling for inspiration. 'How about – her shoulders were like a speckled pebble on the seashore?'

'Oh, I do think that works *much* better.'

Pur-*lease*! My shoulders are nothing like pebbles.

Jack typed it into his laptop. 'Thank you, Joan,' he said graciously.

Kathryn leant forward. 'Is your heroine a Pisces?' she asked him softly.

Jack looked thoughtfully at her and considered the possibility. 'Hmm. Possibly, yes. You've picked up on that. I like the way you're looking at the story in depth.'

Kathryn blushed.

'I can see that you've played around with the tense,' Arthur added.

'Yes,' Jack said, raising his arms, raking his fingers through his hair. 'I like to play around with the tense.'

'This narrator,' Joan said. 'Is he the hero?'

'I don't know, I don't know – that's the problem that I have with the ending, does she go with the arrogant hero or does she choose the nice guy? What kind of woman is she? Is she superficial or is she discerning? I'm not sure yet.' He tapped his chin thoughtfully. 'Does she ruin her life or does she find a happy ending?'

That was it.

'Jack, your characters are so clichéd,' I burst out. 'Arrogant hero versus nice guy? It's a bit one-dimensional, don't you think?' It came out louder than I'd intended.

Neveen said, 'Surely it depends on how he writes it.'

'But look – you're writing about a heroine stupid enough to go out with a hero who in your misguided opinion has got no good qualities whatsoever because she's too – what, dumb to know what he's really like?'

He grinned at me. 'Isn't she?'

I was infuriated. 'Oh – and I suppose at the end he proposes and goes to work in a leper colony or something, does he?'

Jack looked at me steadily, rubbing his dark stubble with the palm of his hand. 'I don't know the ending yet, I already told you that. But I'll keep it in mind as a possible. Thanks.' He typed it up carefully. 'Le-per co-lo-ny.'

'Why are you suggesting a leper colony?' Neveen asked with interest. 'Where is this leper colony?'

'I don't think he would work in a leper colony in this day and age,' Joan said. 'It sounds unlikely. And it's called something else now, isn't it?'

'That's true,' Arthur said. 'I think you'll find, as it's a bacterial infection, leper colonies went out with the discovery of penicillin. Patients are treated in hospital now.'

'Everyone be quiet!' I said. This was taking sarcasm way too literally. 'Forget the lepers.'

Deep breath. In-two-three, out-two-three. Stay calm.

'Okay, let's move on.' I waited for someone else to volunteer to read. Despite the fire, the atmosphere had become decidedly chilly. 'Who's next? Joan?'

'I don't feel my work is quite ready to be presented to the class,' she said stiffly.

Oh, great; I'd offended them all. I looked at Nancy.

'That's it,' she said, suddenly getting to her feet. She was always sensitive to atmosphere. 'All this' – she made a stirring motion, including us all in the mix – 'and you can't see clearly, but what you need to know is that the end is always there at the beginning.'

Joan nodded. 'That's true enough.'

Looking round, Nancy was suddenly distracted by the sight of the blue bottle. 'Pass the sherry, could you?'

Arthur poured a little more into her chicken egg cup and then he cleared his throat. 'You're usually extremely supportive towards us, Lana,' he said reproachfully. 'And it's the first time that Jack has shared his work with us so I feel we should cut him some slack.'

Nancy liked the idea. 'I have some nice embroidery scissors we can use,' she offered.

Faced with the unanimous disapproval of the class I knew what I had to do. Save face, that's what.

'I like a lively discussion, but if it's too lively then I'm happy to tone it down. Jack, the whole leprosy thing, it was hyperbole. I'm sorry if you felt it was a bit over the top.' I put my fist on my heart. This was as near as I could get to an apology without using the word sorry. If anyone dared to point out that being over the top was the whole point of hyperbole I would scream.

Jack was scraping a mark off his floral cuff with his nail.

236

He didn't even look as if he cared so I don't know why the others were so disapproving. He looked up as if he'd suddenly realised that I'd stopped talking.

'Apology accepted,' he said.

And we all relaxed. Kathryn read about Hannah who is staying at the refuge and has found Ryan's grave because Ryan has been dug up by a fox.

Arthur's hero Bob visits the infirmary and when he is told he has syphilis he's devastated because he knows he caught it from his fiancée.

Neveen's heroine receives a letter of apology from the inmate in which he pleads with her to keep writing to him.

It was all very interesting but as usual we seem to have drifted a long way from romantic prose. However, I didn't bother to point it out – I was unpopular enough as it was.

I asked Nancy if she wanted to read.

'Because I love you?' she asked sweetly.

'Yes.'

She smiled. 'No, I will sing for you instead.'

She began to sing a song called 'Scarlet Ribbons', contralto. Joan and Arthur knew it too. Joan picked up the tune, soprano, and Arthur, bass, and encouraged, we all joined in, enthusiastically la-la-ing the words, with Nancy beating time on the arm of the chair.

'And once more!'

'If I live to be a hun-dred . . . Good! What do I owe you?' Nancy asked.

Arthur said it had been our pleasure.

Her clock chimed nine and she got to her feet. 'It's getting late. Time's up. Scoot! Scoot!'

Before she left, Joan handed us invitations to the Egyptian evening in aid of the prisoners' fund, and she and Neveen put on their coats, discussing the food they would serve.

I followed them into the hall.

Without saying goodbye, Jack headed out with Kathryn close behind him.

The mirrors on her velvet jacket flashed and winked as they walked down the path.

CHAPTER THIRTY-ONE

External Conflict

I had determined not to think about Jack and his 'novel' that didn't yet have an ending.

'I'd like you to meet Mark Bridges,' I told Nancy over breakfast. 'You'll like him. I thought we could have lunch together.'

She was vigorously stirring her berries into her porridge, staining it pink. 'Who is he?'

'He's the guy I was telling you about, the one I wrote about in my book. The one who's come back.'

'Your sweetheart?'

'Yes, him. He'd like to meet you.'

That delighted gappy smile!

I couldn't wait for them to meet. I'd described her as eccentric and a bit of a character. Being eccentric and a bit of a character are appealing traits to the Bridges; they are the kind of people they like to invite to parties because they're never boring. Boring is their worst insult and they apply it to anything – politics, cars, the weather.

I hadn't mentioned Nancy's dementia to Mark because inviting someone with dementia to a party is a different proposition altogether, but really, the outcome is the same. By the nature of Nancy's illness, the bit of her brain that was damaged was the same part that is affected by alcohol, so even at her best, Nancy could be sentimental, garrulous, spoiling for a fight or singing gustily. Basically, she was always a large Jack Daniel's ahead of most people.

But she was also childlike and easy to distract with mints in a tin, for instance, or a doll, or a cup of tea. There was nothing wrong with her that sensitive interaction couldn't cure.

So – lunch.

Nancy couldn't chew meat easily because of her missing teeth, so I decided on poached salmon with asparagus and hollandaise sauce, cheese and grapes to follow.

I was stirring the sauce when the doorbell rang.

'I'll get it! It's my house!' Nancy said, hurrying to answer it.

I heard Mark's voice in the hall, volume raised as he does with the elderly, taking it for granted they're all deaf.

I took the pan off the heat, expecting them to come into the kitchen at any moment.

Silence.

I went to see what was going on.

Mark hadn't got any further than the outside step. Nancy was trying to close the door on him, putting all her weight against it, muttering to herself.

'It's all right, Nancy, this is Mark, our visitor, we were expecting him, weren't we?'

She paused in her exertions, pressing her foot against the door so as not to lose ground. 'Were we?'

'He's the guest who's come for lunch,' I reminded her. 'We're having salmon.'

'She took one look at me and pushed me back outside,'

Mark said heatedly through the gap between door and door frame.

Which suddenly reminded Nancy what she was supposed to be doing.

I don't know why Mark decided to stick his head through the gap at that moment, but his bellow of rage as she closed the door on him was straight out of *The Shining*, frightening her so much that she ran through the dining room and up the stairs where we heard the door slam.

Mark stumbled into the hall holding his temples, eyes screwed up in pain. 'Fucking fuck fuck,' he cursed through gritted teeth.

I took him into the parlour and helped him onto the sofa.

Very slowly, with extreme caution, he let go of his skull, as if expecting it to fall to bits on his lap. Gingerly, he poked his fingers in his ears and checked them for blood.

'Want a sherry?' I asked.

'You *never* give alcohol for a head injury,' he said, appalled at my ignorance. Then he lapsed into groans.

'The Royal Free Hospital is only five minutes away,' I said, slightly annoyed at the fuss he was making. Luckily, physically, we can't feel each other's pain but the downside to that is, it often seems as if the other person is exaggerating. 'It's usually about a five-hour wait in A&E.'

'How do my eyes look?'

I stared into them closely. 'Gorgeous, brown and a bit watery.'

He jumped back, getting all worked up again. 'That's what she did,' he said, 'she peered right into my eyes.'

I wondered what she'd seen in there. Indifference, maybe.

'Yes' – I screwed up my nose – 'she does that. I should have said.'

'I could get her sectioned,' he said, 'if I called the police and reported it as an assault. One report, that's all it takes,

241

they have the power to do that if she's a danger.' He put his hand to his tender ear. 'She could be a danger to *you*, Lana.'

'Stop that right now, Mark! When she was trying to push you out of her own home you should just have gone out, let her have her own way. I could have let you in around the back, or in five minutes, instead of trying to bulldoze your way in. She's never even seen you before.'

'But you invited me here,' he said indignantly. 'You should at least have warned me about her.'

'Yes, sorry.' I sat on the sofa next to him. I could see how it looked to a hostile outsider. I could see how it looked to the people she'd bitten; yes, I could see that.

Which, thinking about it, made it all the more remarkable that the Lonely Hearts Literary Society saw it too and it didn't matter.

Mark had put it all into perspective, I suppose. The problem wasn't just about protecting society from Nancy, but protecting Nancy from society, and the CPSO and Ranya the new social worker and the geriatrician and the community health nurse and those who wanted to protect her.

I knelt by him while he sat on the sofa with his head in his hands, feeling around for the precise source of the pain.

Nancy came back down a few minutes later wearing the cerise trilby at a jaunty angle. She was surprised to see we had a visitor, but some faint emotion revived in her, and they looked at each other warily.

'Smile,' I told him. So he did. He had a gorgeous smile. Nancy smiled back and Mark looked a bit startled at the missing teeth.

'Nancy, would you like to come into the kitchen with me and we'll make lunch?'

She was reluctant to leave the visitor. 'Why? You can make it yourself, can't you?'

Don't leave me, Mark mouthed behind her back.

Honestly. 'Mark, come with me to steam the asparagus,' I said. It was like being the mother of two children.

'I'll lay the table,' Nancy offered.

'We've already laid it,' I reminded her.

Nancy went to check it and decided it looked a bit bare, so while Mark and I were in the kitchen she added a few more glasses, a book, a steel ruler and a small plastic basket full of clothes pegs.

'Festive,' I said, bringing in the plates.

Nancy looked down at her food, and then looked at ours. She swapped hers for Mark's, and then Mark's for mine.

'Why do you keep giving me the small one?' she asked indignantly.

Mark couldn't wait to leave.

The last week of October was half-term, and instead of the writing class, we were at Joan's house for the beadwork sale.

Neveen was in the lounge, and once the room was quiet she began telling us about the weekly visits she had made to the prison. Visiting time was one hour, maximum, but the process took all day.

'We queued with local people while two soldiers stood in the towers above our heads with rifles pointing down at us. Oddly we never felt nervous but we did get irritated when they searched everything we had taken and removed a large number of navy sweatshirts intended for the prisoners. We were told they would be returned at a future date and we could try bringing them in again.

'After an hour's wait we walked along tree-lined avenues to a cage enclosure, concrete, with wire walls on all sides where we sat and waited in the sun until the prisoners were allowed in.

'Bala came straight to us. The others in the group spoke to the Nigerians. One of them had not been allowed to come, though he had shaved and prepared himself for our visit. Bala gave us small gifts he had made and in turn we handed over the carrier bags which we and friends had intended as gifts: fruit, cigarettes, toiletries, writing paper, everyday things we thought they might need. After thirty minutes we were told to leave by the guards. Here is a letter from Bala that I have recently received.

'"I am planning for my freedom and as time comes closer I have to arrange things and plan well, prepare myself to face the outside world. We have to pay the fine that is very very important for getting freedom in time. I am hoping that our friends will help. For we need fine for my freedom and others. I need your help for it. Please raise some fund for that purpose. Today I completed nineteen years in prison. Now remain two month. After freedom if any time come to Sri Lanka please come to my home. You can see all Sri Lanka. After I got home you most welcome. Please make a visit Sri Lanka I want to do something for you. Please pray for me to go the time free.'"

Neveen looked up at us from the letter in her hand. 'You can see it has been like riding on an emotional rollercoaster. No month goes by without my heart being touched one way or another. Thank you for your love, and for sharing in their suffering and in their troubles. Bless you, Joan, for holding this evening. Bless you for coming and listening. Thank you.'

The beadwork was laid out on a table in Joan's conservatory; bags and purses, pens, pendants, key rings.

Kathryn had several bags hanging on her arm. She opened one up and showed me the lining. 'Beautiful, isn't it? Feel! Don't you think they've got a good vibe about them?'

Jack had picked up a beaded key ring in the shape of a lizard in the palm of his hand to show us.

'Look at the work that has gone into that,' he said.

We hadn't really spoken since *that* evening so it was a positive step forward, and to show that I too appreciated the craftsmanship, I bought a couple of black beaded bags for my mother and Jo-Ann, and a red one for myself.

In the dining room, Joan's friends had prepared a banquet and Joan was checking everything was good and ready to go. She looked past me and smiled suddenly. She looked beautiful. I turned to see who she was smiling at. It took me a moment to recognise Arthur and even then it was only the blueness of his eyes that convinced me. He had shaved off his beard.

I put my glass on the mantelpiece and I was looking at a framed graduation photograph of a young man when Kathryn came over to join me.

'Did you know who that is?' she asked.

'No, who is he?'

'It's Joan's son Robin. She was telling me about him earlier. He went slightly off the rails when he was younger and they hadn't spoken for years,' she said, 'and then just recently Joan got in touch with him to make amends.' She smiled. 'Lana, do you remember what she was like when she first came to class?'

'Do I! She scared the life out of me.'

'There's such a change in her.'

I agreed and with a jolt of recollection I thought of the drawings of the bird with the inquisitive eyes, Robin the robber, and Joan's grimness towards us and life in general. There you have a perfect example of the power of fiction to transform.

Later, as we were saying goodbye and I was putting my coat on and gathering up my beaded bags, I turned to look for Jack. He was concentrating on counting the money on a card table, various towers of coins and the notes pinned down by mugs.

Neveen was helping Joan to clear up when Jack called her over with some good news.

We were all amazed when we heard it. The evening had started at six o'clock and people had come and gone throughout so the house never felt crowded. I'd estimated that there were about thirty people there but I must have been mistaken. When Joan announced on behalf of the tearful Neveen the amount that had been raised, it came to seven hundred pounds.

CHAPTER THIRTY-TWO

Plans

Mark and I were in Maze in Mayfair having a romantic supper. He was telling me about his next assignment, weaving his fingers into mine. I was giving him my wholehearted attention – he was going to Yosemite to photograph a free-climber, Rachel Ashton, who was scaling El Capitan in the hope of breaking the speed climbing record.

'When are you going?'

'The fifteenth of November. Had to make it after Bonfire Night when the folks have their hog roast. They'd never forgive us if we missed it.'

I was dismayed. 'I can't believe you're going away again so soon.'

He tightened his grip on my fingers. 'Come with me, Lana,' he said.

I felt my heart sink. *I can't.*

What's wrong with me, I wondered. Why not? Well, the writing class didn't break up until November the twenty-sixth and I had to do the reports because London Lit was still paying me. And what about Nancy?

This is what real life is like. People have responsibilities. In a love story, the heroine would never let the practicalities of life get in the way of romance. Here they were, the words I'd been waiting for, and I was saying I can't? Again?

I rubbed my temples, trying to be sensible and get my thoughts straight. But after all, it was Nancy herself who told me that it's not what you'll do for love, but what you'll give up. This was my test and I wasn't going to make the same mistake this time.

'Okay, yes,' I said, looking into his deep brown eyes. 'I'll come with you.'

I would find a solution. As far as the group was concerned, we could Skype each other from anywhere in the world. Somewhere along the way I had lost my role as tutor and become something else, part of the group, making life make sense through our stories. And there was still time for Jack to find someone from the Caring Share for Nancy. Or even for me to find someone suitable that she could get used to having around before I left. She was a lot happier now and hardly disruptive at all. She probably wouldn't even mind.

I knew it was the right answer when Mark smiled that dazzling smile of his.

'Good. I hoped you'd say that,' he said.

A couple of days later, Jack called in on his way out somewhere.

'It's Nancy's birthday on Saturday,' he said. 'I'm taking her to see *Sister Act* in Leicester Square.'

'Really? That sounds great! I'll write it on the calendar,' I said. The thought of them going out and having fun made me feel pale and listless. 'She's in the parlour.'

Nancy was pleased to see him and delighted to hear she was having a birthday at last, because she hadn't had one for ages.

'Almost a year ago,' Jack said with a smile.

'Gosh! Is it that long ago?'

As I listened to them talking about *Sister Act*, I realised I would have the whole evening to myself. The fact that Jack was about to leave us and have fun somewhere else revived the spirit of competition in me.

'Would it be all right if I invited Mark and his parents here for supper that night?' I asked politely.

There were two reasons for this.

It was a way of thanking them for their hospitality in the past. It was also a way of consolidating the fact that I was Mark's girlfriend before the party on November the fifth.

'Do what you like,' Jack said. 'It's fine. It will make no difference to us.'

As he didn't make any derogatory remarks about Mark we seemed to be back on an even keel and it would have been a good time to tell him about my future plans, except that I didn't really want to talk about them in front of Nancy. She might get upset at the thought of change but she wouldn't remember it, and I would have to go through the whole painful process again. And as I hadn't heard back yet from the Caring Share, I decided to put it off until another day.

For her birthday I gave Nancy a pair of pink gloves and a card with a cheerful verse on, which she read out loud to me several times, with meaning.

I planned that evening's dinner party carefully because I desperately wanted the night to go well. I bought a piece of fillet to roast. The menu was horseradish mash, leeks, carrot puree and Yorkshire puddings, followed by cheese, pickled grapes and quince paste.

'Look at you' – Mark grinned, watching me in the kitchen with a glass of wine in his hand – 'it's like going back in time. You're the fantasy wife.'

I liked the sound of that. 'Fantasy wife?'

He looked at me with his dark brown eyes and his grin softened into a smile. 'You know,' he said, 'the smell of roast potatoes . . . you with your hair up and a big smile . . .'

Fantasy wife, I thought proudly, despite being hot and bothered.

I put the baking tray down on a trivet and he came to take a look at the Yorkshire puddings and kissed me on my forehead. 'Don't want to mess up your make-up,' he said.

Judy and Stephen turned up on time, marvelling at the oil painting of Old Mother Hubbard; Stephen all in black and Judy in a ruby dress with draping sleeves. Judy was disappointed that Nancy Ellis Hall wasn't joining us for supper as she would have loved to have discussed feminism with her.

'Feminists,' Stephen said, 'all that bra burning – well, women have got what they want now and are they any happier?'

'Oh, Stephen,' Judy said, flicking her napkin at him, 'you old dinosaur.'

On second thoughts, it was a good thing that Nancy wasn't there.

Stephen was undeterred by our collective disapproval. He went on: 'I like my women like my coffee.'

'You mean you make them strong and bitter?' I asked, laughing merrily. I was on fire that night.

Mark opened the wine and I pulled off the oven gloves. We sat round the table and Mark carved the meat, so bloody it was nestled in a pool of gore, but just right, just perfect. We took it in turns to talk and laughed at each other's stories and said how nice it was to be all together again. It really was.

We were on the cheese when the doorbell rang and for a moment we all froze – Mark holding the wine bottle at an angle, Judy plucking a stem from a grape, Stephen buttering a water biscuit – and we looked at each other inquiringly in the way that you do when the doorbell rings unexpectedly at night – *who's that?*

'I'll get it,' I said; two reasons: one, I was at the end of the table, and two, I was the one living there so technically I was the host. Normally, Nancy would be racing me to the door on the grounds it was her house. I dropped my napkin on the table and went to answer it.

The security light was on, and the man who had rung the doorbell was standing lit up on the path in a dark overcoat, his hands in his trouser pockets. He was frowning until he saw me, and then his face cleared.

It was Jack.

'I thought I'd better warn you that we're back,' he said.

I pulled the door closed behind me – I wasn't sure if Mark could see it from where he was sitting.

'What are you doing here? You're too early.'

He grinned. 'Nancy yelled at the nuns for singing too loudly so we stayed in the bar after the interval.'

'Where is she now?'

'She's in the taxi, haranguing the driver. How long are you going to be?'

I stared at him and turned to look back at the door because, any minute now, Mark was going to come out to see who it was, and why I'd shut the door.

'We're still on the cheese.'

Jack shifted his gaze from mine and he glanced towards the window with a half-smile. 'Oh.'

The heat drained out of me and I hugged my arms, shivering with nerves.

'Can you give us another sort of, ten minutes or so?' I could guess what Nancy would think, finding strangers in her house, and right this moment I didn't want to ruin the night which had, so far, been perfect.

'Sure. Don't rush,' Jack said and he turned to leave.

I was so grateful that I pulled him back to give him a hug. I shouldn't have, I know. I don't usually do that sort of thing. It was out of friendship, and he was so understanding and I was happy he was talking normally to me again. I slid my arms under his jacket, feeling the warmth of him through his cotton shirt, and as he squeezed me back I could feel his heart thudding against mine. The security light switched off and for a brief moment we were safe in the privacy of the night when I heard the door latch turn.

The security light came on again.

Jack released me as Mark stood in the doorway, but we were still standing too close.

'I wondered where you'd got to,' he said. 'Ah. Jack, isn't it?'

Public school had equipped Mark for most situations and I watched his hand rise automatically with the introduction, until he had second thoughts and dropped it again.

'What can we do for you?' The words were more polite than the tone.

'I'm talking to Lana,' Jack said.

Again the heat rushed through me.

Mark was icily polite. 'You'll have to do it another time, I'm afraid. We're finishing supper.'

'I know,' Jack said, as if it was amusing.

It killed me to see them side by side. I felt as if my mind had broken free of my body – I could see myself in my sleeve-less black dress, goosebumps on my bare arms, a step away from a warm room and wine while Jack stood alone with his hands in his pockets, his breath clouding in the cold air. I knew what it felt like to be the outsider, two against one, and I couldn't bear it, so I turned and went back inside, to Mark's parents who were talking softly to each other over empty glasses and who looked up expectantly at me.

'Everything all right?' Stephen asked.

I told them that it was Nancy Ellis Hall's stepson, letting us know she would be home any minute. I knew that Judy wanted to meet Nancy, but if Nancy was grumpy, she might be annoyed at having people in her house.

Just then the front door closed, gusting a puff of cold air all the way from the hall that flapped the Mother Hubbard painting and blew out the candles, and Mark came back in, rubbing his hands to warm them.

Stephen sat down again. 'Seen the opposition off?' he said jovially through the candle smoke.

Mark gave a brief laugh and looked at me curiously. 'Persistent, isn't he?'

I focused on filling my glass, keeping my hand steady, trying not to spill a drop. Then I focused on drinking it slowly. It tasted different, sweeter, as if I had been eating liquorice.

Judy was curious, wanting to know more about Nancy.

I knew she would be impressed.

She changed her opinion slightly when Mark added that Nancy was totally barking mad and she'd slammed his head in the door.

You hear a lot of bad things about boyfriends' mothers. Because they've been there, in the relationship game, I suppose, and they know from personal experience what women are capable of. They can be soft, gentle, manipulative and scheming, but Judy bucked the trend. I liked her immensely. She touched Stephen's wrist and he messaged his driver and shortly afterwards a car came to collect them, and I texted Jack to tell him that the coast was clear.

Nancy was very grumpy as she came in the house. Her hat looked peculiar – it was perched very high on her head.

'We've been in a huge hall crammed with a lot of noise

and singing and we've been driving for *miles*,' she said. 'And I've lost my gloves.'

'They're in your hat,' Jack said.

She took the yellow hat off her head to look with great astonishment and delight. 'How did they get there?'

CHAPTER THIRTY-THREE

The Dream Realised

Judy and Stephen's annual Guy Fawkes hog roast took place on a cold Friday night when the leaves were skittering in the streets and the buildings ricocheted the sound of fireworks.

The driveway of their house was lit up with oil-burning torches and as I went down the side of the house into the garden, drawn by the smell of pork and mulled cider, the steel fire pit was burning with coloured flames and the guests were wearing neon-bright glow sticks around their necks.

I saw Judy talking to a woman the same age as herself. Judy was wearing a black Cossack hat and a glossy, dark fur coat. As usual, she was laughing. When she saw me, she linked her arm in mine and introduced me as Lana Green, the novelist.

'Yes, we met here last year. I adored *Love Crazy*,' said her friend, whose name, I remembered, was Rosalind. She was wearing a flat tweed cap and a tweed jacket with a fox-fur collar. 'It was so absolutely full of fresh air that I felt quite light-headed.'

I laughed and felt an arm reach around my shoulder and Mark slipped a pink glow stick around my neck. 'Darling,

I've been looking out for you and you managed to sneak in unannounced.'

Darling. So there I was with Judy's arm tucked in mine and Mark's arm around my shoulders, and Rosalind's praise warming up the parts of me still exposed to the night air.

'What are you working on now?' Rosalind asked. 'Or is it the kind of thing that writers like to keep to themselves, for fear of letting the daylight in upon magic?'

And they all looked at me expectantly. It's the kind of treatment that always goes to my head.

'I'm going to write about Mark and me,' I said.

'Oh,' Rosalind said, 'you're writing a sequel?'

Judy squeezed my arm. 'She's going with Mark to the US.'

'I suppose you can write anywhere, though, can't you?' Rosalind pointed out.

'Yes,' I said. 'Absolutely anywhere.'

Rosalind stepped a little closer. She was wearing Youth Dew. The whole crisp night smelled expensive.

'I have a story for you,' she said. 'I suppose you hear that a lot.'

'Roger?' Judy asked subtly. 'Oh yes, he's a story if ever you are stuck for a rogue. Mark! Darling! Get this girl a drink!'

Mark steered me towards the drinks table where a teenager of seventeen or so was being charming as he handed out the mulled cider. I cupped the hot glass in my cold hands.

I envied their sense of continuity; to Tim's on Midsummer's Eve! On Simon's boat on the Thames for New Year's Eve! Burns Night with the Tilbrooks! It seemed so safe and predictable, with none of the anguish of planning or feeling left out.

Mark was looking at me in the glow of the garden flares. 'What are you thinking?' he asked.

'I'm thinking about what a lovely life you have,' I said.

'Oh good. I thought for a moment you were thinking about

Roger. Don't let Rosalind talk you into writing about him; most things he does are only half legal and nobody quite knows where he gets his money from except that there seems a never-ending supply of it.'

I had misinterpreted the dress code of fur and feather, which I'd thought was a euphemism for warm clothing. In the light of the pink glow stick, my yellow quilted jacket and Hunters looked conspicuously out of place but luckily writers are known for their eccentricity so I had that excuse to fall back on.

'Excuse me for just a moment,' Mark said, and just then, Rosalind homed in on me once more.

'What qualities would I need to become a writer?' she asked.

'If you want to become a writer, you just need to write,' I said, remembering Nancy's advice of *words, words, words*. 'Simple!'

She looked doubtful and slightly hurt as if I was deliberately misleading her.

'I was thinking of a writers' retreat. Somewhere sunny,' she added. 'I just need that time by myself; long whole stretches of it to write and write and do nothing else but let my imagination roam free.'

'Yes,' I said. 'Boredom is a wonderful way to kick-start creativity. I'm a firm believer in it myself.'

Rosalind raised one shoulder and rubbed her cheek against her fur collar. She gave a short laugh, like a yip. 'Darling, I've never been bored in my life. I'm far too busy. How long would it take for me to write a book?'

'About nine months,' I said.

Just then, Stephen came up and kissed me on both cheeks. 'The caterer is just carving the hog.' Out on the lawn, two men were checking the ignition systems on the fireworks.

'I see you've gone the whole hog,' I remarked.

Stephen smiled. 'Jolly good,' he said.

'Lana was just telling me that it takes nine months to write a book,' Rosalind told him, aghast. 'It's a wonder writers manage to get anything else done.'

I wanted to tell her about the two people I knew who'd written a book in a fortnight, but I felt it might give her false expectations of her writers' retreat.

I wondered whether the infamous Roger was here, and I asked her.

'No, he's not. There was an unfortunate incident last year,' she said. 'You see those blackened Canary palms at the bottom of the garden? Roger set them alight. They're covered in little hairs which turned out to be wildly combustible, so he's *persona non grata* this year. He's gone to his club instead in the guise of protecting the dog from the noise.'

I sipped my mulled cider. That was another endearing thing about them, they told you the most intimate things without any embarrassment or censure.

I thought about my mother and her overwhelming sense of shame when my father walked out. I understood it now because I had been through that same humiliation myself, the knowledge that somebody you love, who knows you better than anyone else in the world, couldn't bear to be with you any longer. I imagined telling Rosalind my story but I wasn't sure I could strike the right note of carefree cynicism. To attach any emotion to the story would not be the done thing at all. That was the secret. Pretending not to mind about things.

Mark's friend Nicole came over and introduced me to George who was a filmmaker.

George was very tall, with a pale face and a mass of dark hair. He asked me whether anyone had optioned the rights to *Love Crazy*. I briefly thought of telling him that it was something I was going to have to check on. I felt that would be the correct thing to do but on the other hand I wasn't really that well practised in keeping my emotions hidden yet so I said no. He asked me who my agent was and when it turned out that he knew Kitty 'by reputation', as he put it, I was so happy that I went to find Mark. He was sitting on the swing chair with a plate full of crispy crackling.

I told him what George had said and he kissed me. 'That's marvellous, darling.'

The 'darling' was ubiquitous, a coverall term for affection, part of the language they used.

I was going to use it myself. 'Isn't it, darling?'

Mark's face shone warm and red in the light from his glow stick but his eyes were bright and distracted, as if he had something on his mind. He looked familiar and alien at the same time. I smiled at him. I was happy.

I wanted to be alone to absorb it all and take notes before I had another drink, but it was impossible to be alone in their company. Mark introduced me to dark-haired Cathy, who read tarot cards. She returned from the table with a bun full of pork and apple sauce and laughingly asked me whether I had been groped by Winston yet.

'No, who's—' I began, but she had turned away. Like the flick of a shoal, everyone's attention was now on a group of men on the lawn, dressed in black, speaking into radios.

'And now for the fireworks,' Rosalind sighed, as if it was some old but necessary ritual.

The first thing to tell you is that I love fireworks. The coldness of the air, the scattering of sparks against the black sky, the ribcage-pounding booms, the huge, dazzling extravagance of colour, the thick pungency of the smoke; all these aspects lift my spirits and the effect lasts for ages. Mark put his hands on my shoulders and steered me towards the steps on the decking. The two men on the lawn stood back, black shapes against the illuminated grass. I turned to look up at Mark. He returned my gaze, gripping my forearms.

'I do love you, you know,' he said.

'I know. You *are* lovely,' I responded warmly, because he was. I did love him, I'd loved him since I first met him and he put that camera lens between him and me and made me beautiful.

We were all standing around in little groups, gasping as the fireworks were released high into the sky, dazzling us, trailing sparks that trickled to earth and died, each explosion overlapping and illuminating the sky, lighting us up with their beauty. Little twisting red bombs swizzled and squealed in the air and hung there for seconds before exploding in a reverberating boom.

At some point during the display the young waiter came around with a tray of champagne glasses and I suppose it was then that I started to wonder exactly what was coming next. Not just to wonder, but anticipate. But my vivid imagination has led me wrong about this kind of thing before.

Mark took two glasses and gave one to me, his eyes dark and glittering. The final flashes faded from the sky and died, and we carried on standing there until Stephen tapped his spectacles on his glass and called for silence.

I knew immediately that Mark was going to propose and I stood, awestruck, waiting.

'Lana, will you marry me?'

I blinked. Rematerialising through the blue smoke, the guests fell silent.

I was surprisingly clear-headed, considering. Why not? I thought. He's a good guy. Fearless. I love his family. And I was absolutely certain that he would never divorce me because his family didn't do that sort of thing – they had a solid self-image and I knew that I would go through life being Mrs Bridges, the romantic novelist, and that I would be admired for it.

And in all this rationalisation I didn't consider for one moment saying no. No one turns down a guy like Mark. And whatever other faults I have, I know a good thing when I see it.

I closed my eyes for a moment, savouring it while his friends and family were all around us with their champagne glasses poised. And I thought again: why not?

'Yes! Of course,' I said, and Stephen took his champagne flute from him and Mark felt in his back pocket and put a ring on my finger, an emerald-cut diamond that seemed to glow as white as ice.

And everybody crowded round, toasting us and congratulating us, kissing me and hugging Mark. Mark put his arm around my shoulders and gave a short speech about what a lucky man he was and it was faultless, an evening that I will never forget.

Despite how it ended.

CHAPTER THIRTY-FOUR

The Dark Night of the Soul

Hug, hug, goodbye! The evening was ending and as people started checking their phones to see whether their drivers or their taxis had arrived, I too had the feeling that the main event was over. Usually I'm the last man standing at any party but this was different. I wanted to keep the evening at that high point of happiness, hold it in my mind so that it would become part of me.

I wanted to go home quietly and relive it.

This feeling brought back a distant memory with startling clarity that I hadn't thought about in years.

My mother would have liked me to have been an actress. She used to take me to the theatre regularly. I enjoyed the ice cream and the occasional surprises from the stage such as the actors bursting into song and I learned to tune out the yelling, or projecting as she called it. But the worst part was going behind the theatre afterwards and watching the actors leave. They didn't all leave together in a celebratory group; they left alone, coming out and sliding into the dark night, startled to have a young girl suddenly thrust a programme at them to sign.

Sometimes it was hard to believe it was them really, even when they took our pens and scribbled a greeting across their photographs, and I was left feeling cheated. What had happened to the glamorous extrovert, the handsome hero? Where had they gone? I wanted *their* autographs, not those of these shadowy impostors.

This was how I was feeling right at that moment, in Stephen and Judy's garden, all dressed up against the cold and staring at the diamond ring on my finger. I was feeling like someone who had been performing in the spotlight for a couple of hours and now wanted to retreat into the dark to enjoy being myself, by myself.

I told Mark that I was going home. He told me to wait because he could arrange for me to have a lift with someone. Then he was shaking hands with an elderly lady and going to find her coat. For a short while I waited for him to come back, and then I gave up and went to thank Stephen and Judy for the amazing evening. Smiles and hugs from me; smiles and hugs from them.

At the front of the house there was some heated negotiating going on. George's car was boxed in and he wanted to drive across the lawn. Mark came over when he saw me, and I told him I would speak to him the following day. Then he hurried back to stop George from tearing up the turf so I left along Hampstead Lane. The city was spread out and glinting like a sparkling treasure in the distance. A long, animated frieze of fireworks flared across the sky, sound trails lingering behind them.

I turned my ring in towards my palm, feeling the diamond with my thumb, closing my fist on it. It was so big I expected to be mugged at any moment.

I suddenly felt amazing. Most of the time it is quite obvious that as a person I have plenty of room for improvement. (I can hear my mother's booming voice: there's *always* room for improvement.) Not tonight, though. Tonight I was perfect just as I was.

It's not a long walk to South End Green, probably only a mile or so, and I was enjoying the fireworks blazing in a constant burst of colour across the sky from east to west and I got all the way to the zebra crossing when I felt my phone buzzing.

I took it out of my pocket and to my surprise I saw that it was Jack. 'Hello!'

His voice was strained. 'Have you seen Nancy?'

I looked at the lights of the city with a sudden sense of dread. 'No. I left her at home watching television.'

'She's not here.'

The sentence was like a thud.

'Oh. Look, I'm on my way back and it won't take me longer than—'

'I'll come and get you,' he said.

I told him where I was, and I carried on walking along Hampstead Lane towards the Spaniards Inn, keeping a hopeful look out for Nancy, imagining her walking along the pavement towards me, happily distracted by the stimulation of fireworks, car lights, children and small dogs. I had got as far as Whitestone Pond when Jack saw me, flashed his lights and made a tyre-screeching U-turn.

I jumped in the car, closing the door, shutting out the night noises.

Jack looked grim. A car headlight bleached his face moment-arily and he looked at me in the half-dark.

'How long do you think she's been gone?' I asked him.

He shrugged. 'I'm not sure. I didn't get there until nine. The fire was out and the kettle was cold.' Braking by the roundabout, he glanced at me. 'How was your evening?' He saw me playing with the ring and he frowned. 'Is that what I think it is?'

I admired it myself, moving my hand to let the light bounce off the diamond like sunlight on ice. 'Mark and I are engaged to be married.'

It seemed like a strange phrase, 'engaged to be married'. I'd imagined telling my parents about it but this was the first time I'd actually said it out loud.

'Bloody hell,' he said.

'How about congratulations?'

'Sure. Congratulations, Lana. I wish you both many years of happiness.'

'Thanks.'

'Well, not him. Just you.'

He put his foot down and turned left down East Heath Lane, slowly following the red tail lights of the cars in front.

To the left of us was the dark and lonely Heath. Nancy wouldn't necessarily have had a destination in mind when she started out.

From the houses on the right, a rat-tat-tat of a hundred-shot barrage made me jump.

'She'll hate that,' Jack said, craning his neck to look. 'You know what she'll be doing, she'll be stomping off somewhere, full of indignation, determined to put a stop to the bangs.'

It was true, Nancy hated loud noises.

'She could be anywhere,' I said, looking across at the Heath again. Even at eighty you can go a long way in a couple of hours. 'What's the plan?'

'If I drop you off at hers,' Jack said, 'you can stay there in case she turns up. I'll carry on looking for her.'

'You know what? She could have made her own way home. She might be there now.'

'What, waiting for us?'

'With her sherry at the ready. "Ooh, there you are!"' I said, mimicking her. '"And who *are* you?"'

Jack chuckled deep in his throat and we relaxed a bit because this visualisation had comforted us. But when we turned into the street we saw the house was still in darkness.

'She might have gone to bed,' I said.

Jack parked up and we went inside, whispering because we didn't want to wake her up.

In the parlour there was barely any warmth left in the grey ashes.

Jack came noisily down the stairs, not needing to say anything.

'What now?' I couldn't bear the thought of waiting there for her, doing nothing. 'If you drop me off by the shops I can check in the pubs and ask people if they've seen her. They know her really well around here.'

'I was going to come here earlier,' he said bitterly. 'But then I thought, I'll go to Ben's for the fireworks and call in on her afterwards.'

I nodded, sharing his guilt. We were supposed to be keeping her safe.

We got back in the car and drove slowly towards the high street.

'What do you think if we give it another half an hour and then we'll call the police,' Jack said.

'Yes, let's give it a bit longer,' I agreed, knowing that we'd be back on a loop again; police, social services, best interests meetings. We'd got complacent, tied up in our own lives, and this was the result.

I dashed into pubs powered by hope. Visualising Nancy, hands clasped behind her back, asking visitors with keen interest whether they were enjoying themselves.

Looking around, asking, coming back out disappointed,

Jack with the car window open, his pale face enquiring, reading my body language, putting the car into gear.

'She's got to be somewhere,' I pointed out, fastening my seat belt. 'Jack, she wouldn't have gone to the ponds, would she? The mud is so slippery.'

He looked at me and raised his eyebrows. 'Like it's not bad enough already?'

But I wanted to fear the worst, for the relief when we found her. Fearing the worst was a gamble, a bet I wanted to lose.

As we were skirting the locked Heath car park a rocket screamed into the air and burst into a chrysanthemum head of white sparks.

As the sky lit up I saw Nancy, pink coat, yellow hat high on her head, standing with a group of boys, long shadows shifting beneath them. 'There she is!'

'Awesome!' Jack punched my arm with relief and bumped onto the pavement and we jumped out of the car.

Nancy was twenty feet away from us, we could hear her laughing happily with the group of boys, in her element at being the centre of attention.

'Nancy!'

She turned towards us. And then I saw she was holding a rocket in her hand.

'Look!' she said, waving it at us triumphantly. 'Look what I've got!'

In the dark car park I suddenly saw the flickering yellow flame of a Bic lighter.

One of the boys stood back. 'Don't blame us! She made us give it her!'

Jack was running towards them. 'Let it go, Nancy,' he urged, but she raised her arm and looked gleefully at the sizzling fuse, her joyful face illuminated by sparks, and with a great *whumph!* of sound the rocket flew from her hand, took off at a tangent and exploded over the pond.

The sound of the startled ducks carried over the silver water.

Nancy grimaced, suddenly diminished, always sensitive to noise.

'Wow, that was close, wasn't it,' I said ruefully, patting my pounding heart. 'Nancy?'

Nancy screwed her eyes shut. The grimace grew stronger, more determined, and her neck corded as she strained like the last man on a tug-of-war team. Her face darkened, and she cried out hoarsely through her clenched teeth, resisting the pain in that empty car park to her utmost ability, eyes tightly shut.

Jack caught her as she collapsed, felled by some internal blow. 'Nancy!' Fear in his voice. 'Hang on in there. Get someone down here, Lana.'

I fumbled for my phone and dialled for an ambulance. The boys had scattered but now a new crowd gathered in on us, caught up in the drama, enclosing and advising in the gloomy dark. A shadowy man suggested an aspirin, and they felt in their pockets and their bags as Jack lowered Nancy down and undid her pink coat clumsily. I put my jacket under her head as he knelt over her and pressed his hands against her sternum and started pumping. Under his breath he was saying *staying alive, staying alive*, keeping the rhythm going.

A police car pulled up, bathing us in blue light, radios crackling. One of the police officers was talking to a boy who looked young and scared.

His friend protested, 'She made us give her a firework, she was a laugh, she just wanted to join in.'

I scrambled to my feet. 'But you *lit* it!' I said in outrage.

'And he told her to drop it,' he said, pointing to Jack.

I stood back, waiting for the officers to take over from Jack and do it properly, but they stood and watched, detached, like people in a nightmare, and he carried on, *staying alive*, bathed in flashing blue light, and I was cursing with frustration because I could see she wasn't staying alive, not at all; she had left as quickly as the boys had when the fun was over.

It was an age before the ambulance turned up, though the Royal Free Hospital was a five-minute walk away, and all that time Nancy was lying on the dead leaves and cold gravel in her coat, her face dark and unrecognisable. Jack stood up slowly and the paramedics lifted her onto a stretcher and we walked up to A&E, to wait.

Interminable waiting in the bright room, sitting side by side on hard plastic seats. The place crowded and all of us listening hopefully as a name was called and sinking back. The murmur of voices. A baby's high-pitched crying. Drunks coming in, snoozing briefly and wandering out, families grouping together, impossible to tell who was ill. I stared at the reflection of the strip lighting in my engagement ring. I twisted it on my finger, sprinkling white reflections across the pale walls.

Jack was sitting bolt upright. I nudged my leg against his, as a friend. 'She'll be all right.'

He looked at me. 'Yeah.' After a moment he said, 'I'm sorry. I've spoilt your evening.'

'It doesn't matter.' I realised it was true. 'It doesn't matter,' I said again.

'If we'd left her in Greenacres it wouldn't have happened.'

'Don't say that.' I was remembering the excited expression on her face when she saw us. 'She was having fun, wasn't she.'

'Yeah.' He smiled ruefully. 'She was having fun.'

We leant against each other for comfort.

The boredom of waiting had plunged us into a state of weariness.

A little later a doctor called Jack's name. We stood up eagerly, but there was no time to hope because his grave face told the story.

I like to think that leaving the world in a cloud of glory is the ideal ending but outside of the Bible, when does it happen that a chariot and horses of fire take a person to heaven in a whirlwind? Nancy had gone in the glory that we'd imagine for her and died as she lived, lively and sociable, the centre of attention, in a blaze of sparks. Not for her the slow fade.

We were called in by a nurse to see her. Someone had put a pink rose on her pillow. I stared at her face closely but she was impossible to recognise with all that life and energy gone out of her. She looked like a sleeping child.

I waited for Jack, then we went back to collect the car and drove slowly to Nancy's house. Jack lit the fire and opened the Harveys Bristol Cream. We sat drinking and talking about her in the firelight, dipping in and out of silence. Loss, laughter, ruefulness.

In the early hours of the morning he fell asleep. I put the tartan throw over him and went up to the green bedroom. I lay on the bed and closed my eyes. I could see the fireworks blaze in Stephen and Judy's garden. I could hear Mark say *Lana, will you marry me*. It was so amazing. My heart started beating so fast, and in the brightness of those lively, glittering words, the rest of the garden was blacked out; the grass and trees; all the guests and even Mark. I would never forget it.

I pulled the duvet around me. I don't know if that's exactly how it happened, but that's how I wrote it happened. That's how it should have happened anyway. The anticipation of daring to hope, that cold and smoky night, and then the slow creep of the dazzling brightness of fulfilment, and then the ring. It is a beautiful ring.

And that's that story about how Mark proposed to me. It was deeply romantic and it took up a whole chapter.

Nancy disappearing and our search for her and her death in the car park; that is a different story told for a different purpose and belonging to a different memory.

CHAPTER THIRTY-FIVE

Downturn

The following Tuesday we were back in the blue classroom in London Lit, listening to the red ticking clock.

Carol Burrows had been very sympathetic about Nancy's death. 'A great loss to the literary world in general and to our literary world in particular,' was how she put it, nursing her hand with its faint, yellow bruise. There was some kudos in being bitten by a famous writer now dead, so we had been welcomed back to the London Literary Society again.

Joan, Arthur, Neveen and Kathryn were subdued by sadness after receiving Jack's email telling them about Nancy and giving the details of her funeral.

Unfortunately, the date was the fifteenth of November, right in the middle of November, the day that Mark and I were leaving for Yosemite, and I hadn't yet broken the news.

'Jack said it was a heart attack. She always seemed so very full of life,' Joan said, smoothing a lock of steel-grey hair around her ear. 'More than most people.'

She looked towards the head of the table at Nancy's empty chair. And because of that, we all looked at it.

'We should go to the funeral together, as a group,' Arthur said. 'If we all contribute, Lana, could you organise the flowers?'

'I'm so sorry.' I felt bad about it, but I was going to have to tell them today anyway. 'I won't be around – I'm going to California with Mark Bridges. Marco Ferrari. He's back in my life.' I showed them my hand, watching the diamond flash. I'd moved out of Nancy's house and into Mark's parents' place for now. (Separate bedrooms; my rules. I hadn't forgiven him for Helga that easily. Mark respected my decision, he said.)

Despite the awful circumstances, I expected some kind of congratulatory response to this bit of news, but they seemed muted with shock.

'But what about Jack?' Kathryn asked in a small, fairy-tale voice.

'He'll have you guys with him.'

'And what about our classes? They do not finish until the twenty-sixth.'

'I know,' I said regretfully. 'I'm sorry to spring this on you, but I've been thinking about it and the way round it is if you submit your work to me by email and I can send you reports for you to discuss with each other in the class. I'll speak to Carol about it. Really, you hardly need me anyway.'

I'd disappointed them and I was truly sorry about it but what could I do? I liked them, not just as students or even fellow writers, but as friends.

Arthur broke the silence. 'Congratulations on your engagement,' he said. 'On behalf of us all.'

'Thank you,' I said gratefully. I glanced at the clock. 'Today I want to talk about—'

Trainers came squeaking down the corridor and I stopped as Jack came into the room. There were shadows under his eyes as if he hadn't slept, and his jaw was shaded with dark stubble, but still, here he was, coming through the door, weighed down by a blue Carluccio's cool-bag.

Arthur started to clap and we joined him.

Jack took his jacket off, hung it on the back of the chair and sat down. His smile was crooked. 'Thanks, guys.'

'The subject today is—' I looked at Jack leaning back in his chair, his gaze skimming mine. The tension smoothed out of his face as he closed his eyes.

'I have something to tell you,' Neveen said. 'In January I am being transferred back to the Marriot in Zamalek. I will be near Bala for his last few months before his release.'

'What good luck!' Joan said.

'I've never been to Cairo,' Arthur said wistfully.

'Nor have I, although I've always wanted to,' Joan added.

They exchanged a meaningful glance.

Neveen smiled knowingly and tapped her nose. 'I understand, and in that case I will book for you the honeymoon suite.'

Joan laughed.

'I have some news too. I've finished my novel,' Kathryn said.

'Wow!'

We congratulated her and there was a lovely feeling in the class. Despite us losing Nancy, there was the sense of a future, a way forward for all of us. Or nearly all.

At the end of the session, Jack waited behind in the empty classroom after the others had left.

'Claudia the CPSO called this morning.'

'Offering sympathy or reproach?'

He raised a dark eyebrow. 'Neither. She wanted the CCTV camera back.' He picked up the large blue Carluccio's cool-bag and dumped it on the table. 'This is for you.'

'Really? Intriguing.' I unzipped the cool-bag. It contained all those bulging Jiffy bags, bound up with plenty of Sellotape.

I looked at Jack hopefully, trying to tone down my excitement and searching his face. 'Nancy's notes?'

'I'm guessing so.'

'You guess? You haven't opened them?'

'No.' He pinched his lower lip.

What a bounty! Pure gold. 'But I thought you wanted to know more about their story, about how they met?'

'Yeah well, I wouldn't feel right reading this stuff. There might be things in there that are private, letters between her and my father, things I definitely do not want to know about. I thought you could do something with them; I don't know. You decide.' He shrugged. 'Do what you like. What you think she'd want.'

I took out the top envelope and felt it. It was soft. Loose pages, I guessed.

I suppressed a shiver of excitement and started to pick at the edge of the Sellotape. Nancy had done a good job of sealing it but I loosened it eventually and hesitated as I glanced at Jack.

'You're sure about this?'

'Yeah, I'm sure. Go on. Open it.'

I looked inside. 'Ah.'

'What?'

'Peach toilet paper.' I took out the bundle of papers, all smoothed out and folded carefully.

The switch of emotion from high expectation to severe disappointment was so unexpected that I started to giggle; couldn't help it. He began laughing too.

'Why did she keep all these tissues?' I asked, wiping my eyes.

'I have no idea,' Jack said.

I started to giggle again weakly and put them back in the cool-bag; so much for the masterpiece.

'I'll go through the rest of them at home,' I said.

As we left the college together that cold night, I hoisted the cool-bag over my shoulder and told Jack that I couldn't come to the funeral.

'Oh?'

'That's the day I'm going to California with Mark,' I said, to prove that I had an important reason for leaving. 'He's doing a shoot of a rock climber on El Capitan. In Yosemite. We've booked the flights.'

'Oh.'

'Obviously I'd have been there otherwise—'

'Yes, sure. Not a problem. Say no more.' He squinted up at the orange city sky and turned up his jacket collar against the wind.

I didn't want to leave him like that. 'Jack – are you really writing a book? Because as I told the others in class, you can email it to me while I'm away.'

He was quiet for a moment. Tucking his hands into the pockets, he said, 'Nah. That's okay. I just wanted to know—'

'Yeah, you wanted to know how your story ended, right.'

'Not my story; our story.' His hair ruffled in the wind. The muffled roar of traffic pulling away from the lights, the whine of a motorcycle. He didn't look at me. 'Well, I know now, don't I? Here,' he said, taking two keys out of his pocket. 'Give him the bicycle back. It's parked over there.'

I knew what he was doing. 'I can't,' I said. 'It's yours.'

Jack gave the faintest smile. 'Well – it was never really mine.'

I wanted to argue with him; to protest. I closed my hand reluctantly around the keys. 'I'll return the money you paid me.'

He shrugged. 'That's okay. Let's say we just call it bike rental.'

As an ending, it left me sad and dispirited, but as the ending was of my choosing there didn't seem anything more to say.

CHAPTER THIRTY-SIX

Resurrection

When I got back to Judy and Stephen's that night, the house was empty so I decided to make a start on emptying the Carluccio's cool-bag in the kitchen. I tore a recycling bag off the roll and tipped out the bag on the worktop. I cut open an envelope with the scissors and took out a wad of rough green paper towels. I looked at them fondly and put them in the bag for recycling.

We'd never worked out why Nancy counted napkins, tissues and toilet roll or why she kept them. While it was baffling, it was also touching. I didn't understand it. Nancy was a good woman, a lively woman, intelligent and interested in people. It didn't seem fair or logical that she had got dementia but life is random and frighteningly unpredictable.

I got into the rhythm of sorting. Newspapers, tissue paper, paper napkins, paid bills, vouchers for the Co-op, wrapping paper, used envelopes, new envelopes. And then, to my absolute amazement, I unfolded a letter on pink notepaper beginning: *My Sweetheart.*

I was so surprised that I folded it up again quickly and laid it on the table, feeling some of the superstitious doubts that

Jack had expressed, because the letter wasn't meant for my eyes. It was private. People's secrets and endearments should die with them.

And yet – where would history be if the evidence of it was destroyed?

I sat on the bar stool to think. It wasn't just the fact of reading Nancy's mail that was putting me off. I was a coward, too; I was missing her and protecting myself from an emotional love story whose ending culminated in death and illness. I didn't want to let in any more sadness right now.

I heard voices outside, and Mark, Stephen and Judy came in, flushed with the cold, surprised to see me surrounded by papers.

'What's all this?' Mark asked, putting his arms around me and pressing his cool cheek against mine.

'Nancy's letters.'

Judy put the kettle on.

Not just Nancy's; Richard Buchanan's too. These were in white envelopes held together with a rubber band. The top one was addressed to Nancy c/o Le Meurice, Paris. I slid it out of its envelope, heart thumping. *My Sweetheart. I couldn't bear to see—*

'Anything juicy?' Judy asked.

'No,' I said quickly, putting it back, suddenly protective.

'Pity. You'd have thought—'

'They're private, aren't they?' I said, hoping for a bit of moral guidance.

Judy glanced at me. 'Yes, that's true,' she agreed with less enthusiasm.

'Don't waste your time on them – you're supposed to be writing your sequel,' Mark said, nuzzling my hair. 'Bin them.'

'Don't bin them,' Judy said. '*Burn* them. It's safer, if they happen to be indiscreet.'

If they were burned, they were gone forever.

'Yes.' I swept the letters and the remaining Jiffy bags back into the cool-bag to look at them later, and put the recycling bags outside like the good future daughter-in-law that I was.

When I came back inside Judy was saying to Mark, 'That's one thing you're not going to have to worry about after we've gone, darling. All our personal correspondence has been by text and email.'

'Glad to hear it,' he said.

Stephen was indignant. 'I always give you birthday cards and Valentine's cards,' he reminded her.

'Sure, you give me cards,' she conceded, 'but they all say the same thing – "I love you". They're not even signed.'

'I don't sign them because you know they're from me,' Stephen said.

I smiled. 'Do you keep them all?' I asked her curiously.

'No, I don't keep any of them – I get a fresh supply every year.'

I laughed, loving her confidence.

I zipped up the cool-bag and took it upstairs. I wasn't going to bin them or burn them. The letters were my responsibility. Jack had told me to do what I liked with them and I hadn't decided what that was yet.

Mark was having a session on a climbing wall the next morning and after breakfast I went back up to the bedroom and tipped the letters out again. I sat on the bed contemplating them. If Nancy and Richard had wanted them to be destroyed, wouldn't they have done it themselves?

After a few minutes I came to a decision – I would curate them. But I would see them as literature rather than reality.

I already knew the story; I was familiar with the overall narrative and the long-term fallout – a broken marriage, a vindictive ex-wife, a guilt-ridden father, a bitter son. I was aware of the plot.

As I was reading the letters, I found the characters. A middle-aged woman falling in love for the first time with her beloved man, who, despite public condemnation, never sees her through anyone's eyes but his own.

Nancy wants him. And despite the age gap, Richard wants her too. But she shares her torment about the fact that she is too old to have children; he loves his son Jack and for that reason alone they know that nothing can happen. Their idea is to love each other for a little while, that's all, and then they will let each other go.

The lies we tell ourselves.

There was a desperate letter from Richard: Penelope has found out.

There had been so many, many reasons his wife should have found out earlier that he'd convinced himself she knew and didn't care. But that's not how it was. Penelope didn't know and, now that she does, she cares enormously.

A yellowed press cutting from the *Camden Journal* was witness to Penelope publicly burning Nancy's books outside Kentish Town station. And another one stating that she had been charged with stealing property from Kentish Town library. Penelope is worse than broken-hearted; she's insulted. It's not just about the infidelity, she says, although that's bad enough. But with an older woman? An uglier woman? A treacherous writer who has blatantly betrayed her feminist principles?

There is a letter from Nancy apologising to Richard because they can't go anywhere without being looked at, without comments being made. And another written after they go to Morocco for a holiday and the curious rug-sellers offer them mint tea and ask if she is his mother and he says no, patiently, over and over while the men remain curious and disbelieving; she thanks him for this.

Through all this, though, I could see that Richard Buchanan loved her. He tells her so. He loves her character and her audacity and her courage. He loves her in bed and out of it. He longs for the days he can be with her.

I opened all the envelopes right then. Nancy had kept everything: notepads and notebooks; spiral-bound, perfect-bound, loose leaf. There were diaries, Filofaxes and address books; cards that had come with flowers, the Order of Service for Penelope's funeral and invitations to weddings, letters, adverts, final demands. Nancy had kept bills and corner shop receipts and charity appeals. One package held Christmas cards, signed and unsent. There were letters that Jack had sent, cards to Daddy, paintings done at school, school photographs, school reports.

I came across Richard Buchanan's obituary, five years previously: *Survived by his only son, Jack Buchanan, and his second wife, Nancy Ellis Hall.*

Jack had told me that the affair happened because Nancy was ruthless and his father was weak; as though they went into it blind and unthinking.

But Nancy understood herself better than he knew.

I could see from the letters that Nancy never expected Jack to forgive her, or for anyone else to, either. She willingly gave up all that she had been for Richard. She shouldered the guilt because it was the price she paid to be with the man she loved and she was proud to pay it. She lived with her own culpability, accepted it and never tried to justify it even to herself.

Ruthless; yes. But in among her letters and notebooks I found treasure that moved me to tears, insights, stories of a love that was solid, constant, reliable; a wellspring for good.

It was afternoon when I surfaced tearfully from the past in a daze, disconnected, a time-traveller.

Through Nancy I'd seen it for myself and understood it at last as she'd described it; love, the divine, that source of deepest, richest joy and laughter.

CHAPTER THIRTY-SEVEN

Settings

Back to my own romance. To give Mark the coveted keys to the bicycle, which Jack had relinquished, is an important scene. You need a good setting in a book, so Mark and I went for a romantic walk across the Heath and from the top of Kite Hill the pigeon-grey city was spread out like a frieze on a pale sky. Mark was talking about Yosemite. Yosemite was cold in November and Mark was making sure we had the appropriate layers for the weather conditions.

'And we need to keep alert for bears,' he said. 'We'll get bear-repellent, pepper spray. They should be ready for hibernation at this time of year but not all of them keep to the timetable. It's been a good berry year,' he added. 'It makes a difference.'

I only heard one word. 'Bears?'

'We have to lock our food in bear-proof containers.'

'You mean like our cabin?'

Mark laughed and pulled me closer, kissing the top of my head. He whispered in my ear, 'You want to know how easily a bear can get into a cabin?'

'Not really.' I didn't remind him that I was even scared of cows.

He went on blithely, 'Mountain lions can be a problem too. The advice is to puff yourself out, make yourself look bigger.'

Baffling. 'Why would you want to do that? Wouldn't a hungry predator prefer his prey to be on the large side? It's asking for trouble.'

We stood looking at the view beyond the trees, his heavy arm on my shoulder, our coats whipping in the wind and our breath clouding in the cold air. It seemed the perfect time to give him the shiny keys to the bike lock.

'Hold your hand out.'

I dropped them into his palm. In my mind's eye, he, the hero, was going to be noble in victory, and perhaps give some heart-warming speech about the power of love.

He looked at them and said, 'What are these?'

'They're the keys to the bike lock.'

'You've got a bike now?'

'No, they're for your bike, the Trek bike. The bike I sold to Jack.'

'Oh, Jack's bike.'

I shrugged his arm off my shoulder and faced him. 'Mark, he's giving it back. It's yours again.'

'Why?'

That's the problem with symbolism; it doesn't necessarily translate to real life.

'I don't know. He just thought you ought to have it back, I guess.'

Mark shrugged. 'Okay. Although I wasn't planning on riding it in the winter anyway and I'm sure as hell not taking it to California.' Being the well-brought-up guy he was, he added, 'But thanks.'

Because I too was well brought up, I said, 'You're welcome.'

It was a bit of an anticlimax, though. I suppose I'd imagined the scene differently. His dialogue needed some improvement – I'd have scrawled through it with a big black line by now.

As we sat on the bench watching magpies squabble in the bushes I suddenly wondered if I was turning into the kind of person who swaps people for a new and similar model, because what I actually wanted Mark to do was run down the hill with me, hand in hand, and go and fetch the bike right now. Then I wanted him to ride off on it and do a big circuit and come racing back along Swain's Lane, put me on the seat and take me for a ride around the block. That now seemed to me to be the appropriate reaction when one is given a bike back.

Well, it was just a bike.

Still, I was irritated by his reaction – not badly enough to actually start an argument, but I had taken him to a high place to look over the city to give him a gift – it cost me not money but a friendship this time round – and he hadn't exactly made it a moment to remember.

As I headed down the path towards the café, suffering from extreme anticlimax and kicking the leaves, I started thinking of our relationship and how independence was our thing. I turned my back into the wind and waited for him to catch up with me.

'Nancy's funeral is on the fifteenth,' I said.

He hooked his arm in mine. 'Is it? That's when we're travelling.'

'I know. But I'm thinking of changing my ticket. I'll fly out on the sixteenth instead.'

'Why? It's not as if she's family, is it?'

I accept that sexual frustration could have contributed to our mood. It was nothing to do with staying with his parents – it had just seemed safer, somehow, to hold back a bit, and my engagement ring was proof that it hadn't put him off.

'No,' I conceded, 'she's not family, but—'

'So it's not as if you actually need to go to her funeral. You were there for her when she was alive. Now she's dead it doesn't matter to her whether you're there or not, does it.'

I couldn't argue with the logic. 'I suppose.'

We hugged by the bandstand and I closed my eyes and leant into him. Mark was the perfect partner. I would marry him and become part of his lovely life where no one thinks badly or lets reality overshadow fantasy; I would travel with him and we could live it all again through my stories and his prints, always showing the best of ourselves.

In his arms I was part of that lovely warm world of Stephen, Judy, Mark and his friends, where nothing awful happened, where they were supportive of my writing and full of praise and admiration; there's nothing nicer than being with nice people and if I was with them long enough, I would become like them – likeable, easy to be with, living an easy life.

As usual, I was packing for the trip right up to the last minute. I'd begun methodically enough but I started getting separation anxiety, trying to stuff a pair of FitFlops into a side pocket of my backpack because you never know, I could easily get fit just by walking to the toilet block and back. Our cabin in Yosemite didn't have an ensuite.

I could hear Mark cursing from his room as Judy tapped on my door, waving a blue packet and a small nylon bag.

'Have you got Imodium? And Mark said he doesn't want this mosquito net, so I thought you might like it. It's a double.'

'I think it will be too cold for mosquitoes. I'll take the Imodium, though. Thanks.' I tucked it in my pocket.

'Are you going to be climbing, too?' she asked, looking at my bulging backpack.

'No, I'm mostly on the support side of things.'

She smiled warmly and patted my cheek. 'I'm so glad you're going with him, darling.' She headed for the door and turned to look at the backpack again, shaking her head dubiously. 'I don't know how you're going to carry that, though.'

Good point. When she'd gone I put the straps over my shoulders and straightened up, taking the strain in my thighs like a bodybuilder. I'd packed Nancy's papers and they weighed more than I'd realised.

Mark came in looking flustered – quite a rare emotion for him. 'Good! You're ready!'

'I hope so. I feel as if I've forgotten something,' I said.

'Got your passport?'

I patted myself down. Passport, laptop, ESTA, pills, notebook. 'Yes.'

'You've got all the important things. Anything else you can get at the airport.' He checked the time. 'The cab will be here in a minute.'

I took a last look around the bedroom and straightened the bed, unable to shake off the hollow, nagging feeling I'd forgotten something vital.

Mark's phone pinged. 'That's the car. You want a hand with that?'

'No, it's fine.' I bumped it down the stairs, gave Judy a goodbye hug and the driver manhandled my backpack into the boot.

I got into the car and sat back on the beige leather seats clutching my laptop bag.

Mark slid in beside me and we looked at each other. He squeezed my knee. 'Happy?'

I nodded and smiled back at him. 'Yes.'

And the driver set off and we waved to Judy until she was out of sight.

CHAPTER THIRTY-EIGHT

The Destination

Jack was standing outside the church by the gleaming hearse, his dark hair gelled back, his face pale, black overcoat blowing in the wind. The last of the mourners was swallowed up in the dark beyond the wooden doorway and Jack watched with his hands in his pockets as the undertakers moved Nancy's casket onto a brass trolley. Cellophane snapped around the flowers like firecrackers in the breeze.

I was hobbling breathlessly down the long gravel path with my backpack bumping against my ribs when he saw me.

He raised a hand to the funeral director and came striding over the gravel path, his dark suit jacket flapping open, his black, silk-lined tie flying. November the fifteenth was a gusty, overcast day.

'Lana.'

'Hello, Jack.'

His face cleared.

He didn't care what I said, whether I said I was sorry, or sorry for him, or offered my condolences or my deepest sympathy, or asked if there was anything I could do, or any of the other various permutations that I could come up with at a time like this . . . any of the permutations that people normally come up with in the same circumstances.

It didn't matter what I said; I was here.

'Mr Buchanan!' The funeral director was wearing dark glasses like an American cop in a film, pumped with self-importance, instructing the pallbearers.

He asked us to 'process behind the casket and let's get this show started'. Then taking his sunglasses off he punched Jack's shoulder, and mustered his men and they hoisted the casket onto their shoulders with a jerk, so surprised at the lightness of it that they almost tossed it in the air.

As we entered through the wooden doors, the subdued church was packed, dense with mourning. I dropped my backpack by the font as the organ started playing 'Jerusalem', and we followed the shiny casket down to the front seats where the other members of the Lonely Hearts Literary Society, one person down, were sitting. They looked up, momentarily surprised, and quickly shuffled up to make room for me with pats and nods.

Neveen took Jack's arm, and Joan gave him a watery, encouraging smile, and after the hymn, we sat back and shifted our legs so that Arthur could get past us to give the eulogy.

Arthur was solemn in his dark suit, solemn but not sombre as he looked across the packed church, gripping the lectern fiercely in his sincerity.

'Throughout her illness, despite her illness, Nancy's life had meaning,' he said. 'Nancy remembered love, but not the grief. She remembered words, but not the story. She found positives in the darkest negatives of life. She is the prism through which we, her friends, have seen what is important in our lives. We are privileged that she let us find the gems within her madness and through them she added magic to our own experiences.'

He looked up and his blue gaze settled on us. 'Twenty years

ago, her books inspired women and will still inspire them; she stopped writing because she thought she'd been compromised by love.' His voice hoarsened, and he paused for a moment before continuing. 'But she was wrong; she was enriched by it.'

Outside the church at the end of the service, we followed the casket down Swain's Lane to Highgate cemetery as the last brown leaves jittered on the branches. We shivered together as Nancy was buried in the same grave as Jack's father, Richard Buchanan, and as the priest finished his reading, Jack threw a handful of earth on the casket, desolate and dry-eyed.

We waited for him as people began to move away, sober but sociable as they greeted him, hugged him and tried to keep the balance right.

There, just off to the left, in a little group by a marble mausoleum, was an odd little bunch of people standing in a man-made mist of cigar smoke. They looked mismatched, like guests at a wedding trying to find common ground.

Writers. I could recognise them a mile off. A plump, white-haired old man, smoking a cigar. A thick-set woman on the arm of a balding guy. I knew them from the Society of Authors. A blonde romantic novelist and a crime writer – Julia and Derek – wearing Versace and sharing handbag wine. Edward, a cravat-wearing documentary maker, next to a short guy wearing a black leather jacket and jeans.

'Isn't that . . . ?' Joan asked, linking her arm in mine.

'Yes. The shortest men always write the longest books,' Kathryn said as the hood of her Scottish Widow cape slipped off her dark hair.

Jack was turning round to look at me in response to something the old man was saying.

Seeing us watching, he stubbed his cigar out in a gilt pocket ashtray and advanced towards us as he tucked it into his pocket.

'Mrs Green,' he said in the booming voice of a preacher, 'sorry to meet you under such sad circumstances. I'm Iain McIlroy.'

'*Miss* Green. And this is Joan Parker.'

'How do you do? I'm *so* glad to meet Nancy's new friends at last. I was her agent for many years. Nice service, wasn't it? The great and good of the publishing world – Nancy wouldn't have wanted it simple.'

'We're going to the pub,' Jack said. 'Iain, come with us. Your driver can hang about for you, can't he? This is Kathryn. She's written a book you might want to take a look at.'

Kathryn was swaying like a sapling in the breeze. She found her hands held firmly by McIlroy's.

The crime writer was battling against the flow of mourners, his arm in Julia's, dark hair flying. He stood out in his black brocade frock coat and black shirt and he was intercepted by Carol Burrows who just loved his work . . . her voice drifted over. 'It would be such a fillip to have a signed copy.'

Jack caught my eye and gave a faint grin as he pushed his hand through his hair. We walked back up to the Flask in Highgate Village and Kathryn grabbed us seats, arranging her black cloak around her. Arthur bought us all brandies and Joan sat next to the log fire.

'Brr!' she said, rubbing her hands together. She picked up the glass, sniffed the brandy and shuddered. 'I need something in this. It's too strong.'

'What do you want?' Arthur asked, taking off his dark jacket and passing it over to her to keep her warm.

Joan draped it over her shoulders and pushed her smooth grey hair back from her face as she looked up at him. 'Champagne.'

'Yes,' he replied with a laugh, 'that'll water it down.' But he was getting to his feet. 'Champagne, Jack?'

Jack looked up. 'Yeah, what the hell,' he said.

Neveen smiled at me. 'Nancy would have loved it, wouldn't she? All those people, and being the centre of attention. Nancy gave love and took it too. She always greeted us with joy.'

Arthur was back with a bottle of champagne and flutes on a tray. He poured it carefully and watched it fizz, rise, settle, fizz as he topped it up. As he handed me a glass, he said quietly and kindly, patting my shoulder as if it was just between us, 'Joan and I knew you would come today.'

'Did you?' I was indescribably pleased by their faith in me.

Joan was stirring her drink pensively. 'Nancy was an extraordinary woman. She saw our needs and didn't turn away from them. I wish we'd known her better, and for longer,' she said. A cloud left the face of the sun as she picked her glass up, and the table was clothed with light. 'To Nancy,' she said, looking out of the window. 'A bird, or a thought.'

CHAPTER THIRTY-NINE

Ideas for an Epilogue

I've thought a lot about the way I ended *Love Crazy*. '*Their adventure wasn't over. It was just about to begin.*'

But of course, the real ending came after that.

So I planned on writing an epilogue.

I would say I met Mark on top of Primrose Hill. As previously noted, in a novel, the setting is everything.

Frost glittered on the path, and I tucked my gloves into my pocket, my breath clouding in the cold air. I had to choose somewhere visually appropriate; where the globes of the lights shone like small moons. I saw Mark coming up the path with his hands in his pockets, his head down, and I felt really bad about what I was going to do.

He was panting when he reached the top of the hill. 'Whoooo,' he said, unzipping his jacket. 'Feel my heart!'

'Mark, I can't. Because I'm just about to break it.'

He zipped his jacket back up quickly. The half of his face that the light fell on looked dismayed. 'For real?'

'I'm sorry,' I said. 'You're perfect for me, and I'm perfect for you but I think we're too much alike. We believe our own images. How crazy is that?'

'Bullshit. It's Jack, isn't it?'

'Yes,' I said. 'It's Jack.'

He took me in his arms and rested his chin on top of my head. I closed my eyes and we stood rocking for a moment.

'If I hadn't gone to the Bahamas,' he said, 'would this be a different ending?'

'If you had come back at the end of that assignment and we were still living in the flat, and nothing had changed, yes, it would have been an entirely different ending.'

'I will never forget you,' he said.

The tears came into my eyes at all that I was saying goodbye to, and I turned a little towards the light so that his photographer's eye would see the line of tears gleam on my cheeks.

He admired them for a moment, took out a white handkerchief and dabbed them away gently.

'I won't forget you, either,' I said.

He gave a sad smile and paused, tilting his head to look at me, probably, like me, wondering if there was anything more that could be added to the scene – but I could be being harsh. Maybe he would be genuinely reluctant to leave. I gave him the ring back and he turned up the collar of his jacket and strolled down the hill in the direction of Regent's Park Road, where the shops are.

I followed the path in a different direction, towards Camden, regretful, but at the same time feeling suddenly lighter.

Of course it didn't actually happen like this.

The truth was, in the taxi, I couldn't shake off that hollow, sick sensation I was missing something or I'd lost something or I'd left something behind and I thought, it's about what you'll give up for love.

But it's one of those statements that works any way you want it to.

298

And I had a strong feeling that, even though I hadn't scraped the surface of it yet, I was closer to knowing what love was through Nancy, Jack and the Lonely Hearts Literary Society than with Mark.

It's not a good reason to break off an engagement, but by the time we reached the North Circular it was over between us.

So our relationship ended with plenty of recriminations and lots of yelling and only the last bit, feeling suddenly lighter, is true.

These are the reasons that I like to write: it's safe. It's so much easier to make sense of the world in fiction, where there are rules and regulations and the writer has total control over people's actions. The problem I've always had with real life is, you never know what's going to happen.

I don't feel too bad about Mark, though. I know that he will find someone else as easily as he found me; maybe Rachel Ashton, the rock climber, or Helga, if she gets perfectly well again because he never was that happy with imperfection; anyway, someone with an image to capture and share his digitally enhanced life with. I'm not bitter, just realistic.

I hoped Jack found love too.

The difference was that one of these trains of thought didn't affect me in the slightest and the other one broke my heart.

CHAPTER FORTY

Treasure

Weeks passed, and I hadn't seen Jack since the funeral when he asked the vicar to let me back into church to get my backpack.

I'd hoped he'd come back to London Lit for the final two sessions under the red ticking clock in the blue room, but although we waited hopefully for him, he didn't turn up.

Give him time, Joan said.

So in his absence we talked about how to write a synopsis, the importance of the elevator pitch, self-publishing versus mainstream publishing and what were we doing for Christmas. We discussed the syllabus for next term and believe me, when they all signed up for it, it was as exciting as getting a second date.

I had swiftly moved out of Judy and Stephen's – they didn't understand it either: *how* could *you?* – and into a tiny rented studio in Kentish Town in what used to be the Old Piano Warehouse yard.

I spent the next three weeks working on an outline of Nancy and Richard's story, and in writing it I grew familiar with what love is about; I learned that it is solid and enduring and gives vitality to life. Love is widespread, humane and not confined to couples. Nancy lived a full life and she lived it on her terms, with help at the end from those who loved her and here I include myself. Writing her story didn't make me feel sad. It made me feel brave. It made me understand my parents better.

When the first draft was finished, I printed it up, and while it was still warm I put it in a Tesco bag and asked Jack to meet me at the Edinboro Castle, early evening.

I saw him before he saw me and I felt a sudden rush of nervous excitement. He was sitting outside in the chilly beer garden when I got there, his elbows on the wooden table, the stripy coloured scarf around his neck. The darkness was lifted by the red glow from the heater which was colouring half his profile, leaving part of him in shadow.

'Hello, Jack.' I put the Tesco bag containing the typescript on the table.

He smiled and looked from me to the carrier and he reached out and tapped my naked third finger which was missing a diamond ring.

'What happened to your hero, Lana? He get eaten by a bear?'

'No. We broke up, actually. The day of the funeral.' I waited for a reaction. 'This is where you chip in with some insightful comment,' I said.

'Why did you break up?'

'We differed on what was important.'

He glanced up at me. 'You differed on what was important,' he repeated drily.

'Basically,' I agreed. How had we got this formal with each other? 'How are you?'

He shrugged. 'You know. Working.'

I thought about the day we first met. 'Still firefighting?'

302

'Yes.' He laughed and glanced at his watch. 'Have you got time for a quick drink?'

'Yes, please.'

He got up to go to the bar and I couldn't take my eyes off him as he went inside. I wanted to be with him. I loved him, I realised. I *loved* him. He came out with the drinks and sat down again in the rosy glow of the outdoor heater. He tapped the Tesco bag and raised his eyebrows.

'Your book?'

'Yes. It's about Nancy. It was true, she did write everything down. I want you to have a look at it before I show it to Kitty.'

He looked confused. 'I thought you were writing a romantic novel.'

I drank a mouthful of wine and shuddered. It was shockingly cold and surprisingly sour, with the flavour of an unripe gooseberry. 'It *is* romantic.'

He shook his head and looked at me in cynical disbelief. 'Yeah?'

I was so frustrated with him.

'I don't understand you, Jack. You think love is a waste of energy but you also said you wanted to know how our story ended – as if you didn't have a say in it. How did you want it to end?'

'How?' He leant forward so that his face was close to mine. Away from the red glow of the heater, the only light in the darkness was the gleam of his eyes. He whispered: 'Like all love stories. Happily ever after.'

'You and me?' I whispered back hopefully.

'But,' he said in his normal voice, 'we probably differ on what's important, right?'

I sighed, sat back and stared up at the black sky. Above us, a thin moon tipped on a cloud.

'How could we ever have a real relationship anyway? You've

never let me into your life. I don't know your friends, or where you live. Was I always just Nancy's carer to you?'

'That's all I wanted you to be,' he said. 'You'd already found your soulmate. And just when I thought we had a chance, Mark Bridges came back and suddenly you were dropping everything to be with him. You were the happiest I'd ever seen you.'

'I know. I was wrong about him. I'm sorry I messed you around.' Everything had changed for me, but nothing had changed for Jack. For him, love was another word for misery and pain. I wanted to pin him down now with the truth so that he couldn't misunderstand himself out of my reach. I took a deep breath. If I couldn't be honest about my feelings, then what was the point? I thought, folding my arms.

So I gave it my best. 'Jack, listen to me. I love you. I love you for the way you loved Nancy and for joining the Lonely Hearts Literary Society. For being nice about my engagement to Mark even though you and Nancy hated him. And for not being surprised when I turned up at the funeral.'

Jack pondered over this speech in silence, eyes narrowed. After a moment he said, 'Yeah, well. Actually you're wrong, I *was* surprised you turned up.' He grinned suddenly. 'So Nancy didn't appreciate the Mark Bridges charm, huh?'

'Nah. She was completely impervious to it.' I couldn't say any more. I missed her so fiercely my eyes filmed with tears.

'Nothing was grey with her, was it?' he said.

The night was cold on my back but luckily the heater was so warm on my face that its glow hid my blush of shame. Well, I'd done it. I'd told him as best I could that I loved him and the conversation had altered course and he hadn't said it back to me or even acknowledged it.

So what? I thought. I'd gambled and lost nothing but my pride. And as I'd discovered, love was worth taking a risk for.

I sat up a bit straighter. It wasn't a barter system. I could love him without him loving me.

'You're smiling,' he said.

'Yeah,' I said, suddenly all business. 'Why wouldn't I? I'm finally writing again.' The rest of the wine tasted mellow as I finished it off. 'Let me know if there's anything in it you want me to change.'

I stood up, said goodbye and caught the bus home.

When I hadn't heard from him after a few days I emailed the typescript to Kitty.

A couple of days after that I got a phone call at eight thirty on a sunny Friday morning while I was eating my porridge in my dressing gown. I assumed it was her.

It was Jack.

'What are you doing?' he asked abruptly. No preliminaries.

'Nothing,' I said warily, putting my spoon down. 'Why?'

'I've read it.' He paused. 'And I get it.'

My heart jumped with relief. 'Oh! Great.'

'I'll meet you in Starbucks in Parkway at nine. Wear comfortable shoes.' He hung up.

I looked at the time. Thirty minutes! Thirty minutes to get ready, made-up and get to Camden? Comfortable shoes?

I got dressed and looked at myself in the bedroom mirror. Yeah well.

It's a bad time of the day for traffic, so I half-jogged, half-walked to Parkway and Jack was standing outside Starbucks, waiting for me. Black jeans, black coat, turquoise T-shirt. He looked tired, but sort of – different.

I greeted him cautiously. 'Is this about the book?'

'It is. Okay, Lana,' he said seriously, 'this is Starbucks. This is where I get my coffee every morning. I have a black Americano with one sweetener in it, which I order on the app.'

Obediently I went inside and we picked up the coffees.

'Carlos, this is Lana.'

'Hey!'

'Hi! Thanks! So where are we—?'

'Come on.'

Jack took me past the ladies' toilets, across the road, past the HSBC, past the Camden Eye, past Sainsbury's, scattering pigeons as I hurried to keep up with him, holding my cup aloft. We weaved through the bus stop queue, crossed Camden Street and went past Costa where he'd bought the bike from me, turned right into Royal College Street. We stopped outside a modern office building and went inside. Jack signed me in and we went to the first floor in a lift.

'In here,' Jack said when the lift stopped.

It was a large, air-conditioned office that I recognised from the website. A white Christmas tree decorated with memory sticks stood in the corner. People were working at tall desks you can stand by. Some looked over from their computers and smiled and said hello, one was making a coffee, one was on the phone. But Jack wasn't finished. We went into an office.

'This is Joe, my partner in the business.'

Joe, handsome, bearded, got up to shake my hand. 'Hey, Lana! Nice to meet you at last.'

'You too.'

'And this is Alaska.'

'Hi there! We've heard a lot about you.'

'And this is Ben.'

'Hi, Ben.'

'This here is my office,' Jack said, holding the door. Huge desk, four monitors, a black leather ergonomically designed chair.

Then we left the office with a wave and went back onto Camden Road. We passed the chemist, went over the canal as we headed back to Camden and Jack pointed out the dry cleaners.

'This is where I get my shirts done.' He pushed open the door. 'Menna, this is Lana.'

She smiled, looking bemused. 'Hello! Pleased to meet you!'

And further on: 'This is where I have my hair cut. That's Raj, the barber. And here, Rawhide, is where I get my shoes mended.' We crossed Camden High Street again and walked back up Parkway. 'That Co-op is my nearest food store, and Whole Earth, for vegetables.'

We turned left by the Edinboro Castle and Jack was still striding ahead of me as if he had a schedule to stick to.

We were walking along Mornington Terrace and halfway down he stopped at a terraced flat with terracotta-tiled steps.

'Come on in. This is my flat.' He took me inside – pointed out rooms in the desultory manner of an estate agent who'd failed to meet his monthly target. 'Study, bedroom, bathroom.' It was airy and modern. 'The kitchen's through there.' A blue mug upside down on the draining board.

In the lounge he stood in front of a pebble-stacked fireplace and faced me with folded arms. The draft manuscript was on the sofa. Jack's stubble glinted in the sunlight, his short hair gleamed. Under the straight, dark eyebrows his clear grey eyes were totally focused on mine.

'Let me tell you about myself, Lana. Sometimes I don't shave,' he said. 'I wear casual for work, unless there's a meeting. I'm untidy but I eat my five-a-day. I work hard. I have holidays. I enjoy my time off. You know where I live and where I work. This is my life. This is me.'

'I understand.'

'Good, because I want to share it with you. But you should know I'm not so keen on independence. I'm not like that. I like being able to depend on people.' He was quiet for a

307

moment and his gaze locked on mine again. 'I know without a doubt I can depend on you,' he said. 'And I want you to know you can depend on me.'

I started to cry and covered my mouth with my hand. They were the nicest words that anyone had ever said to me, and *he'd* said them.

'Come here,' he said, holding me tight and stroking my hair. 'I appreciate the whole hero thing you did on my family, by the way. What's that called again?'

I wiped my tears and looked up at him. 'Characterisation.'

'That's it. Characterisation. The point is, now I've read the book, it's clear to me that I love you.'

Heat flared through me. 'Is it?'

'Yeah, see . . .' Jack laid his hands against my cold cheeks; his hard palms were warm and smelled of aftershave. 'I didn't understand it before. I didn't recognise the positives of love. I didn't realise what love was all about. But I do now.' And he smeared my tears away and leant forward and kissed me, his lips soft on mine.

Happiness soared in me like delirium or the best stage of drunkenness, that moment before you reach for another glass and it all starts going downhill.

He kissed my eyelids, my lips, my throat.

His short hair was like velvet under my fingers.

And for now, that's how it ends.

Almost.

CHAPTER FORTY-ONE

Trilogy

Some days start off perfect: snow is falling gently, people are muffled up, smiling – this was one of those days. I was waiting for Kitty to let me into her apartment block.

As I looked into the ground-floor flat at the tall Christmas tree glowing with fairy lights and spreading its branches over gift boxes, the intercom clicked into life.

'Come on up, Lana,' Kitty said.

The door clunked open and I got into the lift which took me up to her floor. She was waiting for me, glossy dark hair tied back, smiling gently, wearing a navy and ochre velvet shift dress. 'Sit down.'

I dropped the last couple of inches into the tan leather chair, hugged my knees and looked at her hopefully. I was keeping my fingers crossed that this was the resolution of my story and I wasn't going to have to write an epilogue. Sometimes, as discussed at length in the writing class, an ending can go on too long.

I tried to read Kitty's body language as she glanced at her notes.

'*Nancy Ellis Hall: A Love Story,*' she said. 'Lana, it's not just

309

good, it's sellable. And topical. What a life she had! And you've captured it beautifully. I cried, but they were good, life-affirming tears. Anthea loves it. It's going to make us lots of money. Now . . . have you had any ideas about the next one?'

Eh? 'Er . . .'

Kitty glanced at her watch and smiled. She flexed her triceps and stood up. 'Come on! Let's have lunch!'

Acknowledgements

There's nothing quite as exciting as being with experts in their field, and my warmest gratitude goes to Judith Murdoch my agent and Rachel Faulkner-Willcocks my editor, who have helped me make this book what it is.